"There are no vultures out there," Penelope said to group. "There's nothing out there."

"Only an empty car."

"I'm going to look for her," Penelope said. "Freda!" she called. The wind carried her cry over the mountain slopes, but there was no answer.

Freda's car was indeed empty—and unlocked. "The keys are in the ignition, and her purse is on the seat," Penelope shouted. "She can't be far away." She looked around for Mycroft, but he was no longer following her. "Mike!" she shouted. "Mycroft!" She spotted the big gray cat near a stone wall and rushed over to him.

He growled at her approach. Something was wrong. Then she saw blood on his right paw. He growled again.

Looking over his furry shoulder, Penelope found the cause of his concern: He had found Freda . . . sprawled face down in the dirt, a chopping knife plunged deep into her back.

Empty Creek, Arizona, was rapidly becoming the murder capital of the world.

DESERT CAT

GARRISON ALLEN

ZEBRA BOOKS
KENSINGTON PUBLISHING CORP.

For
Mycroft, Archie, and Holmes
Great Cats All

ZEBRA BOOKS are published by

Kensington Publishing Corp.
475 Park Avenue South
New York, NY 10016

First Printing: March, 1994

Printed in the United States of America

THE "CAST"
MORE OR LESS
IN ORDER OF APPEARANCE

EMPTY CREEK, ARIZONA. A small community located in the desert north of Phoenix. It is populated by a curious collection of free-spirited eccentrics, desert rats, cowboys and cowgirls, snowbirds, tourists.

MYCROFT, AKA BIG MIKE, MIKE, MIKEY. An Abyssinian alley cat from Abyssinia who believes he is a lion. He is partial to lima beans and enjoys horseback riding and doing bear imitations. He has an American Express Gold Card and a frequent flyer account.

PENELOPE WARREN. Mycroft's friend and mentor. Penelope also owns a bookstore named after him, Mycroft & Company.

JIMMY BUFFETT. Mycroft's favorite singer. Mycroft is a true Parrot Head.

WILLIAM SHAKESPEARE. Mycroft's favorite playwright. He uses the Bard's collected works as a scratching post.

5

CASSANDRA WARREN, AKA CASSIE, STORMY. Penelope's sister. Cassie is an actress of talent in epic movies under the name Storm Williams, a tribute to her agent's memories of strippers in the old burlesque shows.

ELAINE HENDERS, AKA LANEY. A writer of romance novels set in the old West and Penelope's best friend.

VICTORIA'S SECRET. Laney's favorite mail-order catalog.

WALLY. Laney's cowboy friend and live-in companion, when Laney has not tossed his clothes into the desert, a frequent occurrence.

ALEXANDER. A Yorkshire Terrier and Mycroft's best friend. He lives with Laney and Wally. Alex also enjoys horseback riding, as well as yipping.

THE DOUBLE B WESTERN SALOON AND STEAKHOUSE. Official and unofficial gathering place for practically everyone in Empty Creek. Snowbirds and tourists are unwelcome, however. The town fathers and mothers have been known to hold council meetings at the Double B. There have been weddings and christenings there, and more than one wake to note the passing of a regular.

SAM CONNORS. A police officer and former boyfriend of Penelope. Now, however, he is helplessly in love with . . .

DEBBIE. AKA DEBBIE D, DEE DEE. A waitress at the Double B. Her nicknames are honestly acquired as she possesses what one rejected suitor termed "National Treasures."

THE DUCK POND. An excellent Mexican restaurant which comes by its name honestly also, primarily because the windows and the patio overlook a pond where ducks cruise placid waters. Mycroft once had a memorable encounter with a duck here.

HARRIS ANDERSON III, AKA ANDY. Editor of the *Empty Creek News Journal* and sometime suitor for Penelope's hand. He always plays Abraham Lincoln in the elementary school pageant on President's Day. He would also play Ichabod Crane if there were an Ichabod Crane festival.

LOUISE FLETCHER, AKA THE FIRST LADY OF EMPTY CREEK, QUEEN LOUISE I. Deceased.

HERBERT FLETCHER. A lecherous widower.

TWEEDLEDEE AND TWEEDLEDUM, AKA LAWRENCE BURKE AND WILLIE STONER. Homicide detectives. Of sorts.

JOHN "DUTCH" FOWLER. Chief of the Empty Creek Police Department. He left the Los Angeles Police Department to seek a peaceful sinecure.

RED THE RAT AND DAISY. An old prospector and his pack mule. They are inseparable companions.

DOCTOR BOB. Mycroft's veterinarian. And he has the scars to prove it.

CHARDONNAY, AKA CHAR. A six-year-old Arabian filly who hangs out with Penelope and Mycroft and, of course, Alexander on his frequent visits. A former show horse, Char is sweet, gentle, even tempered, and likes peppermint candies.

KATHY ALLEN. A college student and Penelope's assistant in Mycroft & Company. In Kathy's eyes, Penelope is Wonder Woman. Except for that particular foible, Penelope believes Kathy to be one of Empty Creek's saner citizens.

TIMOTHY SCOTT. A rather mad poet who dedicates his verse to Kathy in more ways than one.

MRS. ELEANOR BURNHAM. Empty Creek's town crier.

FREDA ALSBERG AND MEREDITH STEVENS. Members of the Empty Creek City Council.

ROBERT SIDNEY-VEINE. An aging British expatriate, satyr, and pen pal to Penelope.

MUFFY AND BIFF. Penelope's noble and long-suffering parents. Their real names are Mary and Jameson.

MURPHY BROWN. Mycroft's paramour, a sleek calico who lives down the road.

CRYING WOMAN MOUNTAIN. A dark and brooding mountain on the edge of Empty Creek. It was named for the weeping Indian maiden who is the spirit living in the mountain. Penelope has heard her cry.

MADAME ASTORIA. Empty Creek's resident astrologer and psychic whose real name is Miss Alyce Smith. She would have called herself Mademoiselle Astoria except it is so difficult to spell. She does a thriving business because she is attractive, vivacious, and personable. Everyone likes Madame Astoria. And, many of her predictions actually come true. Eventually.

SPENCER ALCOTT, ESQ. A deal-making attorney with a nautical bent and a Bucky Beaver smile. He always looks ready to tuck into a handy tree.

EMMA PEEL. Not *the* Emma Peel, but secretary and receptionist to Spencer Alcott.

GEORGE BUSH. Not *the* George Bush, but someone wearing a George Bush mask, armed with crazy glue and an apparently inexhaustible supply of pennies and chopping knives.

PEGGY NORTON AND SHEILA TYLER. Police officers.

GEORGE EDEN. An outlandish dresser but an excellent criminal defense lawyer and the main squeeze of Sheila Tyler.

JUSTIN BEAMISH. A private investigator.

RALPH AND RUSSELL. Twin brothers in the employ of Beamish.

THE CHORUS. Abraham Lincoln, Humphrey Bogart, Ingrid Bergman, Sean Connery, Woodward and Bernstein, "60 Minutes," Sean Connery, George Strait, Garth Brooks, Alexander Pope, Richard Nixon, Arnold Schwarzenegger, the duck, Virgil, Thomas Hardy, Ron and Nancy Reagan, Clyde the coyote pup, Emily Dickinson, Peter O'Toole, Omar Sharif, two mockingbirds, assorted bunnies, and a rather large saguaro cactus.

CHAPTER ONE

"I could just kill that woman."

Until this pronouncement, Penelope Warren and Big Mike, the Abyssinian alley cat from Abyssinia, had been sheltered from the cold and rain-swept day before the fireplace in Mycroft & Company, the one reading and the other alternately dozing and listening to Jimmy Buffett as he daydreamed of the old days in the African bush. Although he was also partial to Andrew Lloyd Webber and John Williams, Jimmy Buffett was Big Mike's favorite. But as Penelope often said, "Of course, he's going to like anyone named after a cat food."

But once Elaine Henders rushed through the door of the small bookstore, Jimmy Buffett's rather bawdy lyrics were forgotten for the moment. Laney could overpower anyone, even Jimmy when he was belting it out.

"Laney," Penelope cried. "Have you lost your senses entirely, wandering around in this weather?"

"I had to come into town," Laney said, brushing wet strands of flaming red hair away from her eyes. She opened her raincoat and deposited Alexander, a small Yorkshire terrier on the floor.

Penelope knelt to greet Alex who slobbered happily on her hand before rushing over to Mycroft, yapping and twirling about in his eagerness. Mycroft, all twenty-five pounds of him, tolerantly endured the little dog's effusive tongue. With the amenities over, Alex settled down next to Mycroft. He had learned long ago that one or two slurpy dog kisses were acceptable, but anything more and scratches marred his wet black nose. Alex looked up at Penelope with his placid eyes, anticipating the dog treat that was quickly forthcoming from the stash she kept behind the counter for just such visits.

"I swear," Laney said, shaking her head, "they look like Mutt and Jeff." The Yorkie was barely one-fourth the cat's size.

"Why did you have to come into town, and who do you want to kill?" Penelope asked, although suspecting she knew the answer to the second question.

"Louise Fletcher, of course."

Because of her enormous wealth and a terminal case of nosiness, Louise Fletcher was known around town as the unofficial first lady of Empty Creek, though some referred to the first lady as Queen Louise I.

"What did she do this time?"

"The nerve of the old biddy. As she was picking up express mail at the post office, she asked me ever so sweetly when I was going to stop writing smut. Can you believe that? Smut, indeed."

Laney was the author of a popular and highly erotic series of romance novels set in old Arizona. Like Laney, her heroines resembled a youthful Maureen O'Hara. They were ravishing and frequently ravished. She made pots of money from the books.

"Oh, Laney, what do you care?"

"I don't write smut."

"And what was so important that you had to drag yourself into town in this weather?"

"I missed the mailman, so I had to pick up a package at the post office."

"It couldn't wait?"

"Nope. It's a sexy black negligee for tonight. I thought it wasn't going to get here on time."

"You're such a prude. I don't know why you don't just go into a store and buy one."

"And have everyone know what I'm planning with my cowboy? No, thank you."

Penelope didn't think Laney's cowboy deserved such considerate treatment, but she held her tongue as usual. Wally was . . . well, just Wally, a cowboy whose only visible means of support came on those rare occasions when he loaded his horses into a trailer, packed his duster and guns, and headed down the road to appear as an extra in one of the Western films or TV shows shot on desert locations. Wally was proud that he had almost been given a line to speak in one of the *Back to the Future* films.

"Besides," Laney continued, "would you?"

"I guess not," Penelope admitted reluctantly. "But you're not fooling anyone. It'll be all over town that Elaine Henders is receiving packages from Frederick's of Hollywood."

"Please, it's Victoria's Secret, and I told that old blabbermouth at the post office I'd have his hide if he said one word to anyone. What are you and Andy doing tonight?"

"Nothing."

"Nothing, as in nothing special, or nothing, as in nothing period."

"Nothing period," Penelope replied.

"That man is such a klutz. How can he forget Valentine's Day? I swear he needs a keeper."

"It's not as though we're going steady or anything."

"No one says going steady anymore. That's so old-fashioned."

"I don't think so."

"I rest my case. Sometimes I think you need a keeper too."

Mike, having heard the conversation many times before, strolled back to the fireplace. Alex followed his hero. Side by side, they stared into the fire until they both nodded off.

Laney went over to her books. Despite specializing in mystery novels, Penelope prominently displayed her novels. "Someone bought a copy of *Arizona Maiden.*" Laney always knew exactly how many copies were in the store. Authors were insecure, and she was no exception.

Each time one of her novels was published, Laney would ask Penelope if she liked it. Penelope would say she loved it. A pause would follow. Then Laney would say, "Yes, but did you really like it?"

Now Penelope said, "Kathy took it home to read." Kathy was Penelope's part-time assistant.

"Oh, fie, there goes my twenty-seven cents royalty."

"It's one of the fringe benefits of working in a bookstore. Besides, you don't need another twenty-seven cents."

"That's true."

"Kathy's a big fan of yours."

"Everyone is."

"Except for Louise Fletcher."

"Someday that woman's going to get exactly what she deserves."

Laney rushed out as breathlessly as she had entered.

Penelope went back to reading. Big Mike resumed his nap. While enlivening, Laney's visit was only a brief respite from the otherwise dreary afternoon.

The rain had fallen on Empty Creek, Arizona, all night and continued into Saint Valentine's Day. There were flash flood warnings all through the desert areas and snow alerts in the higher altitudes. Sections of the interstate that traversed the northern part of the state were closed by drifting snow. The creek bed which gave the small community its name was ironically threatening to overflow its banks.

Penelope looked up from *Come Darkness,* the latest woman-in-jeopardy novel by Gary Amo, one of her favorite authors. Her restlessness had nothing to do with the quality of the book and everything to do with the awful weather. It was strange that Louise Fletcher was also a fan of this writer, given that his books were quite realistic and were sprinkled with sex scenes more graphic than any Laney wrote. Well, maybe. Laney could get pretty graphic sometimes. Penelope sighed. This was just another of those strange little quirks common to Louise Fletcher.

Penelope closed the novel for the moment. She looked down at Mycroft—his given name—and said, "Ah, Mikey, you're my buddy."

Mikey twitched his ears in acknowledgment, as though to say, You're my buddy, too, but don't interrupt Jimmy.

Instead of going back to her book, Penelope went to the window and looked out at the streams of water flowing down the main street. Again, she thought of closing early and going home. The rain kept customers away, and the afternoon dragged on tediously. But, Penelope thought, I'd be doing the same thing at home, reading in front of the fireplace.

Mikey suddenly appeared on the window sill. One moment he was in front of the fire, the next instant he was on the sill, as though he couldn't be bothered to rise and stretch and pad across the room, but had decided to transport his body through time and space. This was one of his uncanny feline traits, and it never failed to amaze Penelope.

Outside, the rain beat down.

"So, Mike, do you wish we were back in Africa?"

Big Mike mewed noncommittally. Africa had been all right, of course, an endless source of wonder for a kitten growing into cathood. There were wild dogs and jackals to intimidate, and the mournful whoops of hyenas to be heard in the night. But the place had had its drawbacks, chiefly the lack of availability of canned cat food, liver crunchies, and lima beans. All in all, tumbling out of the bougainvillea practically into Penelope's gin and tonic had been an inspired act for a kitten whose eyes had not yet opened.

It had been Penelope's custom after her last class at the small Ethiopian college where she had taught English as a Peace Corps volunteer to take a drink outside and watch the sun set over what crazed British colonials used to call MMBA—miles and miles of bloody Africa. She had been sitting on the porch of her small staff house when the ferocious kitten had fallen from the purple flowers that crawled up a trellis and along the roof, landing with a little thud. Hissing and baring its tiny teeth, the kitten had raged momentarily—just to get the rules straight at the very beginning—and then had fallen, happily, asleep in

16

Penelope's lap, perhaps knowing even then that he had found his passport to travel and adventure.

Now the big charcoal gray cat with black stripes answered to several names. He was Mycroft on Sundays, on other formal occasions, and in moments of dire stress—"Mycroft, right out of the Christmas tree, now!" He was Big Mike for visits to the veterinarian, whom he terrorized, or when he disapproved of one or another of Penelope's suitors. Ordinarily he was just plain Mike, but Mikey when Penelope was affectionate.

His mentor, a tall, slender, and very pretty young woman with straight blond hair usually worn in a ponytail, was simply Penelope. Only a very special man was allowed to call her Penny—and then only in a moment of helpless ardor. Although Penelope had tried over the years to break her sister of the habit, Cassie still called her Penny. "It's benefit of childhood," she always said, "like benefit of clergy, only better."

In return, Penelope, of course, refused to call Cassie by her own given name of Cassandra and certainly not by the awful screen name Cassie's agent had come up with in a drunken moment at the Polo Lounge while reminiscing about the strippers he had watched in burlesque theaters in his youth. Penelope had giggled hysterically when Cassie's first credit came up on the screen.

AND INTRODUCING

Storm Williams

"I hope the picture's better than your name," she had whispered, before succumbing to the giggles

17

again. It wasn't, of course, but Cassie was as good as the script and the director allowed her to be in the role of a motorcycle moll leading an intrepid band of Harley-riding women on a crusade to clean up a corrupt beach town. After cavorting in various states of dishabille, dispatching one villain after another with a series of well-placed kicks, and escaping one dire predicament after another, Cassie escorted the bad guys to the local jail before leading her triumphant flock into the sunset, presumably to seek out more evildoers.

Mycroft adored Cassie almost as much as Penelope. Whenever she visited, she was a ready source of the lima beans which he also adored. Usually, though, he ignored the videotapes of her movies, which Penelope thought showed discernment.

Fiercely loyal to her glamorous younger sister, nonetheless, Penelope devoted a corner of Mycroft & Company to memorabilia of Cassie's acting career—posters for each of Cassie's films, playbills from the little theaters where she had appeared, video cassettes of her movies, framed publicity stills, and the succession of the head shots Cassie distributed along with her résumé at auditions.

The rest of Mycroft & Company was devoted to books, mostly mysteries; but in a guilt-ridden gesture to the seven years she'd spent earning three degrees in English literature, Penelope did stock some of the classics for the Empty Creek literati—those few who preferred Mycroft & Company to the adult section of the video store next door. The *Debbie Does Dallas* school of film-making was certainly more popular in Empty Creek than *The Mayor of Casterbridge* or *Barchester Towers*.

Inside the warm and comfortable bookstore, Jimmy

Buffett sang of cheeseburgers and paradise and pirates while outside the rain continued to fall. If it went on like this, the adult section next door would be seriously depleted.

Cold endless rain on a gloomy Saint Valentine's Day.

"I guess I *have* been forgotten, Mikey, and you're going to be my big date. What shall we do tonight?"

The cat growled softly.

"Liver crunchies and a bottle of wine by candlelight?"

Mikey looked up, his eyes big, waiting to be scratched beneath his chin.

When the downpour finally ended in the late afternoon, a rainbow appeared in the sky over Empty Creek. The residents then slowly emerged from their hidey holes and splashed through the streets on postponed errands.

A small group emerged from the multiplex cinema down the street, where they had fled from the weather. *Lawrence of Arabia,* the director's cut, was playing on one of the screens. *Casablanca,* the original black and white version, commemorated Valentine's Day on another screen. The other four screenings were the usual Hollywood dreck.

Penelope saw Herbert Fletcher join the small line now forming at the box office. She wondered idly where Louise was.

Other residents tramped into the Double B Western Saloon and Steakhouse for Happy Hour, to wile away the remaining hours of daylight exchanging gossip and lies. The Double B had a shabby weather-worn exterior, a slightly seedy appearance that discouraged tourists and snow birds, sending them to the respectable Duck Pond instead, thereby keeping the Double B reserved for locals.

Madame Astoria, Empty Creek's resident astrologer and psychic, emerged with a push broom and swept puddles of water away from her door.

Sam Connors waved as he passed in his patrol car. Penelope smiled and waved back. They had dated briefly, but Sam had quickly been intimidated by a former Woman Marine who had earned a doctoral degree in English literature and had later served as a Peace Corps Volunteer. Had that not been enough to discourage Sam, there had been the matter of her cat. Given Mycroft's disapproval, Sam and Penelope were not destined to become an item, but they remained friends.

He dated Debbie D now, the cocktail waitress at the Double B who came by her nickname because of a truly memorable chest. Many a drunken lament had been sung for Debbie D of the Double B, for she broke a multitude of young and not-so-young hearts, when she had chosen Sam to be her one and only. Penelope wondered, as she always did when she saw Sam, if the deep scratches Mycroft had inflicted on a sensitive portion of his anatomy still showed and, if they did, how he had explained them to Debbie D. You see, there was this cat. . . .

"God, Mike," Penelope exclaimed, "I love this place. There are so many wonderful and delicious secrets."

Mycroft, who had a few secrets of his own, raised an ear quizzically before returning to his nap.

Harris Anderson III, full-time editor of Empty Creek's bi-weekly *News Journal* and sometime suitor of Penelope Warren, left his cluttered cubicle at the paper's office and marched down the street toward Mycroft & Company.

Penelope saw him coming and fled to a respectable position behind the counter to pore intently through a publisher's catalog, ignoring the bell that rang as the door opened.

Harris Anderson III entered the bookstore, an envelope in his fist and resolve on his handsome face, which disappeared the instant Penelope looked up. Tall and gangling and awkward, Harris Anderson III blushed as he presented the envelope to her. "Here," he practically shouted, "this is for you."

"Whatever could this be, Andy?"

The newspaper editor, still red-faced, backed away from the counter only to stumble over the cat, causing a loud squall. Mycroft delighted in tormenting the shy and maladroit man, always hovering underfoot whenever he was around. Andy bent and disappeared from Penelope's view. "Mycroft," she heard him say. "I am sorry. I didn't see you down here."

He reappeared slowly, all arms and legs. "You know very well what it is, Penelope Warren. I want you to be my valentine."

"How sweet," Penelope said. "I thought you had forgotten me."

"I did." He stammered. "N-Not you, of course, the day. I forgot the day, but Laney reminded me. In no uncertain terms." He clutched the counter for support as Mike rubbed against his legs. "Go ahead, open it. I made it myself."

The big heart on the front of the card enclosed initials. HA & PW. Inside, the sentiment read:

Roses are red.
Violets are blue.

21

There's no one in Empty Creek
As nice as you.
Please be my Valentine.
He had signed it formally: Harris Anderson III.
Penelope smiled. "That's sweet," she repeated. Penelope didn't think a man's face could get any redder, but she was proven wrong when she leaned across the counter to kiss him. His cheeks became a deeper shade than that of any rose in Empty Creek or the entire Sonoran desert.

"You know, I might just have something for you down here," Penelope said, enjoying the look of stunned pleasure on his face.

"I'm such a dunce," Andy cried, slapping his forehead. "I don't have a present for you. I will, though. I promise. I must go."

"Andy, calm down. It's all right. I want you to have this." Penelope proffered a slim package wrapped in paper covered with hearts.

"Save it until tonight," he said. "We'll see each other later?" he asked hopefully.

"We can have a nice romantic evening if you like," Penelope said. "Just the three of us."

"I would like that," Andy said. "I'll shower you with valentines. You, too, Mycroft."

"Come about seven," Penelope said. "Better yet, why don't we meet for a drink and you can follow us out?"

Harris Anderson III nodded before he hastened away.

Penelope watched him lope down the street. A dear sweet gentle man, but Laney was right. A klutz.

* * *

Mycroft waited while Penelope locked the door promptly at five o'clock. He sat, looking distastefully at the puddles, those formidable barriers between him and Penelope's jeep. Normally, Penelope and Mycroft would simply stroll across the street to the Double B, but with Mycroft's aversion to water they would have to drive this evening.

"You're such a baby," Penelope said as she picked him up. "And overweight too." She set him on his spot in the passenger seat. "We'll see what Doctor Bob has to say about that on your next visit. It's diet city for you, babe."

Andy was late as usual, but Red the Rat was leaning against the bar, gazing fondly, if somewhat sadly, at Debbie D's national treasures as she moved gracefully among the tables, taking orders, deftly avoiding the occasional paw that reached out to pat her backside.

Debbie waved cheerfully at Penelope and Mycroft.

"I swear that woman ought to register them things as deadly weapons," Red the Rat said as Penelope deposited Mycroft on the stool reserved for him. "How do, Penelope?" he then asked, remembering his manners. "How do, Big Mike?"

Big Mike mewed a polite howdy to Red, then immediately bellied up to the bar, putting his paws on the smooth polished wood and waited impatiently for Pete to bring him his usual—two ounces of nonalcoholic beer. Mike used to drink real beer, until Penelope came home from a date one night to find him weaving and meowing raucously along with Jimmy Buffet. He had tipped over a nearly full bottle of beer left behind by her escort and had lapped it up eagerly. The next morning, still nursing a hangover, Mycroft went on the wagon.

"I figured we might see you soon, Red."

"Just as I was getting close, too. Cain't take the rain the way I usta. Makes my knees creak, and Daisy gets upset. Starts bellering something awful." Daisy was Red's pack mule. The uncharitable among the Double B's denizens said Daisy smelled better than old Red, a whole lot better, although Penelope could never tell the difference.

Red the Rat had been getting close to finding the lost gold mine of Squaw Hollow—Squaw Holler to Red—for forty years now.

Penelope thought it poetic justice that the mine had been lost for one hundred and thirty years. The rich ledge of pure gold had been discovered by a band of white men after a battle in which upwards of twenty Apache were killed. Before the gold's location could be properly marked, however, the Apache returned with reinforcements and drove the murderous little band off. So the treasure was lost for all time.

"You'll find it, Red."

"Think so, Penelope?"

"Sure. Maybe even the next time out."

When Andy arrived, breathless as usual, he escorted Penelope in a courtly fashion to an empty table. Their passage was marked by hoots from the crowd at the pool table in the back room. Mike, having lapped up his drink, remained behind, curled up on his stool, his nose twitching as he sought to decipher the various odors emanating from Red the Rat's direction.

"Hi, guys," Debbie said. "Happy V Day."

"And the same to you, Deborah," Andy responded.

He was the only patron of the Double B who called her Deborah.

"I saw Sam earlier," Penelope said.

Debbie smiled quickly. "Yeah, he's coming by later when he gets off."

"I think champagne tonight." Andy was also the only patron who ever ordered champagne in the Double B. "In honor of the occasion."

When the champagne was poured, Andy raised his glass. "To the loveliest bookshop proprietor in all of Arizona, indeed, the entire Southwest, the nation . . ."

Penelope interrupted before he could encompass the world and, indeed, the universe. "Thank you, Andy," she said.

"Am I forgiven?"

"Of course. This time, but you'd better not forget my birthday. Or Christmas."

As Penelope and Big Mike drove home, followed by Andy, the rainbow was still there, seeming to end at their small desert ranch. Or did the arc begin there? It was difficult to tell about rainbows, Penelope thought, but she was an optimist. "Look, Mikey," she said, "maybe we'll find the pot of gold right there on our doorstep. Wouldn't that be nice?"

By the time they reached the house, the rainbow was gone, overwhelmed by the night, and instead of riches, they discovered the body of Louise Fletcher on their porch, a huge chopping knife protruding from her back.

She wore a blood-soaked duster.

The three of them—woman, cat, and man—stared at the former first lady and queen of Empty Creek.

Below the house, Chardonnay whinnied nervously from her stable.

No one should be murdered in the rain, Penelope thought, somewhat irrationally she would later recall.

Not on Saint Valentine's Day.

CHAPTER TWO

Sam Connors was the first police officer on the scene. He was followed shortly by more uniformed officers, homicide detectives, crime lab technicians, a man and a woman from the coroner's office, a photographer, the police chief of Empty Creek, the mayor of Empty Creek, and a stringer from the big Phoenix newspaper, much to the dismay of the local editor whose paper was issued only twice a week and would now be scooped. To his credit, however, Andy immediately regretted that thought. The life of Louise Fletcher was infinitely more valuable than any story, a fact that escaped the Phoenix stringer who, perilously close to missing his deadline, made such a nuisance of himself that Sam Connors banished him to his car.

Penelope, never before having had a murder committed on her doorstep, was at a loss. To compensate, she went into the kitchen and made coffee—gallons of it—for the investigating officers, all the while remembering Laney's threat. *I could just kill that woman.* No, it was only a remark. Laney would never kill anyone, not even Louise Fletcher.

Would she?

Mycroft immediately slipped into his Big Mike per-

27

sona, sitting in the window watching the police activity with great interest. He was particularly fascinated by the yellow tape that fluttered loosely in a light desert breeze. Any cat worth his weight could perform wonders with the tape now strung around the porch and the cactus in the yard to protect the crime scene from intruders.

Penelope was soon cornered in the kitchen by a burly detective named Lawrence Burke and subjected to an intense interrogation concerning her whereabouts during the afternoon and evening, her knowledge of the victim, any motives she might have had for disposing of the victim, and various other aspects of her day and her life. It was only later, when she had had a chance to compare notes with Andy, that she discovered he had been taken aside by Willie Stoner, Burke's partner, and asked similar questions. Penelope came to think of the detectives as Tweedledee and Tweedledum.

"Where were you today?"

"I've already answered that."

"Answer it again."

Penelope sighed. "I got up. . . ."

"Alone?"

"What do you mean?"

"Were you alone when you got up?"

"Of course not. Mycroft was with me. Mycroft always sleeps with me."

"Aha." The burly detective poised to make a note. "Who is Mycroft? Your boyfriend out there?"

"Mycroft is my cat."

He wrote *C-A-T* in his notebook. "The fat one in the window?"

"You'd better not let him hear you say that. He would be offended, as I am, by your attitude."

"It's just routine."

"For God's sake, you sound like Jack Webb."

"Lady, just answer the questions. Do you know anyone who wanted to kill the victim?"

Laney's words echoed in her mind. *I could just kill that woman.* "No," Penelope said. She could not bring herself to turn Laney over to this odious man. He would drag her off in handcuffs, maybe even attempt to beat a confession out of her with a rubber hose—or whatever cops used nowadays.

"Okay," Tweedledee said. "Where were you today?"

Penelope sighed again. "I made coffee, fed Mycroft—"

"You don't need to start so early. Start at four o'clock."

"As I told you before, I was at the bookstore. Alone. There were no customers during the last hour. At five, Mycroft and I closed up and went to the Double B, where we met Andy for a drink."

"Is Andy your boyfriend?"

"I suppose you could call him that."

"Well, is he or isn't he?"

Penelope felt like shrieking. "Yes, a thousand times, yes."

"Did anyone see you at the Double B?"

"Pete, the bartender; Red the Rat; Debbie, the waitress. And there was. . . ."

"Torpedoes," the detective muttered.

"Excuse me? Did you say 'torpedoes'?"

"Debbie, the waitress. She's the one with the torpedoes."

"Torpedoes?" Penelope repeated.

"You know . . . big boobs."

"What a vile, cretinous little man you are," Penel-

29

ope said, although Burke was anything but little; a big hairy belly peeked through an unbuttoned bulge in his shirt.

"Hey, watch your language."

Penelope bristled, drew herself up to her full height—she was an imposing and intimidating woman when she wanted to be—and was about to provide a second vocabulary lesson for the detective, using some of the language she had picked up in the Marine Corps, when Police Chief John Fowler entered the kitchen.

"What language?" Fowler asked.

"I got a hostile witness here, Chief. She called me cretinous. Whatever that is. Vile, too. I got it written down right here in my notebook."

"Give me a break, Burke. You couldn't spell cretinous."

In fact, the detective had drawn a representation of one of Debbie D's breasts, although it looked more like a circle with a dot in it.

"And besides," Fowler continued, "Penelope is absolutely right. You are cretinous. Vile, too. Is the coffee ready?" He turned to her. It smells great."

"I'd be happy to pour a cup for you, John, but *he* can't have any. Along with everything else, he insulted Mycroft."

"I was just doing my job, Chief."

"Run along, Burke, see if you can find a clue."

"I didn't want your coffee anyway. It makes me bilious."

Penelope raised her lovely eyebrows. "Bilious?"

"You know—I burp." The detective retreated with as much dignity as he could muster.

Fowler shook his head sadly as he accepted the coffee from Penelope. "I'd make him a crossing guard, but he'd screw that up. They'd get *me* for child endangerment."

"He treated me as though I were a suspect, John. Am I?"

"Of course not. As near as I can tell, you're one of the few people in Empty Creek who actually liked Louise Fletcher. And we don't need suspects. We have plenty of them, including *Mr*. Louise Fletcher."

Penelope ignored the cruel barb directed at Herbert Fletcher. Everyone in Empty Creek knew Louise ran the Fletcher household and empire, just as she had wanted to run Empty Creek, and often did, tolerating no nonsense from anyone, certainly not from her husband. "You know," Penelope said, "I saw Herb this afternoon. He was in line at the movies, just after the rain stopped. I'm afraid you'll have to eliminate him as a suspect."

"Damn, I never get the easy ones. Do you have any idea why she was here?"

Penelope shook her head. "I haven't seen her for a week or so. She stopped by the store and bought a couple of books. Nothing unusual. She likes—liked—mysteries."

"And now she is one."

"Yes, I suppose she is."

The kitchen gradually filled with people. Andy was first, followed closely by Sam Connors and then the mayor, Charley Dixon.

"A bad business," Dixon said, "and bad *for* business."

Penelope thought the mayor's remark was heartless, even if he had been a frequent target of Louise Fletcher's charges of political chicanery, mismanagement of city resources, and general incompetence, but she held her tongue and slipped out of the kitchen. There was nothing to gain by irritating the mayor. Louise Fletcher had done that for years and look what it got her.

In the living room, Penelope stood at the window, idly scratching Mikey's ears, watching as Louise Fletcher's body was wheeled to the coroner's van. "The queen is dead," Penelope whispered as the van pulled away. "Long live the queen."

Mycroft looked up at her with sad eyes. He had liked Louise Fletcher.

Outside, Chardonnay whinnied plaintively; not in mourning for the deceased woman but because she wanted her dinner.

"Oh, good Lord, Mycroft. I forgot Char."

Penelope rushed into the kitchen, pulled a drawer open, and rummaged around for the peppermint candies Chardonnay liked. "I'm going to feed my horse," she announced. "I suppose that will be all right." The men in the room, including Andy, ignored her.

Penelope shrugged and left by the back door to trudge down the path to the stables, making her way by the light of a nearly full moon. It would have been such a romantic Valentine's Day. . . . Poor Louise.

Chardonnay, her golden coat lustrous in the gleaming moonlight, snorted and pawed the dirt as Penelope approached, unwrapping the first of the little candy peace offerings, holding it in the palm of her hand for Char to take. "Forgive me, dear?"

The apology was accepted while Chardonnay chewed the second peppermint and watched Penelope dole out her supper into the big bucket.

"I'll put your coat on after dinner," Penelope told the horse, receiving another snort and contented munching by way of reply.

Behind the stable and corral, the waters of Empty Creek raced, still raging and swirling but no longer threatening to overflow their banks. Beyond, the mountains were dark hulks in the bright moonlight. Stars glittered in the cloudless sky. Except for the rushing water in the creek bed, it was quiet and peaceful, and reminded Penelope of African nights. One of the reasons, perhaps the primary reason, she had chosen to buy her small ranch—the house and stables and a dozen acres of desert and creek bed—had been the quiet, the solitude, the sense of independence and freedom offered by the desert.

She shivered in the chill night air, but she did not want to go back to the house. Not yet.

She had just finished putting the quilted blue blanket on Chardonnay when she heard someone stumble. She turned. It was Andy, of course. He was the only person Penelope knew who could slip on a perfectly smooth path.

"Hi," he said, recovering his balance.

"Hi, yourself."

"It occurred to me that there might be a killer lurking out here."

"He'd have to be pretty dumb to hang around here with all these cops milling about."

"Well, if you want the truth, I just wanted to be with you."

"It hasn't been much of a Valentine's Day, has it?"

"No. It certainly hasn't." Andy took her in his arms.

Surprised but pleased by the sudden display of masculine strength, Penelope closed her eyes and lifted her face to await his kiss.

He missed her lips. The man was *such* a klutz.

"Oh, good Lord, Andy," she exclaimed in exasperation. Penelope grabbed his ears and pulled his face down. A long time later, she said, a little breathlessly, "There. That's how you kiss."

It certainly is, Andy thought, leaning over to do it again.

Back at the house, the investigation was winding down. Chief Fowler was still in the kitchen issuing instructions to the odious Detective Burke who was closely watched by Big Mike. It would not have surprised Penelope to find Mycroft counting the silverware after Burke left.

"Ah, there you are, Penelope," Fowler said. "We'll be out of your hair soon. There's not much more we can do tonight."

"Have you found anything, John? Any indications of who might have done this?"

"Not really. We know she rode out here. We found her horse down the road a piece."

"Great. A woman is murdered on my doorstep and the only witness is a horse."

"Oh, we're canvassing the neighborhood, and we'll continue in the morning. Hopefully, someone will have seen Louise, provide some little bit of information. That's all police work is, really. Gathering information and interpreting it correctly."

"Well, I hope you don't leave the interpretation to Detective Burke."

Fowler laughed. "I'll be supervising this one myself. Whatever else might be said of Louise Fletcher, she was our most prominent citizen."

"Yes, she was," Penelope agreed. "And I'd like to help find her killer."

"Thinking of going into the detective business?"

"I very well might."

"Penelope . . ."

"Now, Andy, I know what you're going to say. . . ."

"What?"

"You're going to tell me to leave it to the professionals, that I might be in danger, that I'm untrained, a woman, all that sort of nonsense."

"Actually, I was going to say I think you'd be a very good detective. I was also going to offer to make you a stringer for the paper and give you a press card."

"You were?"

"Yes, I was, but I don't think I'll make that offer now."

"There, John, you see. Andy thinks I'd be of valuable assistance in your investigation."

"He didn't say that at all."

"It's what he meant," Penelope insisted, "and it's what he will say when he's had a chance to think about it. Isn't it, Andy?"

"Oink, oink," Andy said. "You're a female chauvinist pig, Penelope Warren."

She ignored him. "Well, John?"

"Oh, I don't suppose it will do any harm. You can look at the reports, lab results, that sort of thing."

"Thank you."

"But I don't want you running around by yourself. This is a murder investigation, and if no one else will say it, I will: It could be dangerous."

"I'll be very careful."

"Yes, you will, or you'll answer to me. Is that clear?"

"Yes, sir, Chief Fowler, sir."

"Besides," Fowler said, ignoring her sarcasm, "is there anyone who would like to see you dead?"

"What?" Penelope and Andy chorused in astonishment. Even Mycroft perked up his ears.

Captain Fowler looked pleased with himself. "Now that I have your attention . . ."

"Why would you ask that?"

"There was a penny glued to the handle of the murder weapon. It is possible someone wanted to kill you instead of Louise Fletcher."

"John, that's nonsense. Who would want to do that?"

"I don't know. That's why I'm asking. A penny. Your nickname is Penny. It could be some bizarre message."

"That's bizarre, all right. No one calls me Penny, except my sister, and she likes me."

"It's still a possibility."

"Remote, at best."

"The killer has a twisted sense of humor," Andy said. "When you give someone a knife, you have to give a penny with it. Otherwise, the relationship is severed."

"How did you know that, Andy?" Penelope asked. "You're a constant source of amazement tonight."

Andy blushed. "An old girl friend gave me a chopping knife once."

"What a romantic present," Penelope said. "Why didn't I think of that?"

"She thought I needed a good knife."

"I'm sure you did."

"She taped a penny to the handle. That's how I know."

"But your relationship was severed anyway."

"Oh, no," Andy said. "We're still friends."

"Are you now?" Penelope asked.

"Oh, not . . . not like that, I mean—"

"I know what you mean," Penelope said. "I was just teasing." She turned to Fowler. "There, you see. Andy has come up with a perfectly logical answer. Our killer has a macabre sense of humor."

After everyone left, Penelope, Andy, and Mycroft sat around the kitchen table. Mike was the only one among them who felt like eating. He attacked his Valentine's Day treats with considerable gusto, growling softly in his role as lion, savoring the fresh taste of zebra or wildebeest as the females of his pride looked on with adoration.

Penelope and Andy picked at their food, while the ghost of Louise Fletcher hovered over the kitchen, as disturbing a presence in death as she had been in life. Penelope was forced to admit that, although she had liked Louise, the murdered woman had been only a meddlesome gadfly to many in and out of the community—the members of the city council and the planning commission, the town's employees, developers, environmentalists, the drama society, the school district's supervisor, the chamber of commerce, the women's club, some factions of the country club, senior citizens, and the horsemen's association. Many an individual had been subjected to Louise Fletcher's scathing tongue and imperious manner.

"Damn it!" Penelope cried, causing Andy to jump and Mycroft to miss a beat in shoveling down his food. "To the best of my knowledge, no one has passed an ordinance against being a gadfly."

"When it came to Louise, there were those in local government who would gladly have done so," Andy pointed out.

"Yes, she could be a pest, but still . . ."

"I know," Andy said. "It's very sad. I'm going to miss Louise."

They fell silent.

Mycroft finished eating and sat back to wash his face.

After a while, Andy said, "You know, sometimes *I* call you Penny."

Penelope smiled sweetly. "Do you? I've never noticed. I must have been distracted."

"I believe you might have been."

"Would you like to distract me again?"

"Very much."

"Let's go make a fire and see what we can do about that."

On the couch before the blazing fire, Penelope waited to be kissed again. Andy not only found her lips on the first try this time, he kissed very nicely indeed. He is certainly improving with practice, Penelope thought.

"Mmm," she said.

"Oh, Penny," Andy responded.

"Grrr." Mycroft inserted himself between the couple, interrupting their display of affection. Mycroft firmly believed that when affection was handed out, it should be showered on him first.

"Go away, Mikey," Penelope said.

The big cat padded away in disgust and stood at the door, demanding to be let out.

"Hold that thought, sweetie," Penelope told Andy. "I'll be right back."

* * *

On the way to the door, Penelope decided that if they were going to be in the private-detective business she would be no Miss Marple. No, thank you, ma'am. V.I. Warshawski. Yes, indeed, V.I. was the ticket. Penelope would be smart, tough and sexy, just like the Victoria of Sara Paretsky's creation. But what the hell did the "I" stand for in Victoria's full name? Penelope wondered. Something from Greek mythology, like Penelope and Cassandra. Iphigenia. That was it. Victoria Iphigenia Warshawski, move over. We are sisters in crime now. Penelope Warren is on the trail of a killer.

Opening the door for Mycroft, Penelope knew he was no Yum Yum or Koko, those appallingly cute little creations. No. Big Mike would be a cat detective in the tradition of the Continental Op and Sam Spade, Philip Marlowe, Lew Archer, Spenser and Hawk—hard-boiled on the outside, strong and silent, but with a tender and romantic streak.

Penelope returned to the couch. "Ready for a little more distraction."

"Yes, please."

Just then, Big Mike, the strong and silent cat detective, squalled loudly, angrily.

It was just like the Marine Corps.

In the Beginning, there was the Word. Then the Word was changed, and there was always some poor schmuck who didn't get the Word.

The Word was out in the coyote community—it had been for a long time now—don't mess with that big cat. But the runt of some proud coyote mother's litter hadn't gotten the Word.

Penelope and Andy rushed to Mycroft's rescue, to

find that he was doing very well all by himself. He was in the midst of one of his very finest bear imitations, and Penelope had learned long ago—she thought of it now as rather like a dueling scar—that Mycroft did not like to be interrupted during a performance.

In the light of the moon, Mycroft reared impressively on his hind legs, casting an even more impressive shadow over the confused and frightened coyote pup who skittered away from the terrifying figure and its hideous squall. But the young coyote had courage too. He stopped and looked back.

The bear yowled and reared even higher.

The coyote pup—Penelope had already named him Clyde—fled.

Mycroft sat, staring into the night, waiting for the next intruder. If Penelope was mistress of the manor, he was certainly the Lord High Cat.

Penelope and Andy waited with Mycroft, allowing time for his wild instincts to subside so he might regain the manners for polite society. Finally, Penelope called out tentatively, "Mikey?"

He looked over at her, turned away, made one last survey of the darkness. Then Big Mike strolled genially into the circle of light cast by the porch lamp. As he padded past Penelope and Andy, he looked up rather smugly and meowed several times. Penelope translated: "Taught that little sucker a lesson."

"Yes, you certainly did," she told the cat. "We're going to make a great team."

For the third time, Penelope and Andy settled on the couch.

Mycroft ignored them now, but Louise Fletcher did not. Her specter hovered over the proceedings. Penelope finally pulled away from Andy, thinking yet again of Laney's grim words.

"I'm sorry, dear heart," she said.

"It's certainly not a very romantic atmosphere tonight."

Indeed, it was the very worst Valentine's Day any of them had ever experienced.

CHAPTER THREE

When Penelope Warren enlisted in the United States Marine Corps two days after her high school graduation—to the dismay of her parents and the delight of her younger sister—she did not realize her grave and irrevocable mistake until reveille on her first full day in boot camp. She had planned to enlist on the day after graduation, but she had overslept as usual and so had postponed that fatal move. Had she but known, admitted her true nature, Penelope would have never worn the globe and anchor, the gold and scarlet chevrons and crossed rifles of a sergeant on her uniform sleeves. She would never have thrilled to a rendition of "The Marines' Hymn."

The fact was, Penelope was not a morning person.

If Louise Fletcher had been murdered early in the day, Penelope would not have learned of it until a considerable number of hours later.

Reveille, that cheery, lilting call of the bugle, was hateful to her. Fear of her drill instructors—a fear instantly instilled and deeply rooted—was the only thing that kept her eyes open while standing at attention in the harsh glare of the squad-bay lights that first morning. No. Not morning. It was the middle of the damned night. Didn't the Marine Corps know that? Didn't they care?

Not much.

That Penelope belatedly realized while shivering in the cold foggy air at the Marine Corps Recruit Depot in San Diego.

One, two, three, four.

Goddamned Marine Corps.

Penelope also learned that it was possible to sleep while marching across the grinder—that huge parade ground—while standing in line at the mess hall, while snapping in at the rifle range, even while getting a variety of immunizations and booster shots against exotic diseases. Penelope became a Marine while sleep-walking. She never wanted, ever again, to see another dawn, unless she happened to be coming home at that hour.

Penelope remembered very little of her one thousand and ninety-six mornings—her service included a leap year—in the Marine Corps. She was, however, an excellent Marine in the afternoons. When colors was played at the end of the work day—only the Army has a retreat ceremony—and the flag was lowered, Penelope was a wide-awake, gung ho, John Wayne Marine.

Mycroft would have been a lousy Marine. He was not a morning cat. A world-class sleeper, he was even grumpier—if such a thing can be imagined—than Penelope in the morning. He hated it when she first stirred. He resisted when she attempted to dislodge him from his place beneath the covers next to her legs. He refused to emerge from the bed until she had at least finished her third cup of coffee. Even then, the big cat, from his customary perch on the sun-washed window sill, joined Penelope in staring moodily into space before nodding off again, his paws curled in beneath his big chest.

Fortunately, for woman and cat, Penelope had an assistant, Kathy Allen, a disgustingly cheerful and alert college student who opened the bookshop most mornings. The Empty Creek community had learned over the years that the posted hours of business for Mycroft & Company were meaningless if Penelope was expected to open the doors. Her customers soon adjusted to this little idiosyncrasy, however, just as they adjusted to the quirks and peculiarities of the rest of the Empty Creek citizenry—a populace now depleted by one.

The Queen was dead. Long live the Queen.

Penelope frowned as she remembered the initial shock of the night before, still seeing the glint from the knife. Poor Louise. She didn't deserve such a gruesome fate. No one did.

Mycroft fell from his perch, a frequent occurrence. Penelope told him time and time again that he was too big for the window sill, but he refused to believe her. He landed with a thud and quickly looked around in embarrassment to see if anyone had noticed. Penelope shook her head. Mycroft nonchalantly washed one paw.

Penelope went to the counter and poured another cup of coffee and carried it and the telephone back to the kitchen table, then quickly dialed Laney's number.

"Oh, Penelope," Laney cried, "I just heard. I feel so terrible about what I said yesterday. These awful little men just left. . . ."

"Two detectives who look like Tweedledee and Tweedledum?"

"How did you know?"

"I met them last night."

"Penelope, it's terrible. They practically accused us of murdering poor Louise. Thank God, Wally and I were together the entire evening playing Kidnapped Princess."

Yes, thank God, Penelope thought, although she did not want to hear the details of Kidnapped Princess. Laney had an amazingly inventive mind when it came to sexual fantasies. Maybe she did write smut after all.

"I didn't tell Tweedledee and Tweedledum what you said yesterday."

"You know I couldn't kill anyone anyway, not even poor Louise."

"Laney, I have to go. I'll see you later."

Penelope was relieved that Laney—and Wally—had been eliminated as suspects. Quite a few people had been discounted already—those who were in the Double B or at the movies, herself, Andy, and Mycroft. There were only a few thousand people left to eliminate. Detecting was quite simple, really.

After hanging up, Penelope went to the front door, hesitating a moment before flinging it open.

The yellow tape hung forlornly in a loose circle around the spot where Louise Fletcher had died. A dark and crusted pool of blood marked the exact place of her demise, only some fifteen hours before. By now, Louise had probably had time to reorganize the heavenly choir. It would be just like her to tell God where He had gone wrong. Penelope could imagine Louise issuing orders, a celestial drill instructor. 'Angels, fall in and straighten up. Archangels over here. Heavenly Choir, can't you sing something else for a change?' Penelope had to smile at the thought. Life in Empty Creek was certainly going to be dull without Louise, but it was going to be a whole lot livelier in heaven. Oh, my yes.

Mycroft followed Penelope into the yard. Actually, it was not so much a yard as a cultivated extension of the desert. Instead of grass, there was sand. Instead of flowers, there were cactus, large and small, including a saguaro, its arms stretched high in supplication. The walkway was lined with rocks. All of this territory was Mycroft's fiefdom, and he ruled it fearlessly, as he had the night before when Clyde the coyote pup had challenged his authority.

Penelope and Mycroft inspected the crime scene together. Mycroft circled the blood warily, sniffing distastefully, looking up to report that yes, it was human blood. Penelope agreed.

They extended their inspection beyond the area marked by the tape. Mycroft, now free to play with that yellow curiosity, ignored it entirely, of course. Isn't that just like a cat, Penelope thought, or a human?

While Penelope dealt with the larger picture, finding nothing but the multitude of footprints left behind by the invading army of investigators, Mycroft peered beneath the sage and circled the base of the saguaro, distracted only momentarily by the chirping sparrow sitting high atop the cactus. He found nothing that would aid them in the investigation.

Frustrated, they returned to the house to get ready for work.

Pert, perky Kathy Allen idolized Penelope, looking upon her friend and employer as a combination of Wonder Woman, Superwoman, and Batwoman. Except for that particular failing, Penelope viewed Kathy as sane and normal, at least as normal as a young woman could be in Empty Creek.

After opening Mycroft & Company promptly at ten and brewing a pot of coffee for Penelope's eventual arrival, Kathy pulled her worn copy of *Merry Wives of Windsor* from her book bag and began practicing archaic English because she dearly wanted to move up the hierarchy at the annual Elizabethan Faire, a lusty celebration of spring at which, for the past two seasons, she had been a serving wench, pursued by Timothy Scott, a young poet and juggler who wandered the imitation green fields of England composing odes to the luscious alabaster mounds of pleasure that plumped alluringly above Kathy's bodice.

Now, however, Kathy aspired to a more genteel role than serving wench, rushing hither and yon dispensing flagons of ale all afternoon long and slapping Timothy's wandering hands away. She wanted to be Mistress Kathleen Allen and prepared for her new role, modeling her character after Mistress Anne Page of Shakespeare's *Wives*.

Kathy wandered through the aisles of Mycroft & Company, play in hand, reading aloud—"Sirrah . . . forsooth . . . I pray thee . . . Ay, indeed, sir. . . ."

Stopping before the poster of Stormy's latest film, which was probably playing as the third film on a triple feature in a Southern drive-in movie somewhere, Kathy asked, "Will't please your worship to come in, sir?"

In response to her suitor, Mistress Anne Page replied coyly, "Not I, sir; pray you, keep on." Kathy fluttered her eyelashes at Stormy, before skipping over a few pages to her favorite line which she had, in fact, delivered to Timothy Scott only the night before.

"Alas, I had rather be set quick i' the earth," Kathy cried, "And bowl'd to death with turnips."

This proclamation was delivered when Timothy prostrated himself and begged Kathy to love him as he loved her. "Come, to my bower," Timothy cried, "and let our limbs intertwine to the music of love."

Kathy smiled at the memory. Timothy was quite sweet really, but only a boy, and unfortunately for both of them, Kathy was secretly in love with Harris Anderson III. Despite the early hour, she longingly imagined intertwining her limbs with those of the newspaper editor, feeling his tender caresses on her plump and luscious alabaster mounds as she willingly showered him with kisses. Kathy was ad-libbing soulfully when Mrs. Eleanor Burnham entered Mycroft & Company.

"Come, Master Harris, take me to your bower, I would lie with thee tonight."

"Indeed," Mrs. Burnham harumphed.

In testimony to her good breeding, Kathy immediately blushed. "I didn't hear you come in, Mrs. Burnham."

"So I gathered, young lady, so I gathered."

"How may I help you?"

"You can't," Mrs. Burnham said. "Not unless you have information about the goings on of yesterday evening. I wish to speak to Miss Penelope Warren."

"She's not in yet. What happened yesterday?"

"I have it on excellent authority that Mrs. Louise Fletcher was gunned down right on Miss Penelope Warren's doorstep."

"Good God! Is Penelope all right?"

"Quite all right," Mrs. Burnham replied, but cruelly added, "She had that newspaper editor to comfort her.

There was a great deal of comfort offered, I understand."

Thank God, Penelope was safe, but . . .

Mrs. Burnham nattered on about organized crime, a hail of bullets—all having to do with some casino—but Kathy was not listening, overcome with jealousy as she was at the thought of her lover lavishing affection on Penelope.

"I'll be back, young lady," Mrs. Burnham declared. "You tell Penelope that."

"Yes, ma'am, I will."

"And save yourself for marriage, young lady. Approach the altar in virginal white. You'll never regret it."

Mrs. Burnham marched out, leaving Kathy to fret and worry, in a muddle about Penelope, whom she loved, Harris, whom she also loved, and poor Timothy who was consumed with unrequited passion. Not long after, she was consumed with guilt for barely having thought of poor Mrs. Fletcher.

"I'll enter a convent," Kathy cried.

When Kathy finally heard Penelope's key in the door, she ran to the back and greeted her with concern.

"Thank God, you're here. Finally. Penelope, how awful. Is it true? I just can't imagine how horrible it must have been. Poor Mrs. Fletcher. I was afraid you'd never get here. I wanted to call, but I know how you are in the mornings. What happened? Are you all right? Hi, Mycroft."

Penelope fell back when struck by the torrent of questions. "I see the desert telegraph has been at work."

"Everyone is talking about it."

"What have you heard?"

"Just that poor Mrs. Fletcher was gunned down on your doorstep and—"

"Gunned down . . . ?"

"—and that you would have been killed too if you'd arrived just a minute earlier."

"Gunned down?"

"Mrs. Burnham was in earlier and said you'd found Mrs. Fletcher's bullet-riddled body on your porch. Blood everywhere. Windows shot out. She said it was organized crime—because Mrs. Fletcher didn't want a casino."

"Casino? What casino?"

"I don't know. That's what she said. Casino. I wasn't really listening."

"Mrs. Burnham, as usual, doesn't know what she's talking about. As an informed town crier, Eleanor Burnham would make an excellent plumber's apprentice."

"Mrs. Fletcher isn't dead then?"

"Oh, she's dead all right, but she wasn't gunned down in a hail of bullets. She was apparently killed by a rather large stainless steel, chopping knife with a penny glued to its handle."

"Apparently?"

"Probably," Penelope said, "but we are, as they say, awaiting the results of the autopsy to determine the cause of death."

"Well, you still could have been hurt."

Business was brisk, a steady parade of customers seeking gossip rather than reading material for the weekend, but each felt duty bound to purchase a novel after hearing Penelope's tale. It's an interesting variation on the barter system, Penelope thought. I tell them a horrifying story. They buy another story in exchange. What a terrible way to drum up business!

However, Penelope noticed that a good many of her customers immediately went next door to the video store, their newly purchased novels tucked under their arms.

As promised, Mrs. Burnham returned to demand all the lurid details. Penelope provided the facts of the case as she knew them, which was not really enough for Mrs. Burnham, who seemed more than a little disappointed that there had been no hail of bullets.

"The only guns last night were those carried by the police," Penelope said. "The murder was committed with a knife and by a single assailant. Period."

"That's all you know. Gambling. Mark my words. Gamblers are involved." Mrs. Burnham huffed out without bothering to make a purchase.

"That woman is impossible," Penelope said.

Mycroft, who had fled to the safety of Kathy's lap for the duration of Mrs. Burnham's visit, agreed. He looked after the woman with disdain.

Kathy, her legs now asleep, sighed with relief when Mycroft leaped down. "God, you're fat, Mikey. It's all those lima beans."

Mycroft mewed as he ambled off to the back room to see if his food dish had a few limas in it. He wasn't really hungry, but he needed a little something to sustain body and soul until dinner.

Standing and stretching, Kathy said, innocently but with an aching heart, "It's a good thing Andy was there to be with you."

"It wasn't much of a Valentine's Day, though," Penelope replied. "We fooled around a little bit, but

51

murder is a real cold shower when it comes to romance. What did you and Timothy do?"

Kathy's heart leaped. Their limbs had not intertwined after all, not much anyway. "Oh, the usual. He wanted to fool around. I fended him off."

"Was there another tribute to your bosom?"

Kathy smiled ruefully as she looked down at breasts concealed beneath a shapeless fuzzy pink sweater. "Yes. Now, they're 'Twin fruits to be nibbled delicately in the orchards of love.' " She blushed.

"Your breasts have inspired more poetry than Helen's face launched ships. Can you just imagine what Timothy would do if he had fallen in love with Debbie rather than you? He'd be writing about watermelons in the fields of love."

" 'The greatest teats in all of Christendom on this poor serving wench.' That was another line."

"Oh, Lord. I suppose the boy means well."

"He needs a cold shower."

"How is Mistress Allen coming?"

"Well, and I thank thee, lady."

"Exeunt all. I'm going to see Chief Fowler. If anyone else comes seeking the lurid details, tell them I've gone on a pilgrimage to Jerusalem."

"Aye, dear lady," Mistress Allen said, staying in character.

"Shall I bring something back for lunch?"

"Chicken taco salad from The Duck Pond?" Kathy asked hopefully, dropping her role entirely. The thought of a chicken taco salad from The Duck Pond was enough to send her into ecstasy. That was the bad thing about Elizabethan England. No tacos.

* * *

52

Mycroft Holmes, the older and smarter brother of Sherlock, was one of the founders of the Diogenes Club, where no member was permitted to take the slightest notice of another and talking was strictly forbidden, save for within the confines of the Strangers' Room.

Unlike his namesake, however, Mycroft Holmes Warren was not a member of the Diogenes Club. He grumped around, complaining loudly and registering his displeasure at being left behind by knocking over a small plaster cast of the elder Holmes, a stout replica he didn't like on the best of days as demonstrated by the number of chips and scars on the statuette.

Mycroft was a most forgiving cat, though, and when Kathy went to the emergency supply of lima beans—she knew just how to placate him—he galloped into the back room and twirled happily around her feet in a dance step executed by only cats as electric can openers whirr. There was no sweeter sound in all the world. *Penelope who?*

Penelope, unaware that she had been forsaken for a cat's equivalent of thirty pieces of silver—half-a-dozen big fat lima beans—was ushered into Captain Fowler's office by Peggy Norton, a young and petite police officer with a big gun on her hip.

"Good afternoon, John."

"Penelope."

The commanding officer of Empty Creek's constabulary looked tired. The lines in his face were deeper than Penelope remembered from the night before. Murder was a difficult business, she supposed, even more so when the victim was the most prominent woman in town.

"Have you discovered anything?"

"My people have been out all day. No one saw anything. No one heard anything. The killer was lucky, luckier than we've been."

"There must be something."

"Oh, there's something, all right. The question is, will we ever find it. Half the people in town have a motive. Louise Fletcher was not our most popular citizen."

"Only the richest," Penelope said. "Who stands to gain by her death? Her husband?"

"Apparently, the will leaves everything to Herbert, but you were right. He was at the movies. He went to two, in fact. Verified by the girl in the ticket booth and the people at the concession stand. It seems Herbert has a weakness for popcorn. He bought two jumbo boxes, one for each movie. Even came out for licorice during the second film. Herbert Fletcher may benefit from his wife's death, but he isn't the killer."

"How did he take Louise's death?"

Fowler shrugged. "Outwardly, he displayed all of the proper signs of disbelief, shock, grief. . . ."

"Inwardly?" Penelope asked.

"I think he was relieved to be rid of her. Queen Louise was a royal pain in the ass. I can only imagine what it must have been like to be married to her."

"Herbert, do this. Herbert, do that." Penelope was silent for a moment. "Maybe he just got tired of it and snapped."

"And what about his alibi?"

"Oh, that."

"Do you know how big those jumbo boxes of popcorn are? I couldn't eat one, much less two. I'd remember someone who ate two in the same afternoon."

"It does seem a stumper," Penelope agreed. "I wonder if he puts butter on it. All that fat and cholesterol. And salt. It couldn't be healthy."

"Healthier than a chopping knife in the back."

"I wonder what she was doing at my house."

"Coincidence, probably."

"Yes, probably. May I look at the reports?"

Fowler nodded wearily. "A fresh eye might be good. Maybe you'll see something we've missed."

Penelope spent an hour reading through the various reports. Her annoyance with Detective Lawrence Burke returned once again when she read his record of her interrogation. "In my opinion," Burke had printed in large block letters, "this female individual is hostile and should be regarded as a suspect."

"This super sleuth is stupid and should be regarded as a menace to society," Penelope exclaimed.

Sam Connors, who was sitting at a desk across the room, laughed. "Came to Larry's report, didn't you? I've been waiting."

"The man's certifiable."

"Oh, Larry's a good enough cop. He's just lacking a few of the social graces."

"I'll say."

Penelope read on, wading through the ponderous police prose so common to crime reports, but contrary to expectations, her fresh eye found absolutely nothing.

She replaced everything just as she had found it.

"See you at the Double B later?" Sam asked. "I'll buy you a beer. Make up for super sleuth."

"That would be nice." Penelope smiled. "Can I ask you a question, Sam?"

"Sure."

"Whatever did you tell Debbie about those scars?"

Sam blushed. "Shrapnel wounds," he mumbled.

"What?"

"Shrapnel wounds," Sam said, still blushing. "I told her they were shrapnel wounds."

"You were never in a war."

"From when I was in the bomb squad. She asked how I got them in the butt."

"I think running away from a bomb is a very sensible thing to do," Penelope said.

"You won't tell her the truth?"

"Cop terrorized by cat. No one would believe it."

"Anything happen in my absence?" Penelope asked when she returned to Mycroft & Company bearing two chicken taco salads.

"Mr. Fletcher came by," Kathy said. "He wants to see you. He said it was important."

CHAPTER FOUR

Leaving Kathy to close up, Penelope and Mycroft postponed their evening visit to the Double B and drove out to the Raney Ranch instead. She wondered if Herb Fletcher would change the name of it now that he stood to inherit everything. The Fletcher Ranch just wouldn't be the same.

Set back against the mountains on the edge of government land, the property had been in Louise Fletcher's family for generations, although it had never been a working ranch except when Louise had turned to breeding Arabian horses. Josh Raney, her grandfather, had made his money in printing. Her father—Josh, Jr.—had maintained the printing business and had increased the family fortune through shrewd speculation in the stock market. An only child, Louise had inherited everything. Through her own crafty speculations, she had made it grow.

When Penelope stopped in front of the large rambling Southwestern house, Mycroft leaped through the door before she could stop him. "Mycroft, damn it, wait in the jeep. Not everyone likes cats, you know."

Mycroft didn't know, and didn't much care, so he

marched up the walkway to the house, stopping once to look back over his shoulder as if to ask, Aren't you coming?

Penelope was, indeed, following, determined to snatch up the recalcitrant beast and lock him in the jeep, when Herbert Fletcher opened the door and stepped out onto the large veranda.

"It's all right, Penelope. I like cats."

See, Miss Smarty Pants.

Mycroft went right up to Fletcher to sniff him out.

Herbert Fletcher was a dandy. Rumors had circulated for years about his various mistresses, supposedly kept in luxury with Louise Fletcher's money, but no one had actually caught Fletcher in a dalliance. He was a tall man and still handsome, with all of his hair and his own teeth, a fact he occasionally pointed out while holding forth at the bar of the Double B. He was sixty-two or sixty-three, Penelope thought, and he had not yet begun to stoop. He wore gray slacks that matched his hair, gleaming cordovan loafers with tassels, and a blue silk shirt. His ensemble was crowned with a red ascot.

Penelope thought it an odd touch for a man in mourning. Indeed, it was. Penelope hadn't seen an ascot for years, not since an aging British Council teacher had tried to seduce her in Harar. That ancient and exotic walled Moslem city in eastern Ethiopia had always reminded Penelope of Conrad's "whited sepulcher."

Penelope drifted away for a moment, remembering Robert Sidney-Veine's attempts to seduce her person with both pleasure and amusement. Robert would be about Herbert's age now. Years ago she had found it difficult to take his enticements seriously, not when he perpetually greeted her with "I say, Penelope, old girl." The old girl had been all of twenty-four at the time.

But Robert had remained persistent over the years. Penelope still received lurid love letters from him, each typed on his old Olivetti portable, each invariably beginning with, "I hope this finds you in good health and unmarried." The envelopes—testimonies to the professional expatriate—were postmarked Bahrain or Ghana or Qatar or the United Arab Emirates, but the old satyr continually threatened to come to the colonies and chase her through the desert until she succumbed to his entreaties. Penelope giggled at the thought of running naked through the desert with Robert Sidney-Veine in hot and furious pursuit. That would be a sight for Empty Creek to behold.

Then she frowned. It was strange that Robert hadn't written for Valentine's Day. It wasn't like him to let an opportunity pass him by. Still, the international mails were probably even worse than the United States Postal Service, if such a thing were possible. "I hope the old boy's all right," Penelope whispered.

"I beg your pardon."

"I'm sorry, Mr. Fletcher, I was thinking of something else."

"Yes, we're all a little distracted today, I suppose. It's a terrible thing." Fletcher sniffed, as though on the verge of tears. "Come in, please, come in."

"Thank you."

Mycroft entered the living room, a comfortable place filled with Southwestern style furniture, and explored, leaving a wake of destruction in his path, an excellent sign that he had found Herbert Fletcher wanting in some critical personality trait important to cats. Embarrassed, Penelope trailed along behind Mycroft, picking up the magazines and books he dislodged from end tables and coffee tables—*National Geographic,* of course, *Arizona Highways,* of course, Arizona guidebooks and histories, of course. They were all *de rigueur* in Empty Creek.

"I'm sorry, Mr. Fletcher. He isn't like this usually."

"I suppose cats are just as upset by violent death as the rest of us," Fletcher said, "despite their wild and cruel instincts."

"You said it was important."

"Do you know why my wife came to your house?"

"I have no idea, Mr. Fletcher. I thought perhaps you could tell me."

"Please, call me Herb. Mr. Fletcher sounds so formal."

"Very well, Herb, but I still have no idea what Louise was doing out there. Probably she was riding by . . . met her killer. I don't know. I just don't know."

"Yes, well, I just thought . . ." His voice trailed off.

Penelope wondered what Herbert Fletcher thought. "Do you know why your wife was riding past my house?"

"I have no idea, but Louise never did anything coincidentally. It was still raining when I left for the movies. She was napping, so I left a note for her. She worried so if she didn't know where I was. I expected her to be here when I got back. It was such a shock when that moronic detective arrived. . . ."

"Lawrence Burke?"

"Yes. That was his name. Do you know him?"

"We've met."

"Well, he wanted to go through Louise's papers. I suppose he was looking for one of those ghastly in-the-event-of-my-death letters. Naturally he didn't find one. Louise and I were quite happy. He took her address book." Fletcher began sobbing.

Penelope looked at Mycroft who was sullenly unmoved by the display of grief, though cats are supposed to be sympathetic to pain. Mycroft turned away from her, so Penelope went to Herbert Fletcher to offer what comfort she could. She sat beside him on the couch and patted his shoulder. "I know this is . . ."

Fletcher turned suddenly and buried his face on Penelope's shoulder. She patted his back. He cried louder and held her tightly. "Louise," he moaned. "Louise."

The old lecher's trying to cop a feel, Penelope thought uncharitably and was immediately ashamed of herself. After all, the Fletchers had been married forever.

Fletcher broke away and reached into a pocket to withdraw a silk handkerchief. "I'm sorry, Penelope. I've been trying to remain stoic, but this is so upsetting. I don't know what I'm going to do without Louise. You do understand?"

"Of course. If there's anything I can do . . ."

"Thank you. That's very kind. If you remember anything, anything at all, you'll tell me? I want Louise's killer brought to justice."

"I want that too, Herb, believe me. You said that Detective Burke—"

"That oaf!"

"Yes, we agree on Detective Burke, but did he look closely at Louise's papers, that sort of thing?"

"Not really. He saw me as a suspect. Me. Herbert Fletcher. Can you imagine?"

"No, I can't." Penelope said. She hesitated. "Would you mind if I looked through Louise's things? Perhaps I might spot something that might lead us to the killer."

"Of course not. I'm sure there's nothing to find, though. I've been over everything a thousand times in my head, but you're welcome to take a stab at it. Oh, God," he cried, "what a poor choice of words."

"There, there," Penelope said, looking to Mycroft for assistance, distraction. The cat turned disdainfully away. Thanks a lot.

"I'd rather you didn't look now," Fletcher said. "You understand. I'd rather be alone right now."

"Of course."

"Come tomorrow afternoon. Stay for dinner, if you like. Our . . . my cook does an excellent enchilada."

"I'd like that," Penelope lied, "but I have plans. A date." Because she worked on Saturdays, she and Andy usually went out on Sunday night, although he hadn't asked her yet. "But I'm free in the afternoon."

Herbert Fletcher nodded grimly.

"Well, you were a big help," Penelope said to Mycroft when they were in the jeep again heading for the Double B. "Why didn't you like him?"

Mycroft growled softly as he stood, paws against the windshield, staring out at the passing desert.

After dealing with Herb Fletcher, Penelope really didn't feel like stopping at the Double B, but she had promised Sam she would. Perhaps a beer or two in more convivial company might have a cheering effect.

It certainly had that impact on Mycroft. He brightened considerably when Pete poured his nonalcoholic libation, drinking it down eagerly, looking around afterward with flecks of foam on his whiskers. Mycroft burped. He was a very satisfied cat as he washed his face.

Penelope, however, was besieged by those Empty Creek residents who had not passed through the happy portals of Mycroft & Company during the afternoon. They crowded around her, alternately demanding details and expressing concern for her state of mind. Those who wanted the grisly facts far outnumbered those who offered consolation. Penelope pressed against the bar, looking around at the eager faces.

Sam rescued her. "Make way," he cried. "This lady wants a drink."

Penelope followed him gratefully to the table where Debbie waited, taking her break.

"Hi, guys," Penelope said, throwing herself into a chair.

"What a circus," Debbie said. "You'd think they had nothing better to do. That's all anyone has talked about all day."

"That's it," Penelope declared. "The next time someone is murdered at my place, I'm calling a press conference. I'll make a statement, answer a few questions, and then do my Ronald Reagan imitation."

"What's that?" Debbie asked innocently.

"Pretend I can't hear," Penelope said, cupping her hand around her ear.

"Try not to let it upset you," Debbie advised.

"I've just come from Herb Fletcher. He's the one who's upset. I'm just depressed."

"What did he want with you?" Sam asked.

"How do you know I didn't want something from him?"

"I'm a cop."

Debbie smiled fondly at Sam. "And a good one, sweetie."

"Yes, I am," he agreed. "So what did he want?"

"He asked the same question I've been asking myself. What was Louise doing at my place?"

Sam shrugged. "Coincidence."

"I wonder," Penelope said. "I wonder. Herb said Louise never did anything coincidentally. Anyway, I'll see him tomorrow afternoon. He gave me permission to go through Louise's papers."

"I thought Larry Burke already did that."

"Really," Penelope said.

"I suppose it wouldn't hurt to have a second opinion."

The Double B was crowded for the Saturday night lull between the end of the work day and the beginning of the evening's festivities. George Strait sang from the juke box, trying unsuccessfully to overcome the bursts of laughter, the shouts of long-running arguments, the constant clatter of pool balls.

As Penelope looked around the large room, she wondered if Louise Fletcher's killer was present. The Double B was certainly filled with suspects. No one had liked Louise very much.

"I've got to go, honey," Debbie said. "What would you like, Penelope?"

"A glass of wine, thanks."

"Aren't you afraid to leave me alone with the second prettiest woman in Empty Creek?" Sam asked.

"I think you know what's good for you," Debbie replied. "I'll be right back, Penelope. Whack him a good one if he gets fresh."

"Don't worry," Penelope said, smiling. "I will."

Just then Laney swooped into the bar, looking for

all the world like one of her heroines. She was followed by Wally who had a thin black cigar clamped in his mouth. He didn't smoke; the cigar was to make him look like Clint Eastwood playing the Man with No Name. Spotting Penelope, Laney rushed over. Wally trailed behind, his boots clumping on the hardwood floor.

"Penelope," Laney cried. "Is there any news?"

"Where have you been?" Penelope asked. Laney usually had the latest gossip before anyone else.

Laney blushed. "We spent a quiet day. Didn't answer the phone after we talked. Tell me everything."

Penelope thought Wally must have locked her in a closet or tied her to the bed. That was the only way to keep Laney from answering a telephone—or making calls to her vast network of informants. Maybe his lasso was good for something after all. Penelope looked at Wally with new respect. He might have hidden talents.

"Hi," he said crinkling his eyes.

"Hi, Wally." Penelope tried to crinkle back. That was hard to do.

"Tell, tell, tell," Laney commanded.

"It'll be in the newspaper. You can read all about it. Andy probably knows more than I do anyway." The next issue of the *Empty Creek News Journal* would not be out until Wednesday.

"Penelope!"

"Oh, all right, but there's not much to tell."

After extracting everything she could, Laney dragged Wally off to the dance floor. Penelope sighed with relief. Laney could be so exhausting.

As could the prime murder suspects—two of the five members of the Empty Creek City Council—who next descended upon Penelope. Councilwomen Meredith Stevens and Freda Alsberg now hovered over the table.

"Good evening," Meredith said.

"Evening, Merry. Freda."

"May we join you?"

Penelope nodded in assent, although Merry and Freda were among the last individuals she wanted to be with that night.

An attractive woman of forty-five, Merry Stevens was a hippie who had never quite recovered from the sixties and the heady days of living in Haight-Ashbury while leading the revolution at San Francisco State. She wore granny glasses, granny dresses, and her black hair fell straight to her waist.

Freda, on the other hand, could have been a Valkyrie, one of those handmaidens to Odin who choose the heroes to be slain in battle and then conduct them to Valhalla. Her blond hair disguised the strands of gray and fell down her back in a long single braid.

"Good evening, Officer Connors," the two women chorused as they sat down.

"Council ladies," Sam said. "May I get you something to drink?"

Of course, Merry ordered red wine, the standard potable for aging hippies. Freda asked for a Gibson, very dry, very chilled.

Sam went off to join Debbie at the bar. Penelope longed to follow.

"We were concerned about you," Merry said. "We want to offer our condolences."

"Wouldn't they be more appropriate for Herb Fletcher?"

"Oh, we'll do that, of course," Freda said. "But you

were a victim too. It must have been a dreadful experience for you."

"I've celebrated Valentine's Day in better ways," Penelope said.

"We've talked to Chief Fowler, of course," Freda said, "but we wondered if you have anything to add about the terrible event last night?"

"Chief Fowler knows more than I do, I'm sure." Penelope was puzzled by their interest. Both women had hated Louise Fletcher. Louise had detested them.

Merry and Louise had been bitter enemies despite their obvious agreement on so many social and slow-growth issues. Penelope didn't know why, save that Louise possessed the ability to test even the patience of Job.

But Penelope knew, or thought she knew, why Freda and Louise had despised each other so. One of the old rumors that still swirled about Empty Creek claimed Louise Fletcher had threatened to expose Freda's infidelities if she ran for reelection. Nothing had come of that . . . even if true. But the women had once engaged in a memorable shouting match during the public comment portion of a city council meeting.

Penelope had been present, and she remembered the incident vividly because Freda had threatened Louise Fletcher with a lawsuit, shouting, "And if that doesn't shut you up, I'll find something else that will."

A chopping knife between the shoulder blades was an excellent means of imposing permanent silence. Perhaps Freda the Valkyrie had chosen Louise Fletcher to die in battle, escorting her to the underworld rather than Valhalla.

"So you have nothing to say about last night?" Freda persisted.

"Nothing that you don't already know."

"That's too bad," Merry said. "We hoped you might shed some light on this. We want it resolved quickly. We can't have people thinking some slasher is running wild in Empty Creek. It creates a bad image."

Penelope watched Laney and Wally. They weren't really dancing. It was public snuggling, but it was preferable to sitting around discussing Louise Fletcher's murder with Merry and Freda. Fortunately, Sam and Debbie returned to the table to distribute drinks all around, a welcome distraction.

Then Penelope brightened when Andy entered the Double B. She stood up and waved. "Let's dance," she suggested when he had weaved through the crowd.

"In a moment," he replied. He was distracted, scarcely noticing her presence. "I'd like to get comments from the councilwoman for Mrs. Fletcher's obituary." He pulled a reporter's notebook from an inner pocket and waited, pencil poised expectantly.

"We had our differences, of course," Merry said.

I'll say, Penelope thought, sitting down again, ready to work herself up to a good sulk.

"But I'll miss Louise greatly. Despite our differences, I counted her as a friend. Everything she did was intended to make our community a better place to live."

"Oh, yes," Freda said. "Louise Fletcher was a remarkable woman. We have lost a dear friend. Empty Creek will never be the same. The entire community mourns her passing."

It was appalling—hypocritical—to hear Merry and Freda express their deep regrets over the loss of Empty Creek's first lady.

68

"I'm going to find Mycroft," Penelope said. "Perhaps he'll dance with me."

Mycroft, however, was asleep on his bar stool.

"I'll dance with you," Sam said. "If you'd like."

"Very much, Sam. You're such a gentleman."

Gentleman, yes. Dancer, no.

Laney smiled dreamily at Penelope over Wally's shoulder. Wally was certainly in Laney's good graces—for the moment. I'll have to get her to confess all, Penelope thought, deftly avoiding Sam's left foot. Debbie waved, smiling sympathetically as Penelope led Sam around the dance floor.

"Well, what did you make of all that?" Penelope asked, shouting to be heard over the din of the music. It seemed to be George Strait night at the Double B and someone had turned the volume too loud—again.

"Merry and Freda?" Sam shouted back.

Penelope nodded. It was too much to shout.

Sam drew her close and talked into her ear. "They're trying to find out what you know. Did the same with the chief earlier. Seem a little worried to me."

Penelope drew herself up and talked right back into Sam's ear. She could smell his aftershave lotion. "I don't think they did it," Penelope said.

The music stopped.

"I don't either," Sam said, speaking quietly now, "but they had motive and opportunity. Neither of them has an alibi. They were both home alone. So they say."

Penelope glanced over at the table. Andy was sitting alone now. "It seems safe to return," she said. "Thanks for rescuing me, Sam."

"It was my pleasure."

Andy rose politely as Penelope approached. "May I have the next dance?" he asked.

His notebook was out of sight, but Penelope was not ready to forgive him yet. "I'm sorry, Andy, but Sam has rekindled my passion for men in uniform."

"He's not wearing his uniform," Andy pointed out.

"I know, but if he were . . ."

Laney bustled up to the table, hauling Wally along by his hand. "Andy, why don't you ask Penelope to dance?" she said.

"I just did, but—"

"She refused?"

"Yes, I refused. I asked him to dance before, but he wanted to talk with Merry and Freda."

"I was working," Andy protested.

"I needed rescuing. Anyone could see that."

"Fiddlesticks. The day you need rescuing, Penelope Warren, that will be . . . well . . . that will be the day," Laney declared.

"I'm going home," Penelope said. "I'm tired."

"Will I see you tomorrow?" Andy asked.

"Of course." Penelope smiled sweetly. "But you'd better leave your damned notebook at home."

"I will, I promise."

Penelope turned to Laney. "I'm going riding tomorrow. I promised Mycroft. Would Alexander like to come along?"

"I'm sure he would."

"We'll ride by then."

"I'll have the coffee on."

As Penelope went to wake up Mycroft, she heard Laney say, "You should get a uniform of some kind, Andy. Perhaps a nice cowboy outfit. Then you and Penelope could play cowboy and beautiful Indian maiden. That's one of our favorites. What you do, you see . . ."

The beautiful Indian maiden under discussion gathered up a sleepy cat and left without waiting to hear further details, although she giggled at the thought of Andy wearing boots and chaps.

Of course, she could play the beautiful Indian maiden to perfection.

CHAPTER FIVE

Penelope and Mycroft stopped to order carry-out Chinese food. For herself, Penelope chose spicy chicken, mixed vegetables, and pork fried rice. Ever since Mycroft had eaten a hot pepper by mistake, sending him racing to the water bowl, he stayed away from the spicy chicken, so Penelope ordered a bland and innocuous chicken dish for him. It was one of his favorites when mixed with liver crunchies.

Upon arriving home, Penelope felt guilty about blaming the United States Postal Service for slow delivery when, in fact, she couldn't remember the last time she had emptied her mail box. There, right on what would have been timely for Valentine's Day, was Robert Sidney-Veine's letter. The postwoman had crammed it in along with a variety of catalogs, junk mail, bills, a video tape, and a post card from Cassie who appeared to be on location somewhere in the rainy northwest.

Robert's letter was postmarked from Malawi, a southeast African backwater. When Penelope opened the envelope after pouring a glass of wine, a photograph dropped out. It was of Robert, resplendent in white knee socks, white shorts, white shirt; the epitome of British colonialism, as though the winds of change hadn't been blowing for thirty years and more. The only thing missing from Robert's tropical attire was the pith helmet. Thank God for that, Penelope thought.

He had grown a beard, a full beard tinged with gray, and looked for all the world like Sean Connery. "Mmm," Penelope said. "Sean Connery wouldn't be all bad, would he, Mikey?" She sipped her wine.

The charming and debonair 007 of the cat world purred in agreement, although his taste in companions ran more to the sleek and beautiful calico named Murphy Brown who lived down the road.

Robert stood in front of some kind of memorial. Penelope squinted to read the lettering on the monument. King's African Rifles. Shouldn't that be the Queen's African Rifles, she wondered, and that made her think of Louise Fletcher again. And Herbert. And Merry and Freda. As Mycroft would say if he were a Cheshire cat, things just get curiouser and curiouser. Or was that Alice?

" 'I hope this finds you in good health and unmarried,' " Penelope read. "Indeed," she said, as she glanced down at the photograph of the Sean Connery look-alike all decked out in tropical whites. "Indeed," she repeated, knowing that she was a sucker for beards and Sean Connery.

Penelope continued reading to find that Robert was currently enamored of a certain professor in the classics department at the university. Classics? In bloody southeast Africa. Good Lord. That was certainly new and different.

It seemed that the President for Life had decreed that the only worthwhile education was to be found in classic Greek and Latin literature. And what the President for Life wants, the President for Life gets, including a professor of classics from an American university who is apparently also a charming companion for Robert.

"But, of course, old girl," Robert wrote, "Susan can never replace you in my heart. She lacks your beauty, your grace, your vivaciousness, your wit, your sparkle, your great beauty (mentioned that, did I?), your . . . your . . . your EVERYTHING. Oh, how I long for your EVERYTHING.

"And now, darling girl, my news. At the end of the current university year (it ends in December here), I have decided to take retirement, wending my way slowly home to England for a short stay in the wretched weather of that sceptered isle, and then . . . TO THE COLONIES and that barbaric province called Arizona, doubtless inhabited by a ruthless array of savages, and brightened only by your luster.

"And, dear old Penelope, I shall play devoted pupil to your school marm."

Robert was a passionate fan of Western films, especially those of John Wayne. He had seen *Rio Bravo* seventeen times in twelve different countries, or so he claimed.

"You old rogue," Penelope said, trying to picture Robert in boots and chaps. "I must ask Laney how that game is played." Doubtless, Laney had some wonderful variations. No matter what else might be said about her, she had a delightfully wicked imagination in devising bedroom games. And all this from a woman who was too embarrassed to buy her slinky lingerie in person. Penelope still blushed whenever she recalled Laney's vivid description of Handsome Space Alien Captures Beautiful Earth Woman for Love Experiments. To Penelope, it always sounded like an X-Rated version of one of Cassie's movies.

Which led Penelope to put Robert's letter aside to be savored and answered later. She took up Cassie's post card. Cassie certainly got her money's worth from a post card, filling the message space with her tiny handwriting.

"Dear Penny," she wrote, "On location. Weather ghastly. Haven't seen the sun for days. But I get to play a homicide detective who falls in love with a serial killer (by mistake, of course) and shoots him in the end. It's not as awful as it sounds, and I have more lines than anyone else in the entire movie. It's certainly better than the dreck I'm sending you under separate cover. We wrap next week. Then I'm going to take a few days off. Thought I'd come to AZ and visit for a few days."

Good Lord, is everyone I know coming to visit? I'll have to build a bunkhouse.

"I won't be interrupting anything, will I?"

Just a murder investigation, Penelope thought.

"Anyway," Cassie continued, "I'm coming, so throw all the men out of your house (keep one Studly Do Right for me) and give Mikey a big hug. Love and lima beans to all. Cassandra."

Studly Do Right, indeed. All the women I know are sex crazed.

"Stormy's coming, Mike."

Mycroft was on the kitchen counter, sniffing at the brown paper bag that contained dinner.

"In a minute, Mike, we have to feed Char first."

Mycroft leaped from the counter to the table and watched as Penelope opened the cardboard mailing box for Cassie's latest epic.

"Oh, my goodness, Mikey, look at this."

Penelope held up *Amazon Princess and the Sword of Doom* for Mycroft's inspection. The cover showed Storm Williams brandishing a broadsword with both hands, wearing only soft leather boots and a skimpy white garment that failed to conceal any of Stormy's considerable charms.

Penelope turned the video over to see her sister displayed in still photographs. In one she was tied by her wrists and dangling over a pit filled with alligators or crocodiles—Penelope could never tell the difference—snapping at her heels. Where did this Amazon princess live anyway? In another, Cassie was tied to a stake and about to be burned. Wood rose to her hips. At least, her legs are covered, Penelope thought. The last shot saw Cassie standing over a man dressed in a wizard's uniform, her sword at his throat. Presumably, the wizard was the villain and the Amazon Princess had triumphed.

"I hope we have some popcorn left, Mikey. This is going to be a real howler. I can hardly wait to tell Laney. She can play Wizards and Amazons. Wally Wizard. What a sight to behold."

Penelope laughed and laughed, until Mycroft came over to nuzzle her cheek in concern.

"I'm okay, Mikey," she said, holding her sides, still choking with mirth. "Really."

Mycroft wasn't at all sure that his friend and mentor was all right, so as he followed her to the stables, which he would have done in any case, he stayed underfoot.

Chardonnay huffed and puffed and snorted and ate her peppermint candies. As Penelope made Char's dinner, Mycroft, looking for all the world like the Easter Rabbit himself, deserted her and went to play with the bunnies who gathered at the edge of the light to wait for their handout.

The younger rabbits watched as Mycroft began his stalk, a stealthy, slow pursuit that ended with a sudden rush. The little rabbits, who had been watching the cat the whole time, simply hopped straight up in the air, twisting in midflight to land behind Mycroft. It was a game that pleased all concerned.

Big Mike was an accomplished hunter, and he could catch them if he wanted to, of course, but he had avoided that ever since he had herded one home for Penelope. Showing off his trophy had been fine. Penelope seemed pleased with his hunting prowess. But the rabbit then adopted him, refused to leave his side, interfered with dinner by pigging out on all the liver crunchies, and when Mycroft stomped off to bed in disgust, the rabbit followed, snuggling right up to him, twitching its nose happily as it took up most of the bed. First thing in the morning, Mycroft chased the rabbit out of the house again, telling it in no uncertain terms to stick to carrots and lettuce.

Penelope gave Chardonnay her dinner and then turned to the rabbits. She always tried to bring carrots and lettuce for the cottontails, but with all of the activity the night before she had forgotten. Tonight, to make up for her lapse, she had brought extra helpings and now distributed them evenly around the green patch of lawn surrounding the water sprinkler. The cottontails skittered away from her and then shyly hopped back into the light to nibble at their delicacies.

Impatient now for his own dinner, Mycroft led Penelope back up the moonlit path to the house.

* * *

After dinner had been eaten, dishes washed, popcorn popped, and the movie inserted in the VCR, Mycroft climbed into his tub—also known as Penelope's lap—and, ignoring the *Amazon Princess and the Sword of Doom* entirely, began a long and leisurely bath. Poor Stormy. Mycroft was such a harsh critic.

The movie was a little confusing. Cassie played a Princess Leogfrith who was charged with regaining a stolen sword which possessed magical powers. When Princess Leogfrith wielded the sword, she cut wide swathes through entire armies of inept mercenaries in the employ of the wizard.

In the hands of the wizard, however, the sword's power seemed devoted to removing the already skimpy clothing of Princess Leogfrith's band of Amazons. Indeed, the Princess was the only Amazon who did not bare her breasts during the action, although she seemed to spend an inordinate amount of time plunging through one river or another, emerging to pause dramatically while the camera surveyed the amulet the Princess wore around her neck. Since the amulet also possessed magical powers, Penelope assumed that it enabled Cassie to retain her clothing.

Needless to say, the sword spent two-thirds of the movie in the hands of the wizard.

Princess Leogfrith, when not swimming raging rivers, was constantly pounced upon by the wizard's minions who swooped down from trees like so many demented bats. It always took dozens of men to subdue the plucky Princess who hacked and whacked her way through the incompetent mercenaries, spilling buckets of ketchup along the way, only to be finally overpowered and led away in chains to the wizard's torture chambers—the wizard appeared to have torture chambers for each of the four seasons. When imprisoned, Princess Leogfrith used her amulet to escape and swim another river.

Swim.

Pounce.

Back to the torture chamber.

Swim. Pounce. "This time you will not escape, my pretty little princess," the wizard gloated, despite the fact that he was half the Princess's size.

Escape she did though.

Swim. Pounce.

Just when Penelope thought she could not take another raging river, Princess Leogfrith was led to the stake in the climactic scene, her band of Amazons, all captives now, watching helplessly as she was tied to the stake and pyres of wood were piled high, high enough to conceal her long princessly legs.

As the torch was applied to the kindling and smoke began to rise, Princess Leogfrith used her magical amulet to burst her bonds and leap through the flames.

Bare-breasted Amazons fought and flailed their captors into submission. Princess Leogfrith again took possession of the sword of doom to the wild cheers of her merry little band. The wizard groveled in defeat.

Penelope thought the wizard a little dull for not figuring out that the source of all his trouble was Princess Leogfrith's amulet. But what the hell, it was not her movie. Thank God.

Penelope applauded the credits loudly, awakening Mycroft who had fallen asleep twenty minutes into the epic adventure. As Cassie always said, "The checks clear the bank."

Then, still chuckling, Penelope, accompanied by Mycroft, went outside to sit on the porch. She pulled her windbreaker closed. The night was cold but clear, and looking up into the sky, she could see all the way to heaven, the path lighted by stars.

Everything was right with the world.

Or would be if Louise Fletcher hadn't died almost at the very spot where Penelope and Mycroft were sitting. Penelope shuddered and stood up. "Let's go to bed, Mikey."

Always ready to catch sixty or eighty winks—forty was never enough for a healthy cat—Mycroft agreed, standing and stretching languidly before following Penelope into the house.

Penelope fell asleep as soon as Mycroft had finished kneading the bed covers to his satisfaction and finally settled down for the night.

She slept with a slight smile on her face. An observer might conclude that this woman deserved her hard-earned rest after a long day of righteous labor, but in reality the smile was the result of Sean Connery's attentions to her.

He wore boots, jeans, chaps, a plaid Western shirt, a scarf around his neck, and a big hat. His spurs jingled as he slowly advanced, removing the hat in a courtly gesture and saying, "Howdy, ma'am."

In fact, Sean kept saying "Howdy, ma'am" over and over again, like a broken record. It was rather tedious, but Penelope was willing to endure a modicum or two of tedium to see what would happen next.

Her "sleeping" smile grew broader with each step and each "Howdy, ma'am."

And then, sometime during the night, the telephone rang.

It rang for a long time before Penelope could drag

herself away from Sean and slumber. She finally answered with a mumbled hello which came out something like, "Humph?"

She listened for a few moments, said, "Humph" again, replaced the receiver, and went back to Sean Connery who said, "Howdy, ma'am" as he removed his spurs, hopping from one foot to the other. Perhaps this was going to get interesting after all.

Early the next morning—for Penelope anyway—she saddled Chardonnay and tried to remember her dream of the night before. It was nagging at her, but the harder she tried to remember, the more elusive the dream became. She finally mounted Chardonnay, ensured that Mycroft was snug in his saddlebag, and trotted off to Laney's to pick up Alexander.

Penelope had discovered that Mycroft liked horseback riding in the way she had discovered everything else about the big cat. He wheedled and cajoled and made such a pest of himself that Penelope finally gave in to what she thought a very foolish request, only to be proven wrong.

On the occasion of his first ride on Chardonnay, Penelope told Mycroft, "You're not going to like it. Trust me on this one." But when Char had been saddled and bridled, Mycroft leaped to the saddle—Penelope thought it a pretty damned good leap for such a fat cat—and refused to move until Penelope prepared a saddlebag for him.

Mycroft took to riding immediately and didn't complain once on the way to Laney's, where Penelope headed to show off her strange cat.

And then when Alexander saw Mycroft looking so smug and self-satisfied in his saddlebag, he yipped and yapped and yammered until Penelope was forced to deposit him in the opposite one, where he stood, grinning and waiting for the breeze to ruffle his whiskers.

Even the taciturn Wally had been amazed and had laughed out loud while Laney clapped with delight and then ran for her camera.

Penelope could only shake her head. "You're both weird," she told the animals. Chardonnay snorted and pawed at the dirt. Penelope smiled. "You're just as weird as they are. Happy now?"

Yep.

The equestrian cat and terrier had been much photographed and even written up in the Sunday magazines. Andy had authored a long feature about Mike and Alex and Char. Local television reporters had done human interest stories. The three animals were quite famous in Arizona, and Penelope fully expected Mike Wallace or Ed Bradley or Lesley Stahl to show up on the doorstep one day with a "60 Minutes" camera crew.

Wally was practicing his fast draw with Laney when Penelope arrived and swung down off Chardonnay. Laney clapped while Wally drew the heavy revolver, trying to get it between her hands before she could bring her hands together. Penelope remembered seeing it in an old Western movie, but whoever did it in the film was better than Wally.

"Thank, God, you're here," Laney cried. "I've been clapping for an hour."

"Howdy, ma'am," Wally said.

Penelope pointed a finger at him. "Sean Connery!" she exclaimed.

"Whatever you say, Penelope," Wally said, making his eyes crinkle again.

How did he do that? "No," Penelope said. "I dreamed about Sean Connery last night, but I couldn't remember. He kept saying, 'Howdy, ma'am.' "

Alexander twirled around Penelope's feet, barking furiously.

"I can't imagine Sean Connery saying, 'Howdy, ma'am,' " Laney said.

"Well, he did. It was my dream, so he could say anything he wanted. It was driving me crazy, trying to remember. It's a relief—knowing."

But it wasn't. As soon as Penelope remembered the dream, something else started nagging at her. "Hi, Alex," she said, still wondering what it could be. Something had bumped through her night. She scooped up the little dog and put him in his saddle-bag. Chardonnay twitched her tail at Alex. That shut him up. Alex knew Chardonnay didn't like all the dogly racket, but he nipped at her tail anyway just to show that he wasn't intimidated. It was a friendly nip, though. He really wouldn't know what to do if he suddenly found himself with a mouthful of horse tail.

"Want some coffee?" Laney asked.

"Sure."

Penelope and Laney sat in the shade while Wally continued with his fast draws.

Penelope told her friend about Cassie's visit and about her sister's latest movie.

"Hey, sweetie," Laney hollered when Penelope had finished. "You want me to get you a wizard outfit?"

"Whatcha all talking about?"

"Stormy's new movie. I think you'll like it. Stormy's

83

coming for a visit, and we're gonna have a Storm Williams film festival."

"Okay by me," Wally said, whipping the revolver out. "Bam!" he said.

Alex looked expectantly at Penelope. His ears twitched hopefully. "I'd better go," Penelope said. "Alex looks like he's about to wet his pants again." On his first ride, Alex had been so excited that he'd had a little accident. Well, maybe not so little. Upon returning home, Mycroft had disgustedly tried to bury Alex's half of the saddlebags.

"I'll have brunch ready when you get back."

"Sounds great," Penelope said. "See you later, Wally."

Riding into the desert was one of Penelope's great pleasures. Even her menagerie respected the solemnity of those moments when they left civilization behind.

The bedeviling and evasive business that remained from the night did not mar Penelope's pleasure at riding into the unspoiled land.

The day was bright and clear, the sky was cloudless, and the air crisp with the last vestiges of winter. A big jackrabbit watched solemnly as they passed, streaking away at Alex's single bark. Alex then ducked back into his saddlebag.

Chardonnay climbed effortlessly up the winding trail. Birds filled the air with their lilting melodies, and Penelope leaned forward to pat Chardonnay's neck. "God, isn't it wonderful?" she cried happily.

Only when she had turned Chardonnay and started back down the trail did she suddenly remember what had been nagging at her all day.

Someone had called last night.

"You and that stupid cat stay away from Herbert Fletcher," a woman's voice had warned.

Which, of course, Penelope had no intention of doing.

CHAPTER SIX

"Whoa!"

Stunned with the sudden recollection, Penelope drew Chardonnay to a halt. As Char reached for the leaves on a stubby little tree, Penelope automatically backed the horse away. Char shook her head impatiently. What's wrong with a little snack?

Penelope had heard the warning distinctly.

You and that stupid cat stay away from Herbert Fletcher.

That's what the woman had said. Had she added an "Or else!" Penelope didn't think so. The "or else" had been definitely implied, however. It was not a warning. It was a threat. And that angered Penelope.

Sitting high in the hills above Empty Creek, Penelope saw the vast panorama of her desert community. A red hot air balloon appeared from behind Crying Woman Mountain. It was followed by another and then another, until the sky was decorated by a dozen or more brightly colored balloons—red and green and blue—all floating serenely on their peaceful journey, like Christmas ornaments hung on a blue sky.

From a distance on a clear Sunday morning, the little town looked serene as well. But now someone had betrayed Empty Creek, killing Louise Fletcher, warning Penelope away, calling Mycroft stupid. Someone down there was a killer.

Did I dream the telephone call?

Penelope turned in the saddle and looked down at Mycroft. "Did the telephone ring last night, Mike?"

Mycroft yawned.

Even if Mycroft could talk, Penelope would not have expected much help from him. He could sleep through anything, even the most violent of those furious desert thunderstorms that blew up suddenly and buffeted the house like hurricanes. He would sometimes wake up, look around with interest, and ask, Oh, did I miss something? The jangling of a telephone in the middle of the night would scarcely be an irritant for Mycroft.

Actually, Mycroft did talk. Constantly. He had a wide-ranging vocabulary that expressed a variety of emotions, needs, desires, and affections. It wasn't his fault that humans had not learned to translate the feline language adequately. He probably thinks we're dunces, Penelope speculated.

No, I didn't imagine it, she decided.

It couldn't be a dream—a nightmare, yes, but not a dream. Besides, there was no reason for her to subconsciously call Mycroft stupid. He wasn't. He was a smart cat. His one failing was perhaps an overly inquisitive nature. He had already used up several of his multiple lives because he was consumed with curiosity. Yet a curious mind was a mark of intelligence. Penelope's id and ego would know that Mike was intelligent, or they should. She figured her subconscious was at least as bright as her conscious mind, and she knew that she was one intelligent lady, except for her inability to speak feline properly. However, she had never

87

been very good at languages and had been forced to cram desperately to pass the French and German reading requirements for her doctoral degree.

Nor was Penelope very good at logic. The syllogism "All tables have four legs; all sheep have four legs; therefore, all tables are sheep" made perfectly good sense to Penelope, as it would to any right-thinking human being. This is why she had immediately seen the wisdom of dropping the course in logic and looking for another to fulfill the philosophy requirement for her undergraduate degree. She had wound up taking a course in Aristotle. At least, *he* didn't natter on and on about tables and sheep.

And who needed algebra anyway?

Yes, intelligence took many forms. Unfortunately, Penelope's midnight caller had displayed a singular lack of wisdom. That call had been a mistake. A serious mistake. Penelope was angry at being threatened and having Mycroft described as stupid.

"Mike, Alex, Char. Pay attention. 'Know then thyself,' " Penelope quoted, " 'presume not God to scan; The proper study of mankind is man.' Alexander Pope. Seventeen hundred thirty-three. Thank you very much."

Mycroft, of course, disagreed. He knew that the proper study of mankind should be cats. That was why God created cats. Men—and women—need a higher form of intelligence to guide them through the vicissitudes of life. Douglas Adams had it all wrong in *The Hitchhiker's Guide to the Galaxy*. Dolphins are okay, but it was cats who should have said, "So long, and thanks for all the liver crunchies." Every plumber's apprentice knew that!

Mycroft, now feeling rather peckish after the morning's ride, agreed heartily with Penelope's next statement. "Let's go eat." It was important to eat six or eight times each day to maintain strength and energy. Every plumber's apprentice knew that also.

Laney had prepared a magnificent brunch. There was something for everyone: peppermint candies and a handful of oats to help Chardonnay stave off boredom while she waited outside in the shade; bowls of chicken with gravy for Alexander and Mycroft, who also liked dog food as a change of pace. In fact, no one could find a food group that Mycroft did not relish. As Doctor Bob, the vet, always said, "Mycroft would eat anything that didn't eat him first."

For the humans, Laney's repast consisted of a pitcher of Bloody Mary's made with gin instead of vodka and vegetable juice instead of tomato juice, eggs benedict with salsa instead of hollandaise sauce, blueberry muffins made with apples instead of blueberries, and, unable to find a substitute, real coffee. Laney's meals were always tasty, if somewhat unpredictable.

"You're not eating," Laney complained. "That's not like you. And don't tell me you're dieting. There's not a misplaced ounce on you. I think Wally secretly lusts after you, but he'd better not try anything if he knows what's good for him. What's wrong, Penelope?"

"Oh, fie," Penelope said sipping her Bloody Mary. It was hot and spicy, just the way she liked it.

"Fie?"

"Yes, fie. Double fie. Double damn fie."

"This sounds serious."

"It is."

Mycroft and Alex finished eating and hung around waiting to see if more was coming. When it didn't, they slipped through the dog door and went to keep Chardonnay company.

"Well, tell me about it."

"Somebody called last night. A woman disguising her voice."

"Were you asleep?"

"Naturally."

"I'm surprised you remember."

"I always remember. Eventually. You know that. Anyway, she said, 'You and that stupid cat stay away from Herbert Fletcher.' Then, she hung up."

"Mycroft's not stupid."

"I find it very insulting."

"A jealous mistress," Laney declared.

"Or the person who murdered Louise Fletcher."

"Why would the killer give away her sex?"

"It does seem rather dumb."

"No. It's a jealous mistress. She knew you were with Herb and wants to stop him from going after you. Those stories about Herb Fletcher are true. He's a randy old devil. I should know. He tried to seduce me once."

"No."

"Yes. Don't listen to this, Wally. No, do listen. You should know that other men find me a desirable little bundle." She tossed her red mane seductively.

"You never told me," Penelope said.

"Oh, it was years ago. You were off in Africa or something. He cornered me at a Chamber of Commerce mixer and kissed my hand."

"That doesn't sound like much of a seduction."

"He kissed right straight up my arm. I mean each freckle. I was wearing a sleeveless blouse. I stopped him when he started breathing in my ear. It was a very dark corner. Actually, I started giggling. My ear is very ticklish. Isn't it, Wally?"

"Yes, precious." He pushed his chair back from the table. "Excuse me, please."

"Where are you going? You haven't finished eating."

"Get my gun. Shoot Fletcher. Teach him to mess with my woman."

"Aren't you sweet?" Laney watched him go. "Isn't he a sweet old hunk?" she said turning back to Penelope.

"He's not really going for a gun, is he?"

"Good God, you don't think he's serious? Wally!" Laney raced after him.

I'm living with a bunch of lunatics, Penelope thought. Pleased with the brief respite, she took another sip of her Bloody Mary, reflecting that Laney's hair was an even brighter red than her drink.

"Where's Laney?" Wally asked, sitting down at the table again.

"Looking for you. She thinks you're serious about shooting Herb."

"I went to the bathroom."

"Wally!" The front door slammed.

"Another Bloody Mary, Penelope?"

"Yes, please."

"Wally!" Laney was at the back of the house now. Alex, always a sensitive creature, began howling. Chardonnay joined in with a sympathetic whinny. Mycroft jumped to the top of the barbecue, where his view of the action would be unrestricted.

"Wally! Damn it, where are you?"

"God, I love that woman," Wally said. "Ain't she a pistol?"

"Yes, indeed," Penelope said.

Lunatics. Lovable, but deranged nonetheless.

Penelope bathed Chardonnay and then herself. Mycroft was left on his own. There were limits to his tolerance for coexistence with the human race, and Penelope had tried to bathe him only once, in Africa when the fleas were particularly troublesome and Mycroft was considerably smaller. Like Doctor Bob, she had the scars to prove it.

So Mycroft's baths were now restricted to his visits to the vet's office, where adequate, if rather unwilling, reinforcements were at hand. Doctor Bob's assistants had been known, however, to check the appointment calendar and call in sick when Mycroft was scheduled. The vet had evaded that dodge by having Penelope bring Mycroft in unannounced. He then locked the doors. Mycroft was a healthy cat, thank God, and the ordeal occurred only once a year. Unfortunately, he was due for his physical and booster shots soon.

In the shower, Penelope sighed. First, Louise Fletcher is murdered on my very doorstep and then Mikey has to go to the vet. It's too much for any one woman to bear.

Damn! Penelope had managed to get shampoo in her eyes. It burned.

Well, really. I must have been a real bitch in some previous life.

Herbert Fletcher greeted Penelope and Mycroft politely. He looked tired. There were dark bags under his eyes, new lines etched into his tanned face. Even with his fatigue and grief so evident, Penelope had to admit that the man, although no Sean Connery, was handsome. Laney probably hadn't minded Herb blowing in her ear at all.

Herb Fletcher led them around to the back of the house. "Louise used the guest cottage as her office. It's rather messy, I'm afraid. She was not a particularly neat woman when it came to managing her personal affairs. I tried to help, but you know how Louise could be. . . ."

Do I detect a little bitterness in Herb's voice? Penelope wondered.

"Well, I'll leave you two with it," Herb said. "I'll be in the house if you need anything."

Penelope and Mycroft surveyed the guest cottage with dismay. There were papers, file folders, old newspapers, magazines, and books everywhere.

Mycroft was the first to venture in, moving slowly at first, cautiously sniffing the musty air. By God, this would be a good place to find a mouse or two. He jumped when Penelope threw open a window. Don't make so much noise, he complained with a sharp meow. You'll scare them away.

They confronted a formidable task, particularly since Penelope didn't know what she was looking for. Going to one of the file cabinets, she pulled open a drawer and found legal-sized file folders, each with the name of one of Empty Creek's prominent citizens printed neatly on the tab.

My God.

One of the folders was labeled Penelope Warren.

She pulled it from the drawer and sat at the desk. Her folder contained newspaper clippings and handwritten notes. Penelope recognized the newspaper stories. One was a feature written by Andy on her Peace Corps experiences. Another described the grand opening of Mycroft & Company, and was accompanied by a picture of Penelope and Mycroft sitting in front of the store's fireplace. Of course, there were the stories about the equestrian animals, and their picture as they peered from the saddlebags. Behind the clippings, were notes written on coarse, lined tablet paper. Penelope began reading.

"Penelope Warren seems bright and ambitious. Liberal. Appears to love desert. Good city council candidate? Begin with planning commission? Explore. Frequently seen with newspaper editor. Probably sleeping together. Find better match."

Find a better match? What's wrong with Andy? Well, on the Sean Connery scale of one to ten . . .

Penelope turned the page.

"Sister stars in cheap films. Displays breasts for titillation of ignorant male audience. Herb is a big fan. Disgusting. Sister could be used against Penelope by political rivals. Find better candidate."

In defense of her sister, Penelope said, "What an old prude." Anyway, it wasn't Cassie who did those things, it was someone named Storm Williams, and she didn't do it anymore. That was in her contract now.

Penelope read the folders on her friends and neighbors, feeling for all the world like a snoop.

Laney's contained a single copy of *Arizona Heroine,* her first romance novel. Louise had written "TRASH" in magic marker across the ample bosom of the heroine portrayed on the cover. "Bubblehead and pornographer," was another of Louise Fletcher's comments. "Hair dyed," was her final pronouncement on Laney. That's not true, Penelope protested to the dead woman. Laney's a very good writer, even if she is given to fluttering eyelashes and husky panting. And she doesn't dye her hair.

Louise Fletcher initially called Andy's *Empty Creek News Journal* "Fluff!" A later note, however, in the form of a clipped editorial advocating the need for maintaining desert open space, was labeled "Promising."

Fascinated, Penelope read on through other files, discovering which Empty Creek residents did not pay their bills on time, who was in debt, which teacher was suspected of making sexual advances to a student, who had been hauled into court, who had been arrested as a youth, which couple had had the messiest divorce and custody battle, which recalcitrant spouse was behind in child-support payments.

Through it all, Louise Fletcher traced the labyrinthine pattern of the sexual meanderings engaged in by Empty Creek's desert dwellers. So-and-so was seeing so-and-so. *X* had an affair with *B*. Blank met Blank clandestinely in Phoenix. A married man was seeing prostitutes in Phoenix on the second weekend of each month. Louise knew all about Penelope and Sam and then Sam and Debbie.

"Well, Mycroft, we've certainly accomplished our purpose if we wanted to discover someone with a motive to murder Louise Fletcher. Anyone in town could have cheerfully plunged the knife into the old bag."

But there were mysterious gaps in the dead woman's voluminous musings and railings against virtually everyone in town. Where, for example, were the files on the city council members and the other publicly avowed enemies of Louise Fletcher? Penelope found it more than a little strange that files for Merry Stevens and Freda Alsberg were lacking.

She sat at the desk, wanting desperately to go home and take another shower. She watched Mycroft play with a thick string, expecting him to bat it in the air, toss it across the room, race after it, pounce on it. She had seen him play with string often enough to know how the game was supposed to go. It took a few moments for her to realize this particular string was immobile and protruding from the wall. That was certainly odd.

She got down on her hands and knees beside Mycroft. She tugged at the string. A rather large panel fell free of the wall. Penelope sat back and looked at Mycroft. He looked back at her. He seemed rather pleased with himself. Pretty good, huh?

"Well," Penelope said. "Curiouser and curiouser." It *was* Alice who said it. Penelope was sure of it now. She went to get a pocket flashlight from her purse.

When she returned, Mycroft had disappeared into the black hole in the wall. She saw his big eyes glowing in the darkness as he waited for her to follow.

The penlight revealed a closet that had been boarded over. Mycroft was sitting in front of another four-drawer file cabinet. Pretty damned good, huh?

Penelope felt around, found a door knob on the inside two feet above the floor. She turned it and the door opened. Amazing. What had that woman been up to? Penelope pulled a string, and the closet filled with light. The end of the string had been fashioned into a hangman's noose pulled tight around a campaign button with the former mayor's picture on it. VOTE PHILIP SIMMONS, the button proclaimed. Penelope let it go. Good God. Phil Simmons twirled in his gruesome little noose.

Penelope studied the combination lock on the file cabinet. The arrow pointed to twenty-two. She carefully turned the knob one number to the right and tugged gently. Nothing. She went past twenty-two and back to twenty-one. This time, the lock fell open. People are so lazy, Penelope thought, and Louise Fletcher was no exception.

She slowly pulled the top drawer open. There were the missing files.

"Mycroft, look at this. That woman made J. Edgar Hoover look like an amateur."

Special Agent Mycroft reared up on his hind legs and gave the former mayor's campaign button a good whack.

The special agent had found his suspect.

Penelope, however, had a whole new file cabinet overflowing with prime suspects for murder. She ticked them off as she ruffled through the files—Mayor Charley Dixon, Merry Stevens, others on the council, the planning commission, the town's staff. Everyone was here. . . .

Except for Freda Alsberg.

Penelope replaced everything as she had found it and went back to the big house. Mycroft went directly to the jeep and leaped onto his seat. Detecting made a cat hungry.

"I'm leaving now," Penelope told Herb Fletcher, "but I'd like to come back another time. There's just so much to go through."

"Did you find anything of interest?"

Penelope hesitated.

"Louise was quite a collector, wasn't she?" Fletcher said. "Frankly, I think young Harrison is a good match for you."

"You've read the files then?"

Fletcher nodded. "Louise wasn't a bad woman. She meant well, but information meant power to her. She wanted to be a powerful woman."

He sounded very sad. Penelope wondered if he knew about Louise's hidden closet. Perhaps his wife hadn't been a bad woman, but the files she'd secreted went beyond the bounds of propriety. "May I come again?"

"Yes, of course, Penelope. Come any time. Perhaps we can have that dinner together."

"Perhaps." *Does he intend to blow in my ear too?*

Penelope drove home and hurriedly fed Chardonnay, the rabbits, and Mycroft before jumping into the shower again, grateful for the hot water that washed the dirt of Louise Fletcher's files away.

Almost.

Clean again—almost—Penelope lingered over the decision of what to wear, or rather over the decision of whether she would seduce Andy tonight or not. Deciding that Louise Fletcher had already ruined Valentine's Day and that was quite enough, Penelope elected to provide some material for Laney's latest novel. Having chosen seduction, she dabbed the perfume that drove Andy wild between her breasts and behind her ears—she didn't mind *him* blowing in her ear at all. Then she opened the sexy underwear drawer and went for lacy black.

Poor Andy. He didn't stand a chance.

After ensuring that her purse contained a full travel package of tissues—*Casablanca* was, for Penelope, always a three-hankie movie—she poured a glass of wine and sat in the living room to wait for Andy.

Maybe a good cry and a lusty romp would drive away the memories of those contemptible files.

CHAPTER SEVEN

Penelope cried in all the usual places. She began when Ilsa told Sam to play *the* song. She was still weeping when Sam played it for Rick and when Rick boarded the train in Paris without Ilsa. Penelope sobbed openly and pulled another tissue out when everyone in Rick's Place stood and sang the Marseillaise, drowning out the German officers. Penelope was weak with emotion when Rick and Ilsa parted at the airfield, but she smiled through her tears when Rick said, "Louis, I think this is the beginning of a beautiful friendship."

During the movie Andy held Penelope's hand. At first. Then he shyly snaked his arm around her shoulders. Then he drew her close and kissed her tear-streaked cheek. Then . . .

It's a good thing it's dark in here, Penelope thought. She was surprised at Andy's boldness, but she snuggled as close to him as she could and pressed his hand even tighter against her breast. At this rate, he would be undressing her by summertime.

She was sorry when the lights came up, sad because the movie was over and because Andy had removed his hand. The movie and his caress were *so* good.

Andy smiled at her. "Shall we go home?" he asked.

"No," Penelope said firmly.

Andy was crestfallen. "But I thought—"

"First, I want to go to the Double B for a nightcap. Then I want to dance with you. And then . . ."

"Yes?" Andy questioned hopefully.

Penelope smiled. "Then we'll go home and do naughty things. Would you like that?"

"Oh my, yes."

But Louise Fletcher seemed determined, even in death, to find a better match for Penelope or, at the very least, to make her current match untenable. As they strolled hand in hand from the cineplex to the Double B, Andy asked, innocuously enough, "Did you find anything at the Raney place?"

And Penelope, still awash in the romanticism of *Casablanca* and forgetting for a moment that she was in the company of a newspaperman, a very good newspaperman despite Louise Fletcher's cruel "fluff" comment, answered, innocently enough, "Louise kept files on practically everyone in town."

"Files? You mean—"

"Richard Nixon had nothing on Louise Fletcher. She was a walking dirty tricks department. You should just see some of the things she wrote about people. She used a private detective and everything."

"What a great story!"

"You can't write that, Andy."

"Why not?"

"It would hurt people, for one thing."

"The truth—"

"And for another, it would interfere with a continuing investigation."

"You're not a police officer."

"I might as well be. The woman was killed on my doorstep. I'm going to find out who did it."

"I want you to tell me about those files."

"No."

"Penelope . . ."

Penelope thought that Louise Fletcher smiled spitefully down—or up more likely—as she and Andy bickered. She stopped at the door of the Double B and planted her feet. Like Mycroft, Penelope was never one for backing away from a good fight. Still . . .

"When it's all over," she said, "I'll give you an exclusive." It was a line always used by private eyes in novels. To Penelope's surprise, it worked.

"Promise?"

"Cross my heart." She smiled just as spitefully down—and up, just to touch all bases—at Louise Fletcher.

They entered the Double B holding hands once again, but the specter of Louise Fletcher was right behind them.

Prime Suspect Number One was sitting alone at the end of the bar.

"Why don't you get us a table, Andy? I want to see Phil Simmons for a moment."

The former mayor of Empty Creek smiled as Penelope sat down next to him. She felt a twinge of pity for the man. Just because he was forty years old, unmarried, and lived with his mother was no reason for Louise Fletcher to write those horrible things about him.

"I wonder if we could get together tomorrow, Phil."

"Sure, Penelope. What do you need?"

Hem and haw or be direct? Penelope decided on the direct approach. "I want to talk about Louise Fletcher's murder."

"I've already told the police everything I know."

"I'd like to hear it anyway."

"Come for dinner tomorrow? Mother's making spaghetti. She always makes spaghetti on Mondays. Or Tuesday is meat loaf. Do you like meat loaf? Wednesday is pot roast. . . ."

"Spaghetti's fine," Penelope said quickly. She didn't want to hear Mother Simmons's menu for the week.

"Seven o'clock?"

"I'll see you then."

"She was a vicious old bitch, Penelope, but I didn't kill her."

"I didn't say you did. I just want to find out *who* did." Penelope had always wanted to believe the best about others, but she was beginning to think the murderer had performed a public service.

She agreed to dance with Andy.

Still, Louise Fletcher hovered around her.

The happy couple managed to get rid of the old bag's malevolent spirit only by committing a series of rather lewd and lascivious acts which they both thoroughly enjoyed. Had Louise Fletcher not already been dead, they quite likely would have embarrassed her into expiring.

First, they played Tingling Anticipation of Love in the Jacuzzi Under a Cold Desert Sky Filled with Bright Stars before moving on to Train Station, a game in which the participants got to kiss each other hello and goodbye a lot. When they tired of Train Station, Penelope and Andy segued into You Get the Fritos with its loosely defined rules.

Then, Penelope remembering poor Sam's unfortunate accident, they played Throw the Cat Out of the

Bedroom because Mycroft always watched with such interest—it was like making love in front of a study-hall monitor, and with his penchant for occasional participation, it was better for all concerned to banish him. Mycroft protested, of course, because he was an avid peeping tom and somewhat of a connoisseur of lewd and lascivious acts, but banished he was.

It was time to get back to some serious Train Station. Andy said, "Oh, Penny," frequently and she didn't mind even a little bit.

Penelope awakened late the next morning, thinking that perhaps *she* might have a talent for writing romance novels. Cavorting late into the night had certainly provided interesting raw material for conversion into fiction. She turned over lazily to find Mycroft had, as usual, sometime during the night inserted his furry body between her and Andy. While Mycroft didn't begrudge Penelope the occasional dalliance, he certainly wasn't about to give up his warm bed because of it.

She patted Mycroft's rump and then Andy's. "Nice butts, guys."

Mycroft purred. Murphy Brown, that sleek calico down the road, thought he had a nice butt too. Penelope suspected that Andy might be purring also. She couldn't be sure. Actually, it sounded more like snoring, but Penelope didn't mind. Mycroft snored. She was used to it.

"I'm going to take my still heaving bosom into the kitchen and make coffee," Penelope said much more cheerfully than was usual for her so early in the day.

Her two guys didn't bother to answer.

By the time the coffee pot had hissed and puffed and

bubbled, Andy had tiptoed into the kitchen and embraced Penelope from behind, nuzzling the little hairs on the back of her neck and then her ears.

"Mmm," she purred. She was convinced that she had been a cat in several other lives. "Thanks for last night, sailor," she said.

"My pleasure."

Mycroft padded into the kitchen, still looking slightly out of sorts. There had been the indignity of expulsion from the bedroom when all he wanted to do was watch and perhaps learn something new to show Murphy. And now, not having had a full night's sleep, there was all this chipper activity to behold. Still, it was hard to prolong a grudge, especially when Andy knew just where to scratch a chin and Penelope cracked an egg for him. Well . . . Big Mike allowed himself to be mollified a trifle as he lapped the raw egg.

Life was good after all.

Until Penelope shrieked, rather loudly. Big Mike and Andy abandoned egg and coffee respectively and rushed to her rescue.

By the time they skittered to a halt at her side, Penelope was using the morning newspaper, which she had gone to fetch, to point indignantly at a bright new copper penny glued to her front door.

Apropos of absolutely nothing, she noted that Abraham Lincoln stared placidly to the north, perhaps wishing he were in Sedona, that New Age community in the Red Rock country. At the moment, Penelope also wished she were in Sedona. It was quite peaceful there. Very likely, people in Sedona didn't find bodies on their doorsteps, receive threatening telephone calls in the middle of the night, or find pennies glued to their front doors.

"This makes me very angry." Penelope used her fingernail to paw at the coin. "It'll never come off unless I dig it out."

"I could get you a new door for your birthday," Andy offered hopefully. He didn't want her to get riled. For a woman of English and Scandinavian descent, she had quite the Irish temper.

Having ascertained that Penelope was in no immediate danger, Mycroft hastily returned to his egg. He had seen Penelope's temper also.

"I like this door." Penelope frowned. "You know what makes me really, really mad?"

"No," Andy said, although he fully expected to find out.

"Somebody did this last night. Good God, do you think they were listening at the bedroom window?"

"I didn't hear anything."

"Neither did I, but we were distracted."

"We certainly were."

"Watson would probably call this the Adventure of the Two Pennies."

"Let's hope there isn't a third," Andy said grimly, "glued to the handle of another knife." Of course, either Penelope or Andy *might* have discovered whether there would be, had they remembered to consult with Madame Astoria, whose real name was Alyce Smith. Maybe not, though. Madame Astoria's predictions were sometimes a little iffy.

They left the penny shining brightly in the morning sunlight.

Back in the refuge of her kitchen, her front door firmly locked, an act unheard of in Empty Creek, Penelope looked around at the preparations she had made for breakfast. "I had planned to fix you a nice meal, but I don't feel like cooking now."

"That's all right. Why don't we take a shower and then we'll go to The Duck Pond? I'll buy."

The number seven at The Duck Pond was to die for.

Mycroft leaped to the table and looked at Penelope wistfully.

"No, you can't go, Mikey. You know you've been banned from The Duck Pond. For life, I'm afraid."

Stupid duck, anyway.

It had been quite a scene, one of the more monumental encounters between cat and duck.

"You go first, Andy." After a moment's thought, Penelope followed. "Want to wash my back, sailor?" she said as she slipped into the shower with him.

No one at The Duck Pond held Big Mike's behavior against Penelope. After all, a cat's gotta do what a cat's gotta do. In fact, José María Garcia, who co-owned the restaurant and doubled as the maître d', always inquired after Mycroft. Today, was no exception. "How's Big Mike doing?"

"Quite well," Penelope said. "Thank you."

"Man, he's some kind of cat," Garcia said admiringly as he showed them to a table overlooking the pond that provided the restaurant's name. "Have a good lunch."

Ducks glided past the window.

Sarita, José's wife and a waitress, said, "Hi, Penelope, hi, Andy. How's Mikey?"

"He's fine."

"Cómo está el gato?" Juan hollered from the kitchen. He was José's brother and the cook.

"Muy bien! Penelope hollered right back. *"Gracias."* That exhausted much of Penelope's knowl-

edge of Spanish. She could also say *Dos cervezas, por favor.*

"Margaritas?" Sarita knew that neither Penelope nor Andy worked on Mondays.

"Yes, please," they chorused.

A duck swam close to their window and mooned them. Penelope thought it might be *the* duck. Apparently, he held a grudge. Probably the duck's astrological sign was Cancer. According to Madame Astoria, Cancers held grudges. Penelope was a Cancer.

"I don't like this business," Andy said.

"I think that was a message for Mycroft."

"What message?"

"From the duck."

"What duck?"

"That duck. The one swimming away."

"Honestly, Penelope. Sometimes I really don't know what you're talking about."

"Never mind."

"I was talking about that penny. It concerns me."

"You mustn't worry about me," Penelope said. "I was a Marine." For her, no further explanation was necessary.

"You were a Woman Marine."

"It's the same thing."

"A clerk."

"It's not my fault they wouldn't let me be in Force Recon—what I really wanted to do—or become a tank commander. That would have been good too. Squeak, squeak, squeak. Tanks sound like a family of mice marching down the road. I always found that very interesting. Don't you agree?"

Penelope conveniently forgot that Force Recon Marines rose very early in the morning to jump out of perfectly serviceable airplanes. Tank commanders also arose early to squeak over the landscape.

"No, I'm sorry," Andy said. "That's not enough."

"Were you a Marine?" Penelope asked haughtily.

"You know I wasn't."

"Then you don't know. I can take care of myself," she stated firmly.

"If it makes you happy," Andy declared, "I'll enlist today."

"You're too old, dear."

"You're impossible."

"Yes, I am, rather, but let's not let that spoil a perfectly good day."

Sarita returned with the Margaritas.

"Here's looking at you, kid," Andy said.

Penelope smiled and raised her glass. Andy did a most credible Humphrey Bogart imitation.

After lunch, Penelope went home and devoted the afternoon to doing all of the things necessary to keep her little ranchette functioning—cleaned stables, did three loads of laundry, ordered two bales of hay, thought about dropping in at Doctor Bob's unannounced with Mycroft in tow, but doubted she would be able to catch him by herself. Big Mike was not a cat that could be taken to the vet draped docilely over an arm. Such a visit required planning and reinforcements. Making that decision was a relief. Puttering around the house was much better than upsetting half of Empty Creek by taking Mycroft to Doctor Bob, while greatly amusing the other half.

Andy had been a little disgruntled—and more than a little jealous—when he'd found out that Penelope was having dinner with Phil Simmons. "But I thought—" he complained.

"And you thought correctly," Penelope interrupted. "You are the only man in my life." Except for Sean Connery perhaps, or the Old Boy, Penelope thought, but she withheld that information. "This is business. Phil Simmons is a prime suspect. And don't start in again. I will be perfectly fine. His mother is going to be there."

Mycroft was equally put out at being left behind for the second time that day, but Penelope was not about to take the chance that he would develop an instant dislike for Mother Simmons and maim the poor old woman. As it turned out, Mother Simmons, a frail, birdlike creature who would probably live to be ninety or a hundred, was thoroughly obnoxious as she doted on her only son. Penelope decided that her hostess deserved a laceration or two and regretted not bringing Big Mike along to inflict the lesson.

"Philip was always the brightest little boy in his class," Mother Simmons said.

To his credit, Philip protested. "Mother, Penelope doesn't want my life history."

"Of course, she does, dear. A young woman likes to know all about a man."

Penelope didn't, but Mother Simmons continued anyway.

"Philip was always so good at games and reading and arithmetic and everything."

Nor was the spaghetti very good. Mycroft, always a most discerning food critic, would have attempted to cover it up. Since the spaghetti was this bad, Penelope could just imagine what Mother Simmons's meat loaf would be like. Perfectly dreadful.

Thankfully, the old bag ran down as she served the little marshmallows entombed like fossils in a crusty raspberry jello. Penelope hated jello, crusty or otherwise. She particularly hated marshmallows, little and big alike.

And she soon discovered she was growing to hate mother and son.

Mother Simmons deposited Penelope and Philip on the living-room couch in front of a large screen television. "Well, I'll just leave you two youngsters alone," she said as she dimmed the lights and left the room.

Penelope immediately went to the switch and restored illumination.

"Would you like to see my political tapes?" the former mayor of Empty Creek asked, gesturing with the remote control for the television set.

"Later, Phil. First, I want to hear everything you know about Louise Fletcher."

"I didn't like her. She didn't like me. Louise didn't like anyone."

"And you were with your mother when Louise was murdered?"

"Yes. It was Friday, so it was fried chicken night. Mother always makes fried chicken on Fridays."

"So she said." Chicken surrounded by grease probably, Penelope thought.

"Now would you like to see my tapes?"

"In a minute." Alibi, indeed. That woman would help her son kill and would cheerfully lie about it. "If Louise Fletcher had been killed on your doorstep, who would you suspect?"

Phil Simmons immediately named everyone who had a file in Louise Fletcher's secret closet—and Freda Alsberg who did not—anointing each suspect with a wave of the remote control. "There are more, I suppose, but those are the people who come to mind right away." He paused. "Now?"

Penelope sighed. "Now," she said, "but the lights stay on."

Within a minute, she was already weary of Phil's videotaped political memoirs. After fifteen minutes of them, *she* was ready to kill. An hour later she decided that the only way Philip Simmons could have killed Louise Fletcher was by boring her to death.

"And this is me being sworn in."

Mother Simmons was at his side, looking on proudly.

"And here I am presiding over my first council meeting."

And here I am going to sleep.

"And here I am delivering my first State of the City address."

And here I am contemplating suicide.

"And here is my second State of the City address."

And here I am going home. "Wait!" Penelope cried. "Stop the tape. Back it up."

"Was there a particularly eloquent phrase you wanted to hear again? I could deliver it in person."

"All of it's very eloquent, Phil, but I thought I saw something."

Disappointed, Phil reversed the tape.

"That should be enough," Penelope said. She leaned forward as the former mayor filled the large screen again. There. It was quite clear as the camera pulled back. Freda Alsberg and Louise Fletcher were in a corner of the room, arguing furiously about something, doing much finger pointing and making angry gestures. The camera zoomed in on Phil again.

"I really must be going now," Penelope said.

"But you haven't heard my third State of the City address. Or the fourth."

"Another time," Penelope said. I'll flee the country first, she thought. To someplace that doesn't have an extradition treaty.

Penelope found Andy sitting forlornly on her front porch when she drove in. He rose awkwardly and stood in the glare of the headlights, looking terrified. Actually, she was rather glad to see him. She would have been glad to see Jack the Ripper after an evening with Phil Simmons and his mother.

"I can't help it, Penelope. I was worried about you. I wanted to make sure you got home safely."

"Oh, come on in," Penelope said, relenting. "We'll have a nightcap."

As a good feminist, she felt a trifle guilty for allowing Andy to play Protective Male, but she had to admit that it could be kind of nice, just so long as it didn't get to be a habit. "But I'm not going to play Submissive Female," she said aloud.

"I repeat, Penelope, there are times when I have absolutely no idea of what you're talking about."

"That's good, dear, just the way I like it. I do enjoy a good game of Mysterious Female. Would you like to play?"

"What are the rules?"

"There are no rules."

"I'll be at a disadvantage."

"Of course. That's the point."

CHAPTER EIGHT

Louise Fletcher's funeral was well attended, although Penelope thought most of the people were probably there to ensure that the former first lady of Empty Creek was really dead and in her grave. Potential suspects abounded, like so many albatrosses hanging about Penelope's neck.

Clods of dirt thudded against the coffin as the pseudo mourners filed past the grave. Freda Alsberg wound up to deliver a high hard one to Louise Fletcher's head. Fortunately for the deceased, the expensive mahogany coffin proved to be a very effective batting helmet. Meredith Steven's pitch was more of a change-up, but it was delivered to the general location of the recently departed's head also.

Tweedledee—Detective Lawrence Burke—lurked in the background taking notes. Tweedledum—Detective Willie Stoner—slowly walked past the long line of vehicles parked in the cemetery, writing down license-plate numbers. It was like a bad television movie. A single glance over those in attendance would reveal no strangers, and if there were no aliens in their midst, it seemed logical to assume—even using Penelope's questionable syllogisms—that there would be no alien vehicles either. Perhaps Chief Fowler just wanted to keep Detectives Burke and Stoner away from school crossings.

Standing beside Penelope, who was wearing her black dress—a rarity—and high heels—also a rarity—Andy jotted in his official reporter's notebook. He was covering the funeral for the *Empty Creek News Journal,* but he made his notes unobtrusively. Laney and Wally were on the other side of Penelope.

Herbert Fletcher, seated in a folding chair, was the epitome of stoic grief throughout the brief service. His white handkerchief was used frequently. The couple had been childless and despite the efforts of even the most relentless of Empty Creek's gossips, no one had ever found evidence of other living relatives of Herb or Louise. Doubtless, there were some somewhere, but they probably had not liked Louise either.

Leaving the graveside, Penelope saw that Lawrence Burke was still writing furiously in his notebook. "That's spelled P-E-N-E-L-O-P-E and W-A-R-R-E-N," she said.

"I know that," Tweedledee said.

"I just wanted to be sure."

"Why are you so mean to him?" Laney asked. "He's just doing his job."

"He couldn't find his butt in a telephone booth using both hands, much less a murderer."

"Oh," Laney replied. "That certainly leaves no room for discussion."

With the formal rites concluded, everyone now dutifully drove out to the Raney Ranch for what promised to be a funereal repast. Penelope rode with Andy. "It was a very nice service, don't you think?" he said.

Since they were passing city hall at that moment, Penelope replied, "I think it was hypocritical of the city fathers and mothers to have the flags flown at half-mast."

"That is a bit much," Andy said glancing over quickly. He was a very careful driver and rarely took his eyes from the road. It drove Laney crazy. She constantly pleaded with Penelope to perform a certain lewd and lascivious act on Andy's person while he was driving to see if *anything* would distract him. Penelope refused, not because she had anything against lewd and lascivious acts, quite the contrary, but because she thought Andy might then drive them straight into a saguaro cactus.

In the car ahead—Laney's—a little red convertible with the top down, driven by Wally, Laney was craned around in her seat, red hair flying in the wind, watching.

"Why doesn't Laney turn around?" Andy asked. "She probably can't wear her seat belt in that position."

"I haven't the slightest idea," Penelope replied.

After a second obligatory expression of sympathy to the bereaved widower, the mourners swarmed like hungry terriers over the baked meats. They were cold cuts actually—expensively catered but cold cuts nonetheless. Penelope recalled the reference from *Hamlet* as she watched the elite of Empty Creek crowd the tables laden with food.

Others bypassed solid sustenance in favor of the bar. A funeral in Empty Creek, it appeared, invoked both appetite and thirst.

Penelope and Laney elbowed their way to the food, gathering little morsels for themselves and their men, while Andy and Wally bellied up to the bar in pursuit

115

of strong drink. The couples met at the fireplace to exchange booty.

The huge living room was filled to overflowing with people. As the food and drink took effect, the noise level rose. Despite the solemnity of the occasion, there was laughter and loud conversation as people demonstrated their relief at not being the cause for this gathering.

"She looked so natural, don't you think?"

"Well, the wicked witch is finally dead and buried."

Penelope hoped Herb had not heard that comment. People could be so cruel. She glanced across the room to where he stood with Madame Astoria. He seemed to have recovered from his grief. He was smiling as he leaned over the attractive Alyce Smith and whispered in her ear.

Again, Penelope could not help but think of Hamlet's comment to his fellow student. "Thrift, thrift, Horatio! The funeral baked meats/Did coldly furnish forth the marriage tables." She wondered if . . . That was too cruel. She was just as bad as the others. But Madame Astoria did plant a kiss on Herbert Fletcher that went just past the bounds of propriety for such a somber occasion. Perhaps a visit to our resident astrologer and psychic is in order, Penelope thought.

Freda Alsberg was the next to offer succor to Herb, although Penelope noticed that he winced as the Valkyrie took both his hands in her own. The woman did have a bone-crushing grip. She, too, kissed him and then left, reluctantly, Penelope thought.

Merry Stevens took her place.

What was his attraction to women?

"So, who do you think will be the next Mrs. Fletcher?" Laney asked.

"Good Lord, not Merry Stevens, surely. What could they possibly have in common?"

"They both hated Louise."

"I think Herb is genuinely shocked at Louise's death."

"Really?"

"Yes, really."

"If you were a man, would you want to be married to a woman like that?"

"No, but love takes different courses." Penelope inclined her head in the direction of Wally who was busy explaining to Andy just how to clap his hands so that he could draw his imaginary revolver. "I rest my case."

"Well, perhaps you have a point. We do have our little idiosyncrasies, but you'll notice it's the unmarried women in Empty Creek who are lining up to present their charms to the old rake."

Penelope would not admit to her friend that she had entertained that same thought, as yet another younger, attractive woman approached Herbert Fletcher. If this keeps up, they're going to kiss the skin right off his face.

"Why don't you get in line?" Laney teased. "The inheritance would certainly make you more than comfortable. I assume Herbert inherits all."

"That appears to be the case."

"Go for the millions."

"I'm quite happy, thank you."

"Have you asked Mycroft? Perhaps he would like to be rich."

"He doesn't seem to like Herb. Besides, Mycroft is a very happy cat and not at all greedy."

Just as one of those eerie lulls, when everyone stops

talking simultaneously, descended upon the room, there was a loud clap. Penelope and Laney jumped.

"I did it," Andy cried in the silence.

"You certainly did," Penelope said.

When taking their leave of Herbert Fletcher, Penelope again expressed her sympathy for his loss. "Thank you for coming. I know it would mean a great deal to Louise," he said. "I must see you," he whispered.

"I'll be in the bookshop later," Penelope whispered back. "After I change. Why are we whispering?"

"No one must know."

"Know what?"

"Later, my dear."

Penelope backed away as she saw Freda descending once more. The woman looked for all the world like a legendary Valkyrie swooping out of the hors d'oeuvres to seize her warrior prey.

"It was a wonderful weekend," Penelope said, taking her leave of Andy. "Mostly," she added as they embraced.

"I know what you mean."

"We must do it again."

"Without a murder."

"Let's hope so."

"But wonderful anyway."

"Mmm." Andy was making her breathless again. He was becoming rather accomplished at that. Still, Penelope pulled away, more than a little reluctantly. There was work to be done. She had books to sell. Murders to solve. "Get your rest, sweetie," she said. "And remember to take your vitamins."

"Yes," Andy said thoughtfully. "I think I'd better. Bottles and bottles of vitamins. You're quite an exciting woman, Penny, a regular little sex machine."

Penelope silently agreed. "And you're pretty good yourself, sailor," she said. I must remember to tell Laney how to play Sailor and Sex Machine, she thought.

When the Sailor finally drove off, his chest puffed with pride at Penelope's compliments, the newly proclaimed little Sex Machine cooled her ardor, changed her clothes, gathered up her partner in detection, and headed off in the direction of Mycroft & Company.

They ran into a slight delay, however, in the person of Madame Astoria, who was sitting in her car at the side of the road, crying her pretty little eyes out.

Talk about destiny.

It wasn't that Madame Astoria was such a bad astrologer and psychic—indeed, she had a devoted coterie of followers who wouldn't eat breakfast without consulting her—it was that the time frames of her musings were generally awful. Madame Astoria once asked Penelope who would be coming to see her in a helicopter. For days, weeks, even months, Penelope searched the skies for a helicopter bringing a visitor. It wasn't until two years later that Cassie arrived on a helicopter, flying in from a desert location where she had been filming a swimsuit commercial.

Penelope pulled off the road, backed up the jeep, and looked across the dusty dirt road at the young woman. She could see that Madame Astoria had a flat tire, but she didn't think a flat would provoke such wracking sobs. "Wait, here, Mikey," Penelope said.

Naturally, Mycroft was the first across the road. He

knew just how to console a distraught young woman. Twenty-five pounds of lovable cuddly cat in the lap was just the prescription, better than a teddy bear any day. Who could cry then? Besides, Mycroft liked Alyce Smith. He liked all pretty young ladies. Sometimes Penelope thought that was the only reason Mycroft hung around. He got to meet so many interesting women.

"Oh, Mycroft," Madame Astoria bawled as the cat leaped through the window onto her lap.

Arriving late, Penelope cried, "Alyce, what's wrong?"

"Oh, Penelope," she wailed. "It's so awful."

"It's just a flat tire, Alyce. We'll get it fixed in no time."

"Not that," Alyce moaned. Her sobs were subsiding. Perhaps there was something to that cuddly cat business. Mycroft purred as Alyce stroked his fur with one hand and wiped away tears with the other.

"What then?"

"Life. Everything. It sucks."

"It's a man," Penelope said. "Isn't it?" She wondered who he could be. Surely, not Herbert Fletcher. He was way too old for Alyce.

Alyce choked and whimpered. "How did you know?"

"Alyce, it doesn't take a psychic to figure out that a young woman sitting in the middle of a desert with a flat tire and crying like she's lost her last friend is upset about A, the flat tire; B, a man; or C, both."

"It's so complicated. I just don't know what to do."

"He's married."

"How—"

"Alyce," Penelope said, smiling, "I've never seen you out with anyone. Therefore, if you are seeing someone, you're doing it secretly. That usually means he's married. You see how it works? I'm just observant. Like Sherlock Holmes."

"I don't know how I got into such a mess."

"Do you want to talk about it?"

"I can't, Penelope, I just can't. If it got out . . . Oh, damn, why did I ever fall in love with him?"

Penelope put a hand on Alyce's shoulder. "Come on, let's get you back to town and freshened up. We'll send someone out to change your tire."

Alyce sneezed.

She sneezed all the way back into town.

"I love cats," Alyce said. Sneeze. "I hate being allergic to them." Sneeze. "I'm sorry, Mycroft." Sneeze.

"Why don't you just push him onto the floor," Penelope said. "He won't mind."

"Oh, I couldn't do that." Sneeze. "He's such a good cat." Sneeze. "Aren't you, Mycroft?"

There was a sign in the window of Madame Astoria's office—studio, chamber, suite, salon, den; what did you call an astrologer's place of business?—that proclaimed the availability of gift certificates.

The inside was neatly furnished with an oak table and chairs. Here Madame Astoria met with her clients to do psychic readings and Tarot card readings. There was a computer work station, also in oak, where Alyce fed the vital information—date, place, and exact time of birth—in and then calculated and printed out astrological wheels, compatibility charts, and a variety of other advice and long-range projections. The matching four-drawer oak filing cabinet reminded Penelope of Louise Fletcher's and made her wonder what kind of dark secrets might be kept within this one. Probably

121

things like the compatibility charts Madame Astoria's computer had spewed out for Penelope and a host of suitors, including Sam and Andy. Perhaps I should have her do one for me and the Old Boy.

Or Sean Connery.

Penelope always thought Madame Astoria's parlor was far too automated, far too light and airy, far too twenty-first century for an astrologer and psychic. A traditionalist herself, she would have preferred a dark little place lighted only by flickering candles and punctuated with mysterious incantations and chants, exotic medieval music, and a black cat to serve as Alyce's familiar.

But if that were the case, Alyce would probably be subjected to the modern equivalent of being burned at the stake by do-gooders. It was a good thing a witch couldn't be killed today simply because she used the latest in computer technology. To Penelope, modern information collection, retention, and retrieval were far more sinister than the arcane rituals of witchcraft. Her look at the files compiled by Louise Fletcher, an amateur, had caused her to imagine what those files would contain if compiled by a seemingly benevolent government. Information was power that could easily be abused. In comparison to Louise Fletcher, Alyce was a harmless, youthful eccentric.

Besides, how could you be a good witch if you were allergic to cats?

"There, I feel better," Alyce said returning from the small bathroom in the back room. "But I look a fright."

"You look just fine," Penelope said. Although Alyce's nose was puffy and bright red from all the sneezing, it matched her eyes perfectly, also red and puffed from all the crying.

"Thank you for your help, Penelope. And you, too, Mycroft." Alyce sneezed again, but halfheartedly. "I took a pill," she explained. "I always do when I'm going to see Mycroft."

"I'm a good listener," Penelope said, "if you decide you'd like to talk."

"I'll get through it," Alyce replied. "Somehow."

"Yes, we always do."

Todd, the UPS delivery man, was flirting with the serving wench who aspired to be a gentlewoman when Penelope and Mycroft finally arrived at the bookshop.

"Don't be silly," Kathy said as Penelope entered the back room.

Mycroft, who fancied himself as something of a shipping clerk, immediately leaped onto the stack of boxes Todd had apparently just wheeled in on a dolly. He looked from Todd to Kathy. There must be something interesting going on.

"Who's being silly?" Penelope asked.

"Todd, of course. He thinks I should be the queen of the Faire."

"And why not?" Todd asked. "Kathy would make a much better queen than old hatchet face." Old hatchet face was Carolyn Lewis who always played Elizabeth I, Queen of England, during the annual desert celebration of the Elizabethan Faire.

"I think Carolyn makes a rather good queen," Penelope said. "I've always pictured Elizabeth Regina as hatchet-faced, nothing at all like Kathy."

"Thank you, my lady," Kathy said.

"Well, I think it would be nice to have a pretty queen for a change," Todd said. He eased the blade of the dolly from beneath the boxes carefully, so as not to disturb Mycroft. "Got to run. See you tomorrow."

" 'Bye," the ladies chorused.

When Todd had roared off in the truck, Kathy asked, "How was the funeral?"

"Perfectly dreadful," Penelope replied, going to the telephone books.

There it was in the Yellow Pages. Surrounded by gaudy advertisements for specialists in marital and domestic matters, electronic debugging, missing persons, undercover work, child custody cases, surveillance. Discreet Investigations—the service utilized by Louise Fletcher—was a model of discretion with only an address and telephone number.

Penelope dialed the number. An answering machine picked up after the first ring. Based on the Yellow Page ad, Penelope expected a message on the order of, "You lose, we find," but there was none, just the forlorn beep of a lonely machine. She thought of exercising discretion herself, but after a moment's hesitation left her name and number. "Please call."

Penelope and Kathy spent the remainder of the afternoon unpacking the shipment of books—a replenishment of some of Penelope's favorite women authors, Rochelle Krich's *Fair Game,* Wendy Hornsby's *Midnight Baby,* Patricia McFall's *Night Butterfly*—setting aside special orders, and rearranging shelves and displays to include the latest novels. Mycroft helped for a while, investigating each new stack of books, sniffing, pointing out those that would sell well; but his efforts were unappreciated. After the third "Mycroft, please stay out of our way," he went off, slightly disgruntled, to sleep in the afternoon sun that bathed the window display.

He was still there when Freda Alsberg entered the shop.

Penelope sent Kathy out to deal with the woman, but Freda insisted on seeing her employer. Penelope sighed and gave her clipboard to her assistant. Kathy whispered, "Good luck," as she rolled her eyes.

"How can I help you, Freda?"

"You can start by explaining this." The councilwoman held out a sheet of paper.

Meet me at Crying Woman Mountain. Five P.M. Urgent. Herb.

The entire note was typed, including the name.

"Where did you get this?"

"It was taped to your door for all the world to read. Why are you tormenting that poor man?"

"This is the first I've seen of the note," Penelope replied, thinking that she was the tormented rather than the tormentor. "I don't know what's going on."

"Don't give me that," Freda hissed. "I saw how you were looking at Herbert today. Couldn't you at least have the decency to allow the man to mourn his wife in peace?"

"But . . ." Penelope spluttered.

"You just can't wait to get your hooks on the inheritance. It wouldn't surprise me if you killed Louise Fletcher for that very reason."

"Now listen to me. . . ."

"No! You listen to me. You stay away from Herbert Fletcher. The poor man is distraught."

"You're the one who's distraught. In fact, I'd say

you're crazy. You're the one who hated Louise Fletcher, and I'd very much like to know where you were when she was murdered."

"You dare accuse me . . ." It was the beauteous Valkyrie's turn to splutter.

"You sound like an angry fishwife," Penelope said.

"Just remember what I said," Freda cried, waving a finger in Penelope's face.

Mycroft, awakened by the commotion, hissed at her as she stormed from the shop.

Well.

"What was that all about?" Kathy asked.

"I don't know," Penelope replied, "but I'm going to find out." She went to the desk and looked up Herbert Fletcher's telephone number and dialed it.

No answer.

Penelope looked at her watch. Four-thirty. There was just time to drive to the little park high atop Crying Woman Mountain.

"Want to go for a little ride, Mike?"

Why not? The sun was fading with the afternoon.

"Do you think you should, Penelope?"

"Don't you start in on me, Kathy."

"Just be careful."

"If I'm not back by six, call Sam and tell him where I am."

"Where are you going?" Kathy asked.

"Crying Woman Mountain."

"It's creepy up there."

"Not half as creepy as it's going to get around here if I don't find out what's going on."

As Penelope and Mycroft pulled out, she saw Alyce Smith driving away from her office. At least she got her tire fixed, Penelope thought as she headed in the opposite direction, toward the black mountain that towered over Empty Creek.

One legend said that a beautiful Indian maiden had been brutally murdered at the top of the mountain long ago and that her spirit now lived there and could be heard crying at night. Another legend said that the maiden's spirit lived deep within the mountain and wept at man's destruction of the once pristine desert landscape.

Whichever story was true, Penelope had heard the poor woman's anguished cries often enough. She frequently drove up Crying Woman Mountain to enjoy the solitude and to sympathize with the spirit's plight. It was peaceful there, and despite popular belief, Penelope knew that any malignancy connected with Crying Woman Mountain existed only in the minds of those who dwelt far below its peak.

Penelope found Freda Alsberg sitting in her car in the little park. Penelope pulled the jeep right up to the grill of Freda's car and turned the engine off. The two mechanical steeds sat nose to nose while their drivers glared at each other through windshields and waited for Herbert Fletcher to arrive.

Not to be outdone, Mycroft put his paws on the dashboard and hissed at Freda for the second time that day.

CHAPTER NINE

While Penelope, Mycroft, and Freda waited impatiently for Herbert Fletcher high atop Crying Woman Mountain, he was some miles away in a secluded barn, rollicking in a haystack with Alyce Smith, wooing her skillfully and energetically, and with a strength and stamina quite surprising for a man of his age. For Herbert, it was a most pleasant diversion from the rigors of mourning and burying the former Mrs. Fletcher.

For Alyce, whose allergies did not extend to hay, this brief hour together drove away all the doubt and jealousy she had experienced earlier that day in the aftermath of Louise Fletcher's funeral. Herbert truly loved her, and she returned that love joyfully, even giddily, despite the grim foreboding promised by their respective astrological signs. Herb was a Gemini, and Alyce knew his flirtatious tendencies. Her own sign was Scorpio; she tended toward possessiveness. This was not as good a combination as Scorpio-Scorpio or Scorpio-Sagittarius, but love would overcome such natural disadvantages.

So, the young woman gave of her feelings and her body willingly, endured the tiny pinpricks of hay without complaint, and ignored the implacable and unyielding paths of the planets as they journeyed across the heavens.

The poet once wrote, "Love conquers all things; Let us too surrender to love."

As usual, Virgil was wrong.

Instead of surrendering to the tender and erotic ministrations of her lover, Madame Astoria should have paid more attention to the stars, brushed the strands of hay from her lovely body, and fled just as fast as her slender, coltlike legs could run.

But alas . . .

Penelope looked at her watch—yet again. This is foolish, she thought. Obviously, he's not coming. Besides, Kathy will have the cavalry on the way in another fifteen minutes. She marched over to Freda and leaned into her window. "You can stay here if you like," she announced, "but I'm leaving."

Penelope did not wait for a reply, but marched right back to the jeep, noting with satisfaction that Freda had started her car to follow her down the mountain.

Penelope drove directly back to Mycroft & Company, seeing—also with satisfaction—Freda turn off. At least the pest was gone for the moment. Whatever possessed the woman?

Penelope and Mycroft entered the shop, both feeling more than a little irritated at having been sent off on a wild-Herb chase up the mountain slopes, only to find the object of their search sitting in a chair before the fireplace reading *The Annotated Sherlock Holmes.*

Kathy shrugged helplessly as Penelope stopped to stare at Herbert Fletcher as though he were an unwelcome apparition. Mycroft, intent on a lima bean or two, was paying no attention whatsoever, and bumped into Penelope's legs. In attempting to get out of his way, she then stepped on his tail, not hard but with sufficient pressure to elicit a wild squall of disbelief.

Penelope jumped.

Mycroft's detractors—and there were a few who said he was the fattest cat they had ever seen—had never seen him move when his mind was set. He could go from zero to raging lion in less than three seconds.

He did so now.

A gray blur, he fled to the top of the chair on which Herbert Fletcher was sitting, using the man's lap and chest as a ladder to gain sanctuary from careless feet. Herb screeched with pain. His flesh was not used to being treated like the bark of a tree.

"Mycroft, I'm sorry," Penelope cried as she rushed to comfort him.

Mycroft, now perched on the backrest of the chair, glared.

Herb, who was still seated, turned to glower in his own stead and received a good whack across the fleshy part of his cheek for his trouble. Streaks of blood appeared on his face instantly.

That'll teach you, by God.

Herb Fletcher screeched again and leaped from the chair, holding *The Annotated Sherlock Holmes* like a bullfighter's cape, ready to ward off another charge by what he now considered a demented beast.

"Mycroft, I'm sorry," Penelope said soothingly, stroking his fur.

"What about me?" Fletcher cried.

"I'll get to you in a minute," she retorted. "What are you doing here, anyway?"

"I told you I was coming."

"You left a note telling me to meet you at Crying Woman Mountain."

"What note?"

Penelope turned to stare incredulously at the man. "You didn't tape a note to the door?"

"Why would I do that?"

"Oh, good Lord, Herb, you're a mess."

He was, indeed. Blood from puncture wounds seeped through his cotton shirt. More blood flowed down his cheek. He was gingerly inspecting that portion of his anatomy that had been so recently engaged in provoking a series of little cries from the lovely Madame Astoria. Fortunately for Herb the thick volume of *The Annotated Sherlock Holmes* had shielded him from serious damage in that area.

Big Mike scowled at him and awaited another opportunity.

Penelope, who recognized Big Mike's look, said, "Kathy, take Mycroft in back and give him some lima beans, and when you come back, please bring the hydrogen peroxide." She turned to Herb. "And, you, get that shirt off." When Herb hesitated, Penelope said, "Really, I've seen a man's chest before. Take it off or we'll never get the bloodstains out."

Kathy returned with the first-aid kit. She was trying not to smile. In fact, she was trying not to laugh out loud. She was proud of Mycroft and had slipped him an extra ration of lima beans. "Shall I call nine-one-one?" she asked.

"I don't think that will be necessary," Penelope smiled. "Mycroft has had his rabies shots," she volunteered although she was more concerned about Mycroft. God only knew what he might catch from Herb Fletcher.

"That's something," Herb replied sullenly. He was feeling most put out now.

"Sit down here and lean back. Kathy, would you mind rinsing the blood out? I can never remember if it's cold water or warm water for blood. One of them works."

Penelope turned to her task of patching up Herb Fletcher.

"You smell nice," he said, leaning forward to nuzzle her neck. "What's that perfume you're wearing?"

"Perhaps iodine would be better," Penelope threatened as she pushed him back in the chair. He really is a lecherous old man, she thought. "Now what is all this business about the note?"

"I don't know anything about a note."

"Well, I received one, and it was signed with your name—typed with your name on it to be perfectly correct."

"Well, I didn't type it, send it, or tape it to your door."

"Freda was quite upset about it. Are you boffing her?"

"Am I what?"

"Boffing her. You know, fooling around, making love, doing it with her?"

Herb answered Penelope's question by not answering, but he confirmed her suspicions a moment later. "We had a brief affair of the heart," he said. "It was foolish of me, but Freda can be rather seductive. She wanted me to divorce Louise. I refused, of course. I loved my wife."

"Of course."

"It's true."

Penelope pressed a gauze pad to his cheek and taped it down. "There. The patient will live, but it doesn't

132

hurt to be careful." I must take Mycroft to the vet. Tomorrow. "Now, what did you want to see me about? What's so urgent?"

Herb fell barely short of accusing Freda Alsberg and Spencer Alcott, Esq. of murdering Louise Fletcher, offering the councilwoman's missing file as substantiation.

Damn it all, Eleanor Burnham the town crier had been right. How was that possible?

Much later, Herb Fletcher left Mycroft & Company with bandages on his cheek and damp water stains on his shirt where Kathy had rinsed the blood away. He was not the epitome of sartorial splendor.

Mycroft, who had regained his dignity and composure over the lima beans, sat in the entrance to the back room and watched him go with considerable disdain.

"I don't like that man," Kathy said. "While you were gone, he practically chased me up and down the aisles. He must take hormone shots or something. What were you two talking about so long out here? I tried to listen, but you were whispering. I thought he was never going to leave. And he didn't even buy anything." Kathy finally remembered that she had not been practicing her Elizabethan English and added, "My lady."

"Well, my buxom young gentlewoman-to-be, he shared suspicions worthy of the intrigue of the royal court."

"Oh, goody, my lady."

"I don't think, 'oh, goody,' is a phrase extant in the late sixteenth century."

"I prithee, my lady, share the intrigues."

133

"Much better, but I'm sworn to secrecy."

"Oh, fie." Kathy pouted.

Penelope was not about to bandy Herb Fletcher's suspicions about town, or even Mycroft & Company, without greater proof than he had offered. Still, the papers he'd provided promised an interesting avenue of investigation. Perhaps. . . .

"Come on, Kathy, let's close up and I'll buy you a drink. And I promise to tell all when I can."

Kathy, always easily mollified, curtsied. "Thank you, my lady."

Discreet Investigations did not return Penelope's call.

Kathy, who was still only twenty, could not order a drink at the Double B because no one there paid any attention to her false identification card. Instead, she ordered a diet Coke and contented herself with sipping from Penelope's wine when no one was looking.

Many of the mourners who had been at both the funeral and the reception that followed appeared to have adjourned to the Double B to continue the wake for Louise Fletcher. By now, they were quite loud and rowdy. Despite her unpopularity in the community at large, Louise was having quite the sendoff.

Kathy chattered aimlessly about serving wenches and gentlewomen; deranged poets, especially the young one who had made odes to her bosom a living art form; forthcoming orders at Mycroft & Company; classes at the college; Thomas Hardy's *Jude the Obscure*. It was not Penelope's favorite Hardy novel. Too gloomy. But then, all of his novels were a bit glum.

Penelope listened, but turned away to survey the other patrons often enough for Kathy to sneak her little sips of wine. She didn't think a little wine would hurt the young woman. The French were quite healthy. And after all, Kathy would reach the exalted age of twenty-one soon. A month or two hardly made a difference, except to the law.

Debbie delivered another glass of wine without being asked, winking at Penelope as she put it on the table within easy reach of Kathy. She also put Kathy's order of french fries topped with chili within easy reach of Penelope. The Double B's chili fries were killers.

"Synchronicity," Penelope said.

"I beg your pardon."

"A coincidence in time," Penelope explained. "Earlier, Spencer Alcott's name was mentioned—and there he is. I find that very synchronistic. Sort of."

The attorney was, indeed, seated at a table with several of Empty Creek's leading businessmen. Spencer waved his hands as he made some point or another.

Penelope did not mention the context in which she had heard his name, although she was thinking very hard about what Herb had said earlier.

"If you say so, my lady, but he's here every day."

"His name is not mentioned in my presence every day, though, you see?"

"Not really."

"When is your audition for gentlewoman?"

"Next week. Oh, Penelope, I'm so nervous. What if they don't like me? I'll have to be a serving wench forever."

"How could they not like you? Gentility oozes from your very pores."

"You know how old hatchet face is. She has the final say about everything at the Faire."

"If you are not accepted as a gentlewoman, we'll

stage a coup. I know for a fact that Sir Walter Raleigh and Sir Francis Drake dislike the queen intensely." These men were both English instructors at Empty Creek Community College.

"Ah, there you are, sweet, dear, pure, beloved, angelic, cherished ladies of my heart."

"Hello, Timothy," Penelope said.

"Hi, Timmy."

The gaunt young poet wore a black cape—incongruous over his jeans and western shirt—which swirled when he bowed to Penelope and took her hand to kiss. "Oh, heavenly ambrosia." Timothy turned to Kathy who was already blushing.

"And you of the beauteous mounds, gentle love of my life, I have missed you sorely."

"We had lunch together," Kathy said. "Remember?"

"My dearest, that was generations ago. Endless multitudes of decades in the dim and dusty corridors of time." Again, he bowed and kissed Kathy's hand. "Sweet Katherine, I am your devoted servant, nay, your faithful slave."

"Please join us, Timothy. Would you like a drink?"

"Gracious lady, you intoxicate me with your beauty, overwhelm me with your generous invitation. I am humbled. . . ."

"Sit down, Timmy," Kathy commanded.

Timothy obeyed immediately. "Innkeeper," he cried, "a flagon of your very finest ale."

"I'm not an innkeeper," Debbie said. "Bud Light, as usual?"

"Sure. So, what's happening, ladies?" Timmy asked, beaming. For a dark and brooding poet, he beamed rather easily.

" 'Murder most foul,' " Penelope quoted. So much for beaming.

Penelope used Mycroft's American Express Gold Card to pay. On a tiring flight once, she had idly filled out an application for Mycroft Holmes Warren. Still bored, she had next filled out the application for a frequent flyer account. In due course, the credit card arrived. Since then, Mycroft had been offered a preapproved Platinum Card because of his excellent credit record. He was a generous tipper, especially when Debbie was the waitress.

When Penelope and Mycroft arrived home, a depression had settled over the house. It seemed lonely and empty. They sank into an almost palpable gloom. Penelope supposed it was the aftermath of the funeral.

Feeling very much like a Hardy character, she sighed and went into her evening routine.

Feed Chardonnay.

Distribute carrots and lettuce for the bunnies.

Feed Mycroft, although he had wolfed down the remnants of the chili at the Double B.

While Mycroft was eating, Penelope telephoned, first Laney and then Andy, asking them to help corral Mycroft in the morning for his unannounced visit to Doctor Bob. She whispered so that Mycroft wouldn't catch on to the plan. Sometimes, he was just too damned smart for his own good.

"Oh, Lord, is it that time of year already?" Laney complained. "I really wish Victoria's Secret had something in catproof underwear. I think I'll suggest it."

"Bring Wally too," Penelope said.

"He'll be filled with joy for the opportunity."

Andy agreed stoically, then quickly changed the subject. He much preferred to talk of love. Not liking doctors himself, Andy always sympathized with Mycroft on these occasions.

Finally, Penelope set about feeding herself, although she wasn't very hungry after all those chili fries. She took a Granny Smith apple from the refrigerator, intending to examine the papers Herb had given her in such secrecy.

The documents had originated in the law offices of Spencer Alcott and were stamped CONFIDENTIAL. The cover sheet had a dire legal warning.

THIS MESSAGE IS INTENDED ONLY FOR THE USE OF THE INDIVIDUAL OR ENTITY TO WHICH IT IS ADDRESSED AND MAY CONTAIN INFORMATION THAT IS PRIVILEGED, CONFIDENTIAL, AND EXEMPT FROM DISCLOSURE UNDER APPLICABLE LAW. IF THE READER OF THIS MESSAGE IS NOT THE INTENDED RECIPIENT, OR THE EMPLOYEE OR AGENT RESPONSIBLE FOR DELIVERING THE MESSAGE TO THE INTENDED RECIPIENT, YOU ARE HEREBY NOTIFIED THAT ANY DISSEMINATION, DISTRIBUTION OR COPYING OF THIS COMMUNICATION IS STRICTLY PROHIBITED.

Penelope turned the page. It was difficult to take any warning of Spencer's seriously.

The documents outlined the entire concept for bringing a card club to Empty Creek, including a sample ordinance to be passed by the council authorizing gambling, the strategy and rationale for presentation to the public, and the revenues that would accrue to all concerned. If Spencer Alcott was to be believed—and who would not believe a lawyer who had missed his calling as a used car salesman?—all the riches of the Orient would descend upon Empty Creek.

Freda Alsberg was to be a limited partner.

"Don't you see," Herbert had whispered urgently back at Mycroft & Company, "how it all fits together? Louise was an impediment to their plans."

Penelope had not seen then. She did not see now.

There was probably a conflict of interest and poor, if profitable, judgment on the councilwoman's part, but Penelope still thought the connection between Freda Alsberg, Spencer Alcott, and Louise Fletcher was somewhat tenuous. Why bother to murder Louise Fletcher over the card-club ordinance and risk the potential profits from a gambling establishment? Naturally, Louise would have opposed the ordinance, but her opposition would have been ignored by the members of the city council, who paid little heed to anything Louise did or said. It was the way business was conducted in Empty Creek.

Still, a visit to the law offices of Spencer Alcott, Esq., seemed in order.

Beside her on the couch, Mycroft stirred and stretched and yawned before going over to *The Complete Works of William Shakespeare* to give his claws a good workout. It was Mycroft's way of announcing that he was ready to go outside, please.

Penelope joined him for their nightly meditation in the desert. The moon, which had been full and bright only a few nights ago, was shrinking. In a few more nights, it would disappear entirely, only to reappear as a tiny sliver in a renewal of the timeless cycle. It made

Penelope think of Alyce Smith and wonder if she still cried for her married lover. Which made her think of Andy and wish she had invited him over. Which was a natural progression to her oversexed best friend and Laney's cowboy lover. Which, in turn, led to thoughts of others and they rushed in with a vengeance—Robert Sidney-Veine, Sean Connery, even Stormy.

"What is everyone doing tonight, Mycroft? I'll bet they're all asleep and we're the only people up."

Mycroft looked up at her briefly without bothering to answer. He knew what he was doing as he listened to the night sounds of the desert, swiveling his ears like little radar antennas to pick up the slightest nuances of the teeming life just beyond the circle of light cast by the porch lamp. Someone had to protect Penelope from the coyotes, the owls and night hawks, the mountain lion who was reputed to prowl the slopes of Crying Woman Mountain.

If Penelope had bothered to pursue the matter by calling all of her friends and acquaintances, she would have awakened Andy who was dreaming about a woman very much like herself, would have discovered that Stormy was drinking and dancing the night away at the wrap party, and would have interrupted the stimulating game of Imperial Roman Princess and Greek Slave in progress in Laney's bedroom. It would have been difficult to reach the Old Boy in Malawi, for he was enjoying a rather nice curry lunch with a certain classics professor at the Shire Highlands Hotel. Alyce Smith, however, was awake and at home and trying to decide whether or not to wear white to her wedding.

What was Sean Connery doing?

Penelope sighed.

Mycroft stirred and rubbed his face against her ribs.

"You're a good buddy, Mikey," she said as she put her arm around him and hugged.

Mycroft purred until it was time to go in, when they discovered another penny had been glued to the front door.

What kind of woman would want a door for her birthday?

This is really becoming quite tedious, Penelope thought. Mysterious phone calls in the night, anonymous notes, someone lurking about with a tube of glue, pennies. Where is it all going to end?

Which made her think of Herbert Fletcher.

Again.

That was becoming quite tedious too.

"Semper Fi, Mac," Penelope shouted into the night.

CHAPTER TEN

Damn cat.

Mycroft awakened with suspicions because of the early and highly unusual hour Penelope threw herself out of bed, disturbing and miffing him in the process. Those suspicions were confirmed when she went through the house closing doors, cutting off as many avenues of escape as possible. He recognized the signs and retreated beneath a big chair in the living room, refusing to come out, even when Penelope tempted him with fresh chicken livers, a favorite delicacy that surpassed even lima beans. The condemned cat refused every entreaty, although he did take a little snack when Penelope left the room. He needed strength for the coming ordeal.

Mycroft growled when he saw the big wooden traveling cage that had been specially constructed for his journey from Addis Ababa to Phoenix, with layovers in Cyprus, London, and Washington, D.C.

Penelope looked around. Everything was in readiness, except for the reluctant help recruited for the occasion.

Andy soon arrived, a testimony to his courage—or a hidden streak of foolishness.

Penelope offered him coffee while they waited for Laney and Wally.

"I saw the penny on your door," he said. "And then there were none."

"You're mixing your metaphors," Penelope said. "The ten little Indians declined in numbers. The pennies are multiplying like rabbits."

"I still don't like it," Andy said gravely. "You may be in danger. You're very isolated out here. Perhaps you should move in with me until this is over."

"What, and give up my freedom and independence?"

"It's just temporary."

"Ah, so you're saying you don't want me around for the long haul."

"That's not what I meant and you know it. I just meant—"

"I know what you meant, Andy, and you're sweet for offering, but—"

"I know, I know. You can take care of yourself."

"And I have Mycroft. He's quite a good guard cat."

Andy got down on his hands and knees to peer under the chair.

Mycroft hissed.

"He's upset," Andy said. "Perhaps we should do this another time."

"Coward!"

"I am not."

"Am too."

"Am not."

The doorbell rang, interrupting their litany, but Laney threw the door open before Penelope could answer it. Alexander rushed into the room, circling happily, skittering from Penelope to Andy, then back to Penelope and under the chair to join Mycroft.

"Why on earth do you have pennies stuck to your door?" Laney asked breathlessly. "Sorry, we're late, but I couldn't get the handcuffs off Wally. Something's wrong with the damned key."

"Laney!"

"Well, it's true."

As evidence of her veracity, Wally came in and held up his left wrist sheepishly. Handcuffs did, indeed, dangle from his wrist. "She's a pistol, ain't she?"

"She's certainly something," Penelope said. She started giggling. And then she laughed. And laughed some more. Until she cried.

Even Mycroft edged forward to see what all the hilarity was about before retreating again. He knew exactly who he would like to handcuff.

"Aw, Penelope." Wally scuffled his feet uncomfortably.

"I'm sorry," she said, wiping tears away, "but you have to admit it's funny." She turned to Andy. "Do you have your camera in the car? I think it's worthy of a front-page photo, don't you? Noted romance writer subdues lover."

"Penelope," Laney cried, you wouldn't!"

"Well, I was thinking of a series on the sexual mores of Empty Creek," Andy drawled. "This would certainly start it off right."

"Oh, Lord, I'll kill myself. Romance writer forced to suicide by friends—how is that going to look in the headlines?"

"Better get a picture of the late lamented Elaine Henders, Andy. For her obituary."

"This is serious, Penelope. After we catch Mycroft, we need to get them off. I was afraid we'd have to go to the police station." At the thought of public spectacle, Laney's cheeks grew as bright as her flaming red hair. "Oh, God, do you think Sam Connors makes house calls?"

"I'll help," Andy offered. "I'm good with keys."

"Are you now?" Laney asked. "Is this a new side of the respectable newspaper editor?"

It was Andy's turn to blush. "Not like that," he stammered. "Just keys in general."

"If you say so."

"I say we get this circus started."

"I brought Alexander to be a friendly and calming influence."

"Mycroft is more likely to have Yorkshire Terrier for breakfast," Penelope said. "Now this is the plan. Andy, you cut off escape to the kitchen. Laney, you and Wally just lift the chair. I'll grab Mycroft and get him in the cage."

Laney groaned. "Why don't I think this plan is quite as simple as it sounds?"

"Trust me. Everyone ready?" Penelope received nods from each of the participants. "On three, then."

Penelope counted.

Laney and Wally lifted the chair. Penelope pounced and caught Alexander who was delighted to be captured. He gave Penelope a big wet kiss.

Mycroft, meanwhile, dashed between Andy's legs in a gray blur, setting a new land speed record for the distance between the chair and a backup refuge under the kitchen table.

The chase was on. From the kitchen back to the living room and twice around the couch, under the chair again, to the kitchen table, and then to the top of the refrigerator where Mycroft was finally cornered by the winded posse as Alexander provided a medley of yips and yaps for the sound track.

"I swear he just does this because he likes the

chase," Penelope said when she had slammed the door of the cage.

Alexander pleaded Mycroft's case by frenzied barking at Penelope.

"Shut up, or I'll take you, too." The threat had little impact.

"Now, can we please get the handcuffs off Wally?"

Penelope carried Mycroft to the jeep as Andy busily worked away with the key.

When Penelope carried Mycroft's cage through the door labeled Cat Entrance, the cry went up. The dogs, content in their own waiting room on the opposite side of the reception area, barked to assist in the warning—"Mycroft's here."

It echoed through the building, was passed on.

"Mycroft's here."

"Lock the doors."

Mycroft growled, a deep guttural sound.

"My God, what do you have in there?"

Penelope turned to find a woman scrunched into the corner of the waiting room, as far away as she could get from the cage without actually leaving the building. Her cat scrambled for cover behind her.

"Just my cat," Penelope said, smiling at the terrified woman and her equally terrified cat. "He's quite sweet, actually."

A smiling Doctor Bob greeted Penelope and Mycroft heartily. Despite the scars inflicted over the years, Doctor Bob was quite fond of Mycroft. "How is that lion today, anyway?"

The vet was followed into the examining room by Harriet Oliver, a young assistant. She was obviously new or she wouldn't have entered the room with such a sprightly gait.

The examination went well after Penelope dragged Mycroft out. She held him firmly by the scruff of the neck while Doctor Bob poked and prodded, delivered the necessary booster shots, listened to his heart, felt his muscles, pronounced him healthy.

And then a mistake was made.

Harriet left the room to fetch a cat treat. Unfortunately, she left the door slightly ajar.

"We're almost done, Mikey," Doctor Bob crooned in his soft and calming voice that animals—except for Mycroft—responded to so well. "All we have to do now is take your temperature."

Mycroft decided that his temperature was just fine, or would be, if everyone just left him in peace.

"I can't hold him," Penelope cried.

A well-meaning citizen, hearing the commotion and perhaps looking to see if he could be of assistance, opened the door to the dog waiting room just as Mycroft raced down the hallway with Penelope, Doctor Bob, and Harriet in frantic pursuit.

Mycroft turned the corner and skidded to a halt.

He was surrounded by dogs. Big dogs. Little dogs. In-between dogs. Fat, happy, innocent, tongue-lolling creatures, instantly aroused by the appearance of a cat victim in their midst.

Barking bedlam!

Mycroft surveyed the room and the dogs lunging at their leashes.

Cat heaven.

What an opportunity.

Carpe diem.

And Mycroft seized, wading in enthusiastically.

147

Hissing and spitting, hair standing straight up, he delivered a right to the German shepherd, a left to the schnauzer, another right to the poodle with the pink ribbon on her head who was making a puddle on the floor. Perhaps thinking of his friend Alexander, Mycroft pulled his punch on the full-figured Yorkie, before leaping to the receptionist's counter to survey the carnage in his wake.

Legends were made of less.

When the wild melee was over, there were a number of irate dog owners, chagrined and embarrassed by the poor showing of their canines.

Penelope was rather disposed to pity the poor critters. After all, it had been a surprise attack and none of them had expected to run into a vicious, snarling lion straight from the African veldt.

Doctor Bob was gracious when Mycroft had finally been recaptured and carried forcibly to his own side of the building. He even treated the scratched and wounded dogs without charging Penelope for it. Fortunately, the deep psychological scars Mycroft inflicted on the ill-fated canines were not visible, or Penelope would be paying for their therapy.

"Goddamnedest cat, I ever saw," one hapless dog owner said, shaking his head, as his German shepherd cowered.

Mycroft accepted the tribute as his due. If Penelope ever took up needlepoint she was going to have to inscribe it on a pattern.

He was, indeed, the goddamnedest cat anyone ever saw.

And he never did get his temperature taken.

* * *

Back in the jeep, Mycroft stayed in the box for a while, pretending to sulk, although Penelope left the door open. He was very good at sulking, even when the victorious skirmish with the dogs had put him in a better frame of mind.

The staff gathered to wave goodbye. Like Doctor Bob, they were all fond of Mycroft, especially now that they wouldn't see him for another year unless they stopped by the Double B.

Or so they all hoped.

When Kathy saw the big cage in the jeep, she rushed from Mycroft & Company to offer comfort. "Mikey, baby, are you okay?"

Meow, meow, meow, Mycroft complained, telling her of the various indignities heaped upon his person. Meow, meow, meow. Just wait till you hear what I did to them though.

"He's just fine," Penelope said. "I can't say the same for assorted friends, vets, and dog owners, however, and I'm a wreck. I'm considering taking up strong drink."

Mycroft emerged from the cage and allowed Kathy to cuddle him. He purred loudly. All in all, it had been a most satisfying morning to his way of thinking. A little workout or two always got his blood flowing.

Meow. What's for lunch?

"Mycroft & Company," Penelope said into the phone.

"Hi. How's Mycroft?" Andy asked.

"Much better than I am," she answered, stroking

the big cat fondly. He was stretched out on the counter, helping her order books. All was forgiven. "Did you get the handcuffs off Wally?"

"Yes. Just needed a little oil."

"Laney should keep her toys in better working order."

"That's what I said. Someone should write a book about her."

"A thousand and one fantasies."

"See you later?"

"Sure, sweetie. Let's jacuzzi the night away. Don't forget the handcuffs." Penelope hung up on a startled gasp.

Laney was the next to call.

"Did everyone survive?" she asked.

"Names are being withheld until the next of kin are notified."

"That bad, huh?"

"Pretty gruesome, but Mycroft had a wonderful time."

"That's nice. Penelope, you're not going to tell anyone about the handcuffs, are you?"

"Just Mrs. Burnham. That should get it all over town by three o'clock at the latest."

The law offices of Spencer Alcott were decorated in what Penelope could only describe as early flotsam and jetsam—weather-beaten old crates, angular pieces of driftwood, sections of cargo net, part of a lifeboat, crossed oars, and a harpoon. The top of a credenza was covered with sand, tiny starfish imbedded in it. It was quite a feat of interior decoration since the nearest ocean was several hundred miles to the west.

"Penelope Warren to see Mr. Alcott," she said to

150

the receptionist seated behind a nameplate that proclaimed, EMMA PEEL. Surely, that can't be her name.

"Do you have an appointment?" Emma Peel asked.

"We spoke no more than fifteen minutes ago," Penelope replied.

"Oh, yes, Penelope Warren. It's right here. Please have a seat. I'll see if Mr. Alcott can see you now." Emma Peel wagged her derriere as she disappeared behind a door.

Penelope looked for a spot free of nautical knick-knacks and finding none, decided to stand. She heard giggling from behind the door. Was everyone in Empty Creek sex-crazed? Perhaps it's a phase of the moon, Penelope thought. Or the water. There must be something in the water.

The door opened, and a smiling Emma Peel emerged. "Mr. Alcott will see you now," she announced, brushing her hair back into place.

Spencer Alcott inspired seasickness. Even his clothing had a sea-going motif—blue deck shoes fashionably lacking socks, white ducks, and a red polo shirt. The ensemble was topped off by a yachting cap perched jauntily on his head. It was emblazoned CAPT. and had scrambled eggs on the bill.

Penelope needed a good dose of dramamine just looking at him.

Alcott greeted her with a hearty handshake and a Bucky Beaver smile. "Miss Warren," he exclaimed, "how good to see you." He looked like he might like to nibble on Penelope or a handy tree.

"I appreciate your taking the time to meet with me, Mr. Alcott."

"It's my pleasure. Please, be seated, Penelope. And call me, Spence. Everyone does."

"All right, Spence. I'm investigating the murder of Louise Fletcher."

Spence frowned. "Isn't that a job for the authorities?"

Penelope offered her practically brand-new press pass. She would never understand why on earth it was done in hot pink. It certainly did brighten up a room, though.

Spence was not impressed.

Is it the color? Penelope wondered.

"I don't know what I can tell you, Miss Warren. I didn't know the woman."

It certainly didn't take long to get back to formality. "That's not what Louise Fletcher says. She left a detailed record of several conversations with you."

"If such records exist, they are fabrications." He looked ready to bite her with his Bucky Beaver teeth.

What would Woodward and Bernstein ask now? Or for that matter, Robert Redford and Dustin Hoffman. "That's it?" Penelope said rather lamely. Woodward and Bernstein frowned. Deep Throat frowned. Redford and Hoffman frowned. Even Penelope frowned. I am not a crook; Richard Nixon said it.

"That's it," Spencer Alcott, Esq., said.

The *Empty Creek News Journal* certainly wasn't going to win a Pulitzer Prize for investigative journalism at this rate.

"Why would Louise Fletcher lie?"

"Why would I lie?"

"Because you're distributing largess"—oh, Lord, did I really say largess?—"to every politician in town to get your card club approved. Freda Alsberg, at least, is a partner."

"Campaign contributions. Absolutely proper."

"Louise Fletcher called them bribes."

"Louise Fletcher was crazy."

"I thought you didn't know her."

"Only by reputation. Now, if you'll excuse me . . ."

Penelope thought he might say that he had to go gnaw on a tree. Or Mrs. Peel. Those teeth were very disconcerting.

". . . I have work to do," he finished.

Penelope rose. "I'll be back," she promised.

"I shall look forward to it."

Impasse. What would Woodward and Bernstein do now?

Penelope left Spencer Alcott, Esq., to stare after her thoughtfully.

At the door, Penelope turned back to the young receptionist. "Excuse me," she said. "Were your parents fans of "The Avengers," by any chance? Or of Diana Rigg?"

"Who's she? Is that a rock group? I never heard of "The Avengers." Are they any good?"

"It's an old TV program from the sixties. How did you get your name?"

"I was named for my grandmother."

"Oh."

It was difficult to imagine the real Emma Peel as a grandmother.

"He's stonewalling," Penelope told Big Mike when she returned to the bookshop. "I just hate that."

"Who's stonewalling?" Kathy asked as she came into the back room of the shop.

"Spencer Alcott—Bucky Beaver."

"Oh." Kathy retreated. Penelope was going to be in one of her moods again.

Meow, Big Mike said.

"Meow, indeed. That's what I should have said."

When Chief John Fowler entered Mycroft & Company, he found Penelope and Mycroft dozing in the chair before the fireplace. It had already been a very full day for both of them. The bell at the door awakened Mycroft, who stared up at Fowler with placid curious eyes. When Mycroft stirred, Penelope roused herself from an enjoyable dream in which Andy had been nibbling away at various portions of her anatomy with big Bucky Beaver teeth.

"Oh, John, I didn't hear you come in."

"I can see that. It's a good thing I'm not a shoplifter."

"Who would steal books?"

"Dishonest readers, I suppose."

"You didn't come to discuss my security measures. How can I help you?"

Fowler took the small corpulent bust of Mycroft Holmes and examined it carefully. "There's a nick in it," he said.

"Mikey keeps knocking it over. I keep the good ones in back, out of his reach. Sometimes I don't think he likes his name. Would you like a Mycroft Holmes for your desk?"

Fowler shook his head as he replaced the statuette. "I've been getting some telephone calls, Penelope."

"About me?"

"You've agitated some people."

"I can't imagine who."

"Councilwoman Alsberg for one. Spencer Alcott for another. They think you're prying and that you have no right to do so."

"And you've come to arrest me." Penelope offered her wrists for handcuffs. "For prying." She giggled as she remembered Wally's recent adventure with handcuffs. Whatever were that pair doing last night?

Fowler smiled and shook his head again. "No," he said. "I just came by to warn you to be careful. I'd hate to have you upset the wrong person. I don't want anything to happen to you. One murder is enough for me."

"Have you made any progress?"

"No. We're stuck."

"And the more time that passes, the less likely you are to catch whoever did it?"

"That's usually the way it works. I don't like the thought of a murderer walking free in my town. I want this guy, Penelope."

"You're convinced it's a man? Louise threatened to expose Freda's involvement with Alcott's scheme for a card club."

"Both Freda and Spence told me about that. They've done nothing illegal as far as I can tell."

"I've always thought that honesty—to a point, of course—was an excellent deception."

"Oh, I'm not ruling them out, I'm not ruling anyone out, but it seems a poor motive for murder. Louise would have been an irritant to their plans, but nothing more than that. Now they stand to lose a fortune."

"And Herbert Fletcher gained a fortune."

"But has an alibi."

"That does cloud things."

"Well, I'd better be going."

"Thanks for stopping by."

"Be careful, Penelope."

"We're through detecting for the day. Aren't we, Mycroft?"

"I heard about his visit to Doctor Bob."

"Already?"

"It's all over town. How many dogs did he fight anyway?"

"Three, but it wasn't really a fight."

"Only three? I heard ten. I suppose it'll be twenty by tomorrow. I could use him in my K-9 unit."

"I don't think he'd like the regimentation, but I'm sure he'd be very good at police work."

"The dogs couldn't stand the competition anyway."

Mycroft purred. Damned straight.

Penelope almost dreaded their nocturnal commune with nature, but Mycroft wanted to go outside and she didn't want Andy to know that she was fearful. It wasn't going into the desert night that bothered her, it was using the front door. She didn't want to find another of those damned pennies on it.

"Come on, Andy, let's meditate." She took his hand and led him outside, glancing casually back at the door. The mad penny gluer had not struck again. There were still only two pennies on the door. The Abraham Lincoln twins, standing guard, eternally vigilant.

Equally vigilant, Mycroft prowled around the circle of light while Penelope and Andy meditated in a rather unusual fashion.

CHAPTER ELEVEN

Mycroft awakened more readily than usual, poking his nose out from underneath the bed covers, wrinkling it as he sniffed the air. Yes, the faint tangy scent of adventure was definitely there.

He emerged to let Penelope know of the good things in store, nuzzling the tousled hair that framed her face. After all, there are times in any self-respecting cat's life when eating and sleeping are no longer enough.

No response.

He pushed his cold nose against her cheek.

"Mmmph," Penelope said.

Wake up, damn it. Places to go. Things to do.

He walked up and down her legs and stomach.

Still sleeping, Penelope pushed him away.

He poked her cheek with his big right paw. His claws were withdrawn, of course. He only wanted to awaken her, not maim her.

That got to her.

"Mycroft, damn it," Penelope cried. "There are people trying to sleep around here." She sat up in bed.

Mycroft nodded. About time.

Penelope crabbed her way awake and stumbled into the kitchen to put the coffee on.

After a hearty breakfast and a good bath, Mycroft made a pest of himself, pacing back and forth, getting underfoot, complaining loudly, demanding to be let out. He was ready for adventuring.

Despite her entreaties, Mycroft refused to go to work with Penelope. When the mood strikes, there is nothing to be done but follow the quest for adventure. This trait is called stubbornness in a human being but independence in a cat.

Usually.

"Stubborn damned cat," Penelope said, surrendering and going off to town alone.

Mycroft set out across the desert to call on his lady love.

Herbert Fletcher—damn the man!—was again ensconced in the big easy chair before the fireplace at Mycroft & Company. A fresh bandage hid the scratches Mycroft had inflicted.

Fair-mistress-to-be Kathy Allen was behind the counter—for safety. "Good morrow, my lady."

"Good morrow, Mistress Allen," Penelope replied politely, although she failed to see anything good about a day that started with Herbert Fletcher. He was becoming as much of a nuisance as Louise had been. What now?

Fletcher rose nervously as Penelope entered the shop, bending and craning his neck to look past her, as though he expected the cat from Hades to fly at him.

"You needn't worry," Penelope said. "Mycroft is taking the day off."

Without preamble Fletcher then launched into a tirade. "The damned woman is hounding me," he cried. "Stalking me, following me everywhere, calling me at all hours, threatening me. She's abusive. The woman's obsessed."

"Which woman? Freda?"

"Of course, Freda. Who else could it be?"

"What evidence do you have?"

"Evidence. What do you mean, evidence? I just told you what she's doing. I'm beginning to fear for my life. I think she's got a gun."

"A shotgun, no doubt," Penelope said.

Kathy giggled from her post behind the counter.

"That's not funny," Fletcher said.

Penelope thought the image of Herbert Fletcher marching to the altar with Freda's shotgun in his back was funny, but she shrugged and let it go. "Do you have any witnesses?" she asked instead.

"She's too clever for that. As soon as I had a tape recorder next to the telephone, she stopped calling."

"You could get a court order, I suppose."

"That would make me quite the figure for ridicule. Please, your honor, stop the woman from tormenting me."

"What can I do?" Penelope asked.

"Lido Isle," Herbert Fletcher said, giving a whole new meaning to the term *non sequitur*.

"Pardon me?"

"Check into Lido Isle. It's some kind of corporation, I think."

"Why me?"

"You have research qualifications."

"In literature."

"It's the same thing. Digging through musty old documents."

"I have allergies."

"So do I."

It was true. Penelope had a convenient—if bogus—

159

allergy for every occasion. They were quite useful when it came to avoiding unpleasant occasions. A sneeze, an apologetic smile, and the comment "It's your aftershave lotion" avoided an unwanted kiss when dating. One persistent candidate for her affections gave up shaving and colognes of every description. Penelope's sensitive skin then developed an allergy to beards and mustaches.

Her curiosity was piqued on this occasion, however, and she decided to hold the allergies in reserve. "Oh, all right," she said. "I'll do it, but I can't guarantee how long I'll hold up. Musty old documents bring out the worst in me."

"I think you'll find yourself amply rewarded."

"Where did you come across this corporation?"

"Louise told me about it." He sniffled at her memory.

"Recently?" Penelope asked.

As befitted a small-town newspaper, the offices of the *News Journal* were modestly housed on the second floor of an office building standing, like everything else in Empty Creek, at desert's edge. The public entrance was guarded by one Harriet MacLemore, a robust and gargantuan woman who for years had failed to grasp the simple concept that a newspaper served its community. Mac, a former longshorewoman who claimed she could do wheelies with her fork lift, jealously protected the editorial and advertising portals from public intrusion, reluctantly allowing entrance only after a rigorous grilling as to purpose, intent, and reason for violating the sanctity of the *News Journal.* One Chamber of Commerce wag complained, "You need a goddamned court order to place a goddamned ad." The faint of heart never got past Mac.

Even before receiving her honorary press credentials, Penelope always bypassed Mac by using the employee entrance at the back of the building.

Andy's telephone rang just as Penelope entered his office. He waved to her and grabbed the phone. "News desk, Anderson!"

Penelope admired the way he responded on the telephone. He sounded like a real newspaperman. It was just as she imagined H. L. Mencken or Ernest Hemingway in his reporting days might have answered. "News desk, Hemingway!" Not that Andy wasn't a real newspaperman, of course, but away from the office he was gentle and soft-spoken, not at all gruff the way he was when answering the phone. Penelope believed there was probably a required course in journalism school called "Gruff 101—Telephone Answering Techniques."

"News desk, Warren!" she said when Andy hung up. It wasn't the same. She tried again. "News desk, Warren!" Better, but not by much.

"What *are* you doing, Penelope?"

"Trying to answer the telephone the way you do, but I think I've hurt my throat. I'm a failure. Edna Buchanan doesn't have to worry about me."

"You're much prettier than Edna Buchanan."

"But she has a Pulitzer Prize."

"That's true, but you have me."

"I'd rather have a Pulitzer."

"Penelope!"

"Just kidding, dear heart. What do you know about Lido Isle?"

"It's in Newport Beach," Andy replied. "In California."

161

"Not that Lido Isle. This Lido Isle. In Arizona. A corporation of some sort."

Andy shrugged his shoulders. "Never heard of it."

"Don't you run legal notices?"

"Yes, but I never read them. All that fine print? No normal person reads legal notices."

"Louise Fletcher did. At least, I think she did. Unless she's communicating with Herbert from the spirit world."

"There you go again, Penelope. I never know what you're talking about."

"Really, Andy. You must learn to follow conversations. If you're going to be the love of my life, you have to be able to get into my mind as well as my bower."

"Bower?"

"It's a euphemism, nicer than bed."

"You weren't at all euphemistic last night during meditation."

"One never is," Penelope said, smiling wickedly, "not during meditation."

"Oh."

"Now, back to Lido Isle. Herb thinks this corporation might have some valuable information. Can you look it up in your legal notices?"

"Of course. Why didn't you just say so?"

"I did."

Andy turned to his keyboard and rapidly typed in a series of commands. That was another thing Penelope admired about him. He was an excellent typist, much better than she was. He would make someone a good secretary.

"Nothing," Andy said.

"Damn, I thought this would be a good place to start."

"I guess you'll have to call the secretary of state's office."

At least the telephone was better than musty records. "Well, thanks anyway, sweetie."

"You're welcome. Where's Mycroft?" Mycroft always enjoyed a visit to the *Empty Creek News Journal*. There was so much mischief to be made in the cluttered offices, and he liked sleeping on top of Andy's computer. Trust Mycroft to pick out the most expensive bed in sight.

"Oh, he's in one of his moods," Penelope said. "Wanted a day off, I suppose."

"The desert won't be safe for man or beast with Big Mike on the prowl. Aren't you worried?"

"Mycroft can take care of himself, but I do worry about him a little."

"I meant you should be worried about man and beast."

Back at Mycroft & Company, Penelope called the secretary of state's office, only to learn that Lido Isle, Inc. was a subsidiary of a California corporation. Four telephone calls later—to the secretaries of state in California, Florida, Virginia, and New Jersey—Penelope found that the trail of Lido Isle, Inc. disappeared into a maze of secretive laws in a tiny Caribbean nation. Freda Alsberg's name appeared in no records of Lido Isle or the large companies which swallowed it up like a fish in the food chain.

"Fie!" Penelope said when she had finished talking to New Jersey. "Double fie!"

"Trouble, my lady?"

"Confusion, Mistress Allen, confusion. What comes to mind when you think of New Jersey?"

"Nothing."

"Exactly. What does New Jersey have to do with the price of eggs in Empty Creek?"

"I don't know."

"Neither do I. I'm beginning to wish Louise Fletcher had found a more convenient location to be murdered." Penelope sighed. "I'm going over to the civic center. If Herbert Fletcher returns, lock him out."

"Gladly, my lady."

A search of property records revealed that Freda Alsberg had sold ten acres of desert to Lido Isle, Inc.

So what? It wasn't illegal to sell property.

Freda had made a profit on the sale, quite a substantial profit according to the records.

Well, it wasn't illegal to make a profit on a business transaction. Fleecing the competition was the American way.

The sale had been handled by Spencer Alcott, Esq.

So what again? It wasn't illegal—although it should be—for lawyers to wheel and deal.

Penelope moved on to campaign contribution reports. In each of her two campaigns for the City Council, Spencer Alcott had contributed the maximum amount of money to Freda Alsberg. The other members of the city council had received lesser amounts.

Nothing illegal. Contributions bought ready access, not votes. Except . . .

Freda was apparently prepared to introduce an ordinance which would make gambling at a card club legal in Empty Creek.

Everything was circumstantial so far. Except . . .

Except what?

Penelope returned to Mycroft & Company feeling more than a little frustrated with it all.

At least the shop was busy most of the afternoon. Penelope and Kathy took turns dealing with customers, ringing up sales, unpacking an order that had just arrived. During the slack moments, Penelope busied herself with putting the new arrivals on the shelves. Still, Herbert Fletcher, Freda Alsberg, Spencer Alcott, and Lido Isle nagged at her.

And she missed the damned cat.

When Penelope finally went home—early, because she *was* worried about Mycroft—she found a very pleased male cat preening himself, a female cat named Murphy Brown with a satisfied expression on her face, and a most distraught woman, one Josephine Brooks, agitatedly pacing back and forth in front of the happy feline couple.

The cats blithely ignored Josephine.

Penelope wished she could do the same as she pulled the jeep to a stop and climbed out. "Hi, Jo. What's up?"

"He's done it again. That's what."

"Done what?"

"They eloped, and he seduced Murphy Brown. She's probably pregnant again. You should get him fixed."

"They didn't elope. They're right here. And Mycroft is not getting fixed. It's not natural. You should keep better track of Murphy. Besides, look at the little trollop. She's promiscuous, a regular little Jezebel. If there was any seducing going on, Murphy had a paw in it. It's not like she's a virgin or something."

"It was all set," Jo wailed. "She was going to mate

165

with a champion. The kittens would have been beautiful."

"Their last litter was beautiful," Penelope protested.

"They were alley cats. No breeding, no heritage, no papers."

"Real cats, in short, not some dumb inbred creatures who wouldn't know one end of a mouse from another."

"I'm never going to have a champion at this rate."

"Don't take it so hard, Jo. We'll find good homes for them all. Come on, we'll have a nice glass of wine together."

"Well . . ."

"Blue ribbons aren't everything," Penelope said. "We have to think of their happiness."

"They do look happy. . . ."

"I hope they practiced safe sex," Penelope said.

After two glasses of wine, Jo was resigned to another litter of nonchampionship-caliber kittens and went home with Murphy Brown tucked beneath her arm.

The new father-to-be promptly curled up and went to sleep leaving Penelope with no one to talk to. After a few indecisive minutes, she decided to answer Robert Sidney-Veine's missive from Malawi. A reply was long overdue.

Leaving Mycroft to sleep off passion and ardor, Penelope went into the small bedroom she had converted to an office and fired up the computer. After staring at the screen for a moment, she started typing.

TO : The Old Boy
From: The Old Girl

Mycroft and I were delighted to receive your

latest *billet doux.* I, of course, was heartbroken to learn of your liaison with a classics professor. Thinking of you in the arms of another, I weep myself to sleep nightly, consoled only by dreams of that handsome brute, Sean Connery. (Tell me, do you conjugate those awful Latin verbs beneath the mosquito net in your tropical bower?)

Still, I manage to keep body and soul together through work and the constant attentions of Harrison Anderson III. And the strangest thing happened only a few days ago.

Murder was committed on my doorstep.

Louise Fletcher, the town busybody and a woman of enormous wealth, was stabbed to death. Her husband, who inherits everything, would be a prime suspect except for an unimpeachable alibi. The authorities are stymied, so I've taken up the chase. I suspect everyone.

The telephone rang. Penelope stopped typing and looked at it distastefully. She really wasn't in the mood for speaking with anyone.

It rang again.

She sighed and answered it. "Hello?"

"Penelope Warren, this is Louise Fletcher."

"What?" Penelope cried.

The voice on the telephone ignored Penelope's question.

"You will only hear this message in the event of my death. You are the only person I can trust."

It took a moment for Penelope to realize that she was listening to a recorded message, another for her to start taking notes hurriedly as the deceased Louise Fletcher spoke.

"Silent Night. Page three hundred thirty-six. Look at the cover, Penelope Warren. *Silent Night.* Avenge my death, Penelope Warren."

Louise Fletcher stopped speaking.

Penelope listened until the dial tone buzzed in her ear.

Good God!

She turned back to the glow of the green letters on the computer screen and typed:

Old Boy, the most extraordinary thing just happened. Your classics professor would no doubt understand. A voice from the underworld just spoke to me. I must go!

Penelope saved the file, exited the program, turned the computer off, and listened to its fading whine. It sounded like a vacuum cleaner wheezing to silence. A reluctant housekeeper, Penelope was not that familiar with turning a vacuum cleaner on or off, but that's what the computer always sounded like to her. And to her, the machines were quite the same thing. The one sucked up dirt, the other sucked up information.

Staring at the now black computer screen, Penelope realized that thinking of vacuum cleaners was somewhat irrational in view of the most extraordinary thing that had just occurred. She forgave herself for the absurdity, however. It wasn't every evening that the sheeted dead squeaked and gibbered in the streets or, in this case, into Penelope's telephone. In Shakespeare's *Hamlet,* the appearances of the sheeted dead were portents of momentous events yet to come and foreshadowed the death of Julius Caesar. As Horatio sought to explain the warlike appearance of the ghost, he said, "A little ere the mightiest Julius fell,/The graves stood tenantless, and the sheeted dead/Did squeak and gibber in the Roman streets."

Louise Fletcher's disembodied voice on the telephone had sounded for all the world like a ghost telling Penelope to avenge her death. Hamlet's father.

Penelope went to a bookcase and extracted a paperback copy of Gary Amo's novel, *Silent Night*. Returning to the desk, she opened the book to page 336 and read. The page began in the middle of a word. Penelope turned back and found "chal-" on the previous page. It continued:

"lenge to the mountains and the gods who live there. All others tread timidly.

"Although it can never be his, man has given names to the landmarks of the Superstitions. Black Mountain, Bluff Spring, Haunted Canyon Spring, Weaver's Needle, Fish Creek Canyon, Massacre grounds, Hell's Hole Spring, Geronimo Head, Battleship Mountain, Rough Canyon, Windy Pass, Angel Basin, Whiskey Spring, Castle Dome. The names seem an apology for man's inability to tame this wilderness— and more. The names are an admission of fear.

"For the Superstitions abound in murderous legends—tales of death, beheaded corpses, unidentified skeletons, unexplained disappearances, and endless traps for the unwary. The Apache were probably the first to see the mountains, long before the Spanish arrived in their endless quest for El Dorado. Fierce and warlike, the Superstitions matched those first warriors who adopted them as their own, made them sacred as the home of their gods. Their arrows could not fail as they fell on other hapless tribes—the Pima and the Maricopa—raiding and plundering at whim. The Pima and the Maricopa saw the Superstitions as evil. They figure in the Pima legend of the Flood, a white line on the mountain called Superstition marks the high water mark of the Flood, the foam staining the mountain. When the Spanish came they called it *Sierra de la Espuma*—the Mountain of the Foam. They sought the gold and were driven out by the Apache. But even the Apache finally abandoned the mountains after a monumental battle with their ancient enemies within the sacred domain of their gods. The mountains were now taboo. Some say a few wild Apache still roam the mountains, protecting them from intruders.

"Legends persist, too, around the Lost Dutchman Mine, reputed to be found within two miles of Weaver's Needle, the highest peak in the superstitions. A thou-"

It ended there. What was Louise Fletcher talking about? What did her murder have to do with the Superstition Mountains?

Penelope looked at the cover of the book. It was dark and forbidding, on it a house very much like Penelope's own—a Southwestern-style desert home with a tiled roof and a heavy wooden door. Penelope looked closely to see if the artist had glued pennies to the wood. Lightning streaked through the night sky, crackling above a gloomy mountain. A saguaro flanked an open window at which a curtain floated ominously. The only cheery aspect on the cover was a gaily decorated Christmas tree visible in the open window.

"Creepy," Penelope said to Mycroft who had suddenly appeared on the desk beside the computer.

And who in hell was Louise Fletcher's accomplice? Someone had had to play the tape into the telephone—unless there were telephones in the beyond. Perhaps it was like being in jail and you were allowed one call back to earth.

There would be one hell of a toll charge.

CHAPTER TWELVE

A very long, very white limousine with darkly smoked windows eased to a halt in front of Mycroft & Company precisely at one o'clock. It was an unusual sight in Empty Creek, where the taste in transportation ran mostly to horses—even Mycroft & Company had a hitching rail—jeeps, pickup trucks, or trendy convertibles. It was also rather peculiar that the limousine just sat there, taking up what seemed to be the entire block.

"Penelope," Kathy called. "Come look at this."

What now?

Penelope, with Mycroft, had arrived only ten minutes earlier, after tossing and turning much of the night, then spending a restless morning thinking about that bizarre telephone call from one Louise Fletcher, deceased, and staring at the cover of *Silent Night,* seeking the elusive clue that would reveal the meaning of Louise's message. Penny suspected that Mycroft's thoughts had run more to memories of kitty love.

Penelope sighed and carried her heavy coffee mug to the front. Mycroft was already at the door, standing upright against the window, looking out.

"Who do you think it could be?"

"I don't know."

"I'll bet it's the Mafia," Kathy said.

Penelope found Kathy's statement unsettling. Spencer Alcott's proposal for gambling in Empty Creek might very well attract organized crime interests. Once again, she sighed heavily. What a way to start the working day.

The three of them peered out at the limousine.

"Why would the Mafia come to Mycroft & Company?" Penelope asked. "I don't think the mob reads very much. I don't remember ever seeing Al Pacino with a book. Or Marlon Brando for that matter. If they are Mafia, they're probably going to the video store. No doubt they had a sudden urge to see *The Godfather* again."

Penelope found it disconcerting that she couldn't see whoever was in the limo, not even the driver. Although its wheels were planted firmly on the ground, the large automobile looked like an alien craft hovering menacingly out there in the street. Perhaps they had come to rent *Aliens III.*

The driver's door opened slowly, and a tanned young man emerged. Being rather tall, he was emerging for quite a long time. He adjusted his mirrored sunglasses, straightened his jacket and tie, and slowly looked over the entire neighborhood before walking toward Mycroft & Company.

"Do you think he's got a gun?" Kathy asked.

There was a distinct bulge beneath the left shoulder of his jacket. Penelope was sure of it. "I hope he's going to rent a video," she said nervously.

Penelope and Kathy backed away from the door. Penelope had to return to get Mycroft. The Godfather of the Empty Creek Cat Family wasn't intimidated.

The dark young man entered the store.

Still holding Mycroft, Penelope asked politely, "May I help you?"

The alleged mobster surveyed the bookshop disdainfully, an arrogant smirk just parting his lips. When he finally deigned to reply, he said only, "Penelope Warren."

"I'm Penelope Warren."

"My boss wants to see you," the chauffeur said. "Out in the car."

"And who is your boss?"

"Don't make me come back and get you, lady."

He left the shop abruptly, slamming the door. The bell tolled mournfully.

" 'And therefore, never send to know for whom the bell tolls; it tolls for thee,' " Penelope said.

"John Donne," Kathy offered. " 'Devotions XII.' Shall I call the police, my lady?"

Penelope shook her head. "Let's go, Mycroft. Even if it is the Mafia, they're not going to shoot down an unarmed woman and her cat in the streets at high noon. It just isn't done in the best criminal circles."

"It's after one, my lady," Kathy pointed out helpfully.

"Well, at high one-fifteen then." Penelope gripped the heavy coffee mug firmly as she walked to the limousine, looking back to ensure that the Godfather was following.

The rear door of the limousine opened and a pale but elegant arm emerged, offering a champagne flute filled to overflowing.

"Bubbly, Penny?" her sister asked.

Penelope almost dropped the coffee mug. "Cassie!" she screamed.

"Not so loud, dahling," Cassandra Warren drawled,

174

settling into her best Tallulah Bankhead imitation. "You'll wake the dead."

"What are you doing here?" Penelope cried.

"Didn't you get my card? I told you I was coming."

"Yes, but I thought it was next week."

"You really must check your mailbox more often, Penny. God knows how long my card's been sitting there. Well, here I am."

"Yes, you certainly are. What are you doing in a limousine?"

"A little reward to myself for finishing another film without killing the director. Get in, dahling, we'll demonstrate our conveyance, won't we, John?"

John smiled shyly from the driver's compartment which seemed to be about a mile away. "It would be my pleasure."

"He scared us to death."

"Just our little plot to provide excitement to your otherwise dull life. You needn't worry about John. He's gay and ever so sensitive. Wouldn't harm a fly."

"No!" Penelope exclaimed.

"Yes, dear lady," John said. "It's true, I'm happy to say."

"Stormy!" Kathy shouted as she raced from the shop. "Stormy!"

"Hey, Kathy." Cassandra jumped from the limousine and hugged Kathy. "It's good to see you."

"Oh, you too. Penelope didn't tell me you were coming."

"I meant to," Penelope said.

"She didn't even know when I was coming. I wish you would remind her to empty her mailbox once a month, at least."

Mycroft had been ignored long enough. He rubbed against Cassie's legs.

"Mikey precious, did I forget you?" Cassie reached down and swept the cat into her arms. She showered him with kisses and hugs until he squirmed to get away.

"Kathy, run and close the shop. We're going for a ride."

Kathy looked at Penelope. "My lady?"

Penelope shrugged helplessly. Cassie always took Empty Creek in a thundering charge. Resistance was futile. "Why not?"

With the store locked and a note posted informing potential customers that Mycroft & Company would reopen at three o'clock, the women climbed into the limousine and settled into the back seat.

Mycroft nested happily among them.

"Where to, Stormy?" John asked.

"Oh, just out into the desert. Someplace remote."

"I know the perfect place."

"Champagne, ladies?"

John drove down the main street of Empty Creek. As the limousine cruised through town, passers-by stopped to gawk. Penelope noted with satisfaction that Eleanor Burnham nearly dropped her shopping bag—her jaw did drop. The town crier would have many a restless moment until she found out who was in the limousine and why.

"Muffy and Biff said hello and want to know when you're coming home. They also want to know when you're going to get an answering machine."

"Football season is the answer to the first question, and never is the answer to the second. You know how much I detest the twentieth century and its appliances." That reminded Penelope that Discreet Investigations had still not returned her call. So much for answering machines.

"I don't know how you can stand football," Cassandra said. "I much prefer basketball. The uniforms are so much simpler and more revealing."

Penelope was devoted to her undergraduate alma mater, San Diego State University, and its football team. If a game wasn't televised, she blithely flew off to San Diego. Even Mycroft had to participate during football season, wearing—albeit reluctantly—his not-so-little red and black Aztec sweater on game days. Mycroft also had a scarlet and gold sweater emblazoned with the Globe and Anchor for celebrating the Marine Corps birthday each November tenth.

"I suppose we'll all have to make the trek to San Diego," Cassandra complained.

Penelope smiled sweetly. "Attendance will be taken, especially for the BYU game." The Brigham Young University Cougars were the hated rivals of the SDSU Aztecs. "Aztecas," Penelope cried, "Aztecas, Aztecas. Sis, boom, bah. Aztecas, Aztecas, Aztecas. Rah, rah, rah." Her season tickets were in the alumni section, and that was the only cheer the graduates could manage.

Penelope finished her champagne and held her flute out for more.

Kathy, who didn't understand Penelope's passion for football any more than Cassandra did, asked, "How long are you staying, Stormy?"

"Oh, just a few days. I'm filming a commercial next week."

"Not another one of those ghastly swimsuit things," her sister said.

"It wasn't ghastly at all," Cassandra protested.

"I wish I could do a swimsuit commercial," Kathy said wistfully.

"You have the figure for it," Cassandra observed, "and as soon as you finish school, I'll help you get started as an actress. But you have to graduate first."

"You sound just like Penelope."

"It's not often my sister is right, but she is in this case."

"Yes, Stormy."

For John, the perfect place appeared to be the summit of Crying Woman Mountain. As he deftly guided the long car along the twisting and turning road, Penelope, Cassie, and Kathy giggled and tippled in the rear compartment.

"I wonder if this is what the first lady feels like as she's whisked through the streets of Washington?" Cassie mused as she wrestled with the cork in another bottle of champagne.

"I doubt that the first lady drinks while on the nation's business," Penelope replied, thinking of Louise Fletcher. She frowned. "Besides, this isn't whisking. We're barely moving."

"In any case, the secret service would assist her with the cork."

"Let me," Penelope said, taking the chilled bottle. With a single motion, she popped the cork free. "It's easy. Twist the bottle, not the cork."

"I didn't know that," Kathy said as she lifted the car phone. "It works." She turned to the television set.

"Penelope was always good with mechanical things," Cassie declared. "Despite what she says about the twentieth century."

"I would hardly classify a champagne cork as mechanical," Penelope retorted.

"So," Cassie said, "tell me all about the men in your lives. Did you save one for me?"

"And me?" John said.

"You pay attention to the road," Cassie ordered. "There aren't enough good men to go around now."

"You sound like a Marine Corps recruiting slogan."

"I should have followed in your footsteps."

"Muffy and Biff would have killed you. I only got away with it because I didn't tell them what I was doing."

"Thanks to you, they practically had armed guards following me around the day after I graduated from dear old Peninsula High."

"My class is having its fifteenth reunion this year."

"Are you going?"

"Good grief, no."

"Why not? I'll bet that cute Dicky Harris will be there."

"Along with his second, or is it his third wife. No, thank you."

"He always liked you best."

"Can you see me as the wife of a computer salesman?"

"Well, not really, but he's done very well."

"Oh, good Lord," Penelope exclaimed as the limousine topped the last crest and pulled into the small park high above Empty Creek. The beautiful vista from the mountain peak was marred by the presence of another car. "Freda's here. Damn. I don't want to see her again."

"Why not?" Cassie said. "We'll offer her a glass or two of bubbly. Mellow her right out, no matter what she's done."

"She thinks I'm trying to steal her lover—her former lover, I should say, or one-time lover if he is to be believed."

"Whatever are you babbling about, Penny?"

"You see, Louise Fletcher was murdered on my doorstep," Penelope explained.

"And Mrs. Burnham thinks it was the Mafia," Kathy said, "only she had it wrong. Mrs. Fletcher wasn't gunned down. She was stabbed to death."

Cassandra Warren stared incredulously from her sister to Kathy and back again.

"With a chopping knife," Kathy added lamely.

"There was a penny glued to the handle," Penelope said in an attempt to elucidate for a movie star whose attention span had been addled by too many meetings with illiterate producers whose own attention spans were severely limited. "And two pennies glued to my door."

Cassie looked down at Mycroft who had climbed onto her lap some time ago. "Do you know what they're talking about, precious?" she asked.

Mycroft, who was following the conversation with interest, knew exactly what they were talking about, but made no reply. He was quite content in Stormy's heavenly lap and wasn't about to upset a good thing by getting involved in sisterly vagaries.

"Perhaps you'd better start at the beginning," Cassie said.

"That is the beginning," Penelope said. She was now perched on the jump seat looking through the tinted windows for Freda. Freda's car appeared to be empty, and there was no sign of the councilwoman anywhere.

"John," Penelope said, rather more loudly than was

180

necessary. Despite the length of the luxurious automobile, he could hear her quite distinctly.

"Yes, ma'am?"

"No one can see in, right?"

"That's correct, ma'am."

"Oh, please stop with the ma'ams. You sound just like Sean Connery."

"I do?"

"In my dream. Sean Connery kept saying, 'Howdy, ma'am.'"

"He did?" John looked about, perhaps seeking an escape route. Men were so much simpler to deal with.

"Yes, he did. My name's Penny. I mean Penelope. Cassie's the only person who calls me Penny."

"Do you have a fever, Penny?" Cassie asked. "Should I call a doctor?"

"It's all true, my lady," Kathy said in an attempt to rescue Penelope. "I mean, I don't know about Sean Connery, but everything else is true. Louise Fletcher was murdered with a chopping knife."

Penelope twisted about. "Well, we're not stepping one foot out of this car until she's gone."

"But I thought she was gone," Cassie said. "Murdered."

"That was Louise Fletcher, not Freda Alsberg."

"John, you've delivered me to a lunatic asylum."

"Yes, ma'am," he agreed.

"Cassie, please try to follow the chain of events. It's quite simple really. Louise Fletcher was murdered. Her husband, Herbert Fletcher—"

"He's a lecherous old goat," Kathy interjected.

"Yes, he is, but please don't interrupt."

"Sorry, my lady."

"Freda thinks I'm after Herbert Fletcher now, because of his money. He inherits quite a sum, by all accounts."

"Oh, really? Perhaps I should meet this Herbert Fletcher. He might want to invest in films. Is he good looking? For a lecherous old goat, I mean?"

"Cassie, please. Freda had a brief affair with Herbert. On the other hand, Herbert thinks that Freda and Spencer Alcott conspired to murder his wife because she was opposed to gambling in Empty Creek."

"What kind of motive is that? You might as well start killing everyone opposed to bingo."

"Spencer Alcott has a proposal for a card club in Empty Creek. Freda, a limited partner in the club, is going to introduce it through the city council, you see."

"No, I don't."

"Oh, Cassie."

"Where is this mysterious Freda?"

"Out there somewhere, I suppose."

"Penny, dearest, out there is a desolate mountain slope. There are probably rattlesnakes, gila monsters, and a variety of other icky creatures."

"It's too early for snakes."

"And what about the other little icky creatures?"

"They say a mountain lion lives up here," Kathy interjected.

"Well, that settles it," Cassie said. "John, lock the doors. We're not getting out of this vehicle. If Freda Whatever-her-name-is wants champagne, she will just have to come to it."

"We could just go," Penelope offered.

"We wait. I want to see this Freda woman. And while we wait, you can explain exactly what is going on here. In English this time, please."

It took another fifteen minutes and another glass of

champagne before Cassie had the somewhat convoluted course of events clear. Penelope did not feel up to adding that a dead woman had made a telephone call to her.

"And you and Mycroft are hot on the trail of the killer," Cassie said when Penelope finished the tale and gulped down the remainder of her champagne. "Do you think that's wise?"

"Don't you start, Cassandra Warren. I'm sick of everyone worrying about me."

"I was only thinking of Mycroft. If anything should happen to you, I'd have to take him in, and I'm not at all sure he'd like the film world. What with having to wear sunglasses and designer flea collars and all."

"He doesn't have fleas."

"He would after one meeting at Disney. Probably worse. Those people are impossible. What did you think of the Amazon bunch, by the way?"

"It was a howler," Penelope said honestly.

"Yes, it was. And dare I ask?"

"Mycroft hated it, as usual."

"Oh, Mikey, shame on you. Auntie Cassie tries so hard to please."

Penelope squirmed around on the jump seat. "Where do you think she could be? There's no place to go up here."

"Maybe the mountain lion got her," Cassie said.

"That's just a legend," Penelope said.

"Perhaps she's in the bushes with someone," Kathy suggested.

"At her age?"

"Timmy's always trying to get me to come up here at night."

"Timmy has a terminal case of lust."

"You know," Cassie said thoughtfully, "she might

have fallen. Broken her ankle or something. She's probably lying in pain somewhere, watching the circling vultures and waiting for merciful death."

"There are no vultures out there," Penelope said after looking out. "There's nothing out there."

"Except an empty car."

"I'm getting worried," Penelope said. "I'm going to look for her."

"Good idea," Cassie agreed. "Kathy, bring the champagne. The poor thing may be dying of thirst in this heat."

"It's seventy degrees," Penelope said, "if that."

"One never knows. John, bring your gun."

"I don't have a gun, Stormy," he replied.

"You don't? What about a tire iron or something?"

"All I have is a triple-A card."

"Well, bring that. I'm sure it'll be useful if we have to open a locked door or something."

Penelope stepped from the limousine. "Freda?" she called. The wind carried Penelope's cry over the mountain slopes, but there was no answer. She turned to look at the assemblage now gathered behind her. Penelope shrugged.

Freda's car was indeed empty and unlocked. "The keys are in the ignition and her purse is on the seat," Penelope said. "She can't be far away." Penelope took a deep breath and mustered her very best command voice. "Freda!"

No answer.

Mycroft sniffed the wind.

"I guess we'd better spread out and search for her," Penelope said. She started toward the low stone wall that enclosed the tiny little park.

Footsteps followed her.

Penelope turned. Cassie, Kathy, and John were clustered in a tight little group. Cassie smiled. "I think it's better if we all stick together," she said.

"Where's Mycroft?" Penelope asked.

"He was right here," Cassie said looking around quickly. "I just put him down."

"Mycroft!" Penelope shouted. He was nowhere to be seen. "Mycroft!"

The others took up the cry. "Mycroft!"

Penelope got down on her hands and knees to look under Freda's car and the limousine.

"He was just here."

"We'll find him," Penelope said grimly. Damn cat. Thinks the whole world is a litter box.

"There he is," Kathy cried, pointing to the stone wall.

Penelope rushed to Mycroft. He growled at her approach. Something was wrong. Penelope was sure of it. Good Lord! Could he have been bitten by a rattlesnake? Surely, it was too early in the year for the snakes to come out of hibernation.

"Mikey, what is it?" Penelope asked softly. She saw blood on his right front paw.

Mycroft growled again.

Looking over his shoulder, Penelope found the cause of his concern.

He had found Freda Alsberg.

"Oh, God," Cassie cried.

"Go back to the car, Cassie," Penelope said. "Call nine-one-one."

"Is she dead?" Kathy asked.

Penelope clambered over the wall and slid down the slope to Freda, who was sprawled face down. She shuddered as she took the woman's wrist. It was still warm, but there was no pulse.

"I'm afraid so," Penelope said. There were tears in Kathy's horrified eyes.

Abraham Lincoln stared placidly at Penelope from the handle of the chopping knife plunged deep into Freda Alsberg's back.

CHAPTER THIRTEEN

From the top of Crying Woman Mountain, it was a beautiful sunset, but no one cared.

The color of the western sky slowly changed from one soft shade of red to another, gradually deepening to a dark red that lingered for the longest time. Even when night finally fell, red streaked the distant horizon. Unfortunately, it was the color of blood. Freda Alsberg's blood.

For Penelope, the routine that followed violent death was sickeningly familiar. The others watched with morbid fascination as police officers went through the methodical investigation of the crime scene.

The chief took charge of the operation. Fowler was grimly efficient. He shook his head and frowned at Penelope. "A bad business," he said.

She nodded somberly in return. Empty Creek was rapidly becoming the murder capital of the world.

Larry Burke and Willie Stoner were quick to arrive and equally quick to separate the little party that had discovered the body. Penelope was grateful to get Stoner this time. He was slightly less odious than Tweedledee who, remembering his last encounter with

Penelope, quickly chose Cassandra to interrogate. John and Kathy were allowed to sit in the limousine while they awaited their turn. Tweedledee made John run up the window, however, to isolate Kathy and Mycroft in the passenger compartment.

Penelope shook her head. Detective Lawrence Burke was such a dunce.

Mycroft was upset at being imprisoned in the car when there was so much investigative work to be done. After all, he was the one who had found the body. Big Mike stalked back and forth along the rear window and growled irritably, even ignoring Kathy who still wept at the shock of her sudden introduction to murder.

"If this keeps up," Penelope said, "we're going to have to ban chopping knives."

"Huh?" Willie Stoner asked in the finest tradition of the Empty Creek Detective Bureau.

"But if chopping knives are banned," Penelope continued, "only outlaws will have chopping knives."

"Huh?" Stoner repeated in an attempt to penetrate to the key question.

"Oh, never mind."

Stoner changed his tack. "Hah?" he said.

Penelope took this to mean, What were you doing here? Or perhaps, How did you happen to find the body?

"Mikey found Freda," Penelope announced. "He got blood on his paw."

"Mikey's the fruit?"

"A complete interrogative," Penelope said. "Imagine that. Well, not exactly complete, but intelligible words strung together in a comprehensible manner." Where did Fowler find these cretins anyway? "Mikey's the cat," Penelope explained. "John's the fruit, but you shouldn't say that. It's not politically correct. You should refer to him as a gay person, if you must refer to his sexual preference at all. I really must speak to the chief about instituting some sort of sensitivity training for you people."

"Larry said you were a feisty broad."

"Is that what Detective Burke says?"

"Well, not in those words, maybe."

"Tsk, tsk, Detective Stoner. Sensitivity training is definitely in order. But for the moment, you tell Detective Tweedledee to keep his opinions of my backside to himself."

"Huh?"

"This will go much better if I ask the questions and provide the answers. Tell me if I go too fast for your speeding pencil."

Ignoring the occasional "Huh?" from Stoner, Penelope then provided a succinct narrative of the events that had led them to be here atop Crying Woman Mountain.

When dismissed, Stoner wandered over to the limousine to begin his questioning of the chauffeur. "Don't you dare call him a fruit either," Penelope warned.

Andy screeched to a halt, cried, "Oh, my God;" greeted Stormy with a hug; gathered as many details as were known; and after the briefest peck to Penelope's lips, raced off again to tear apart the front page he had just finished putting together. "I'll see you later," he said over his shoulder as he ran back to the car.

"Drive carefully," Penelope shouted after him. He waved an acknowledgment and was gone. Penelope turned away from the sunset and faced the darkening eastern sky, trying to make her mind as black as it was becoming. But her thoughts raced as fast as Andy's car sped around the twisting curves of the road. Shivering in the cold breeze that had blown up, she tried to make sense of the recent murder.

"Someone is killing the women of Empty Creek," she told the wind. Then she shivered again, not from the cold, but from the realization that there might be a serial killer at work.

Who would be the next to die?

Night had fallen before the questioning was completed and the foursome, with cat, was allowed to depart the mountaintop.

"Don't leave town," Tweedledee warned.

"Idiot," Penelope shot back. "You think we're going to flee to the Mexican border in a white limousine?"

"Just don't leave town. I can have you arrested as a material witness."

"And I'll slap a false arrest suit on you so fast you'll think all the Harpies of hell have descended upon you."

"Jeez, what'd you say now?"

"Look it up. In a dictionary. That's a book with words in it. Drive on, John. Take us to the Double B."

"Yes, ma'am."

Mycroft & Company never did reopen for business that day.

Being on duty, and somewhat shattered by the afternoon's events as well, John declined to join them for a drink, so a threesome with cat entered the Double B to find the news of Freda Alsberg's untimely death had already spread. A cruel wag had added a comment below the luncheon specials still listed on the black-board:

CHILI $4.50

STEAK SANDWICH $7.95

HAWAIIAN CHEESEBURGER $4.95

MURDERER	EMPTY CREEK PD
2	0

Kathy went off to the ladies' room to inspect tear damage to her eyes and Mycroft went to his accustomed bar stool, leaving Penelope and Cassandra to those clamoring for details. Storm Williams's position as Empty Creek's adopted movie star would have put her at the center of attention anyway. Her added notoriety as a codiscoverer of the latest murder victim did not detract from her welcome.

Since the alternative would have caused mayhem in the Double B, Penelope and Cassandra—and Kathy when she returned from the loo—patiently answered all questions.

"Yes, it's true. Freda was murdered."

"Same method, different knife."

"Just finished filming. It'll be out this summer."

"Crying Woman Mountain."

"Just over the little stone wall."

"I'm doing another swimsuit commercial."

"No suspects."

"Have to wait for the coroner's report."

"No, except for the knife in her back she didn't appear to be violated."

The questions finally subsided, and the regulars of

the Double B got back to the serious business of drinking and dulling the pain of their most recent loss.

It was left to Red the Rat to provide Freda's epitaph. "Damned shame, I say. She was a fine figger of a woman. Mature, but a fine figger, anyway."

"What a welcome," Cassandra said when they were alone at the table. "Absolutely distressing. Poor John. He'll never want to drive me again. And that detective—what's his name? A real neanderthal. Are you listening to me, Penny?"

"Yes, of course," Penelope replied, although she had been engrossed in some muddled thoughts of her own having chiefly to do with suspects, or rather the lack of suspects now that Freda the Valkyrie was dead. "You were talking about Tweedledee, or was it Tweedledum?"

"Tweedledee, I think. The fat sloppy one?"

Penelope nodded. She loved her glamorous younger sister. They were the best of friends, but Cassie did have a tendency to rattle on and on, especially when Penelope was trying to think.

"He was positively undressing me the entire time he was questioning me."

"Me, too," Kathy said.

"Torpedoes" Penelope said, glancing across the room to where Debbie stood at the bar.

"How did we get on the subject of submarines?" Cassandra asked.

"He admires torpedoes, which is his euphemism for large breasts. I'm sure he was awestruck by your torpedoes. Yours too, Kathy."

"Not my mind?" Cassie exclaimed. "Good Lord, I hope he never sees *Space Vampires.*" It was one of

Storm Williams's early films, a little epic in which the plot revolved around two groups of vampires from the planet Dorian who spent ninety-two minutes of running time on screen, competing to see who could get the heroine out of her space suit the most times.

"I'm sure he's at the video store right now, slavering over the cover."

"It's a pretty sexy cover," Kathy said.

Cassandra blushed. "What a disgusting thought. I wish I'd never made that movie."

"Muffy was mortified."

"Poor Mother. One daughter leaping from Corps to Corps and the other displaying all of her considerable charms for the camera. Do you know, I still get fan letters from Europe. *Space Vampires* is very popular in Germany. The Teutonic mind howls for a sequel."

"They just want to see you in that Life Force contraption again."

"It was rather erotic, but uncomfortable. All those wires and things."

"It looked like a high tech chastity belt," Kathy said.

"Well, it was rather. You see, the vampires couldn't get to me while I was in the Life Force Machine."

"Laney and Wally are fond of playing Space Vampires. Laney wanted to know where she could purchase a Life Force Machine for her very own. She absolutely clamored for one."

"How is dear sex-crazed Laney?"

"Ask her yourself. Here she comes with her faithful cowboy companion."

"Stormy! I didn't know you were coming," Laney exclaimed. "Penelope didn't say a word. How are you?"

"Mostly fine. How are you?"

"Sex-crazed as always, thank God. I need to do constant research for my novels."

"You see," Cassandra said smugly.

"That's a funny special," Wally said.

"What's funny, dear heart?"

"Murderer two, Empty Creek PD zero."

"Freda Alsberg was murdered today," Penelope said.

"Oh, my God!"

Laney plopped heavily onto an empty chair. Then Wally asked the first sensible question Penelope had heard all day. "What's going on?"

"I don't know." Penelope replied.

Herbert Fletcher entered and approached their table, leering at Cassandra as he weaved through the bar. "Penelope, dearest. Who is this charming lady?"

"Surely, you've met my sister before, Herb. Cassandra Warren."

"Of course, the film star. I'm a big fan, but we've never met. I would have remembered such a stunning creature. I'm enchanted, dear lady." Instead of shaking the proffered hand, Fletcher raised it to his lips and kissed it.

"And you must be the lecherous old goat I've heard so much about," Cassandra said, withdrawing her hand quickly.

Herbert Fletcher spluttered indignantly. Penelope had never seen anyone splutter quite so beautifully before. It was like Wally's ability to crinkle his eyes, probably a God-given trait.

"Where have you been this afternoon?" Penelope asked.

"I took in a matinee," Fletcher replied.

"Then, you haven't heard?"

"Heard what?"

"Freda Alsberg was murdered."

"Oh, my God!" He slumped in the chair beside Laney.

"I was shocked, too," Laney said, taking his hand. "All of us were."

"I just can't believe it. First Louise and now Freda. She was such a wonderful woman. Poor Freda"

Hypocrite, Penelope thought. Only yesterday you were trying to pin Louise's murder on her. Well, it seems poor Freda now has the perfect alibi. But he did seem genuinely shocked at the news. Penelope wondered what he would say if she told him his wife had called her on the telephone.

"You go to a lot of movies," Penelope said.

"One must fill the time," Fletcher replied. "It's lonely."

"Poor dear," Laney said.

And getting lonelier, Penelope thought, deciding to check on Herbert Fletcher's alibi. Even a brief romantic involvement with him seemed to be a dangerous thing.

"What was playing?" Penelope asked.

"My Fair Lady," Fletcher replied.

"How ironic."

Andy drew up a chair from another table and collapsed next to Penelope. "What a job. What a mess. Poor Freda."

"I'll get you a drink, Andy."

"I'll do it."

"No, let me. What would you like?"

"A scotch. A double."

Penelope raised her eyebrows.

"It saves a second trip to the bar," Andy explained.

Penelope smiled. "I wasn't questioning your choice. It's been a hard day on everyone."

Especially Freda.

In reality, Penelope wanted a few moments away from the clamoring guests at her table, perhaps even an out-of-body experience in which she could float unseen and unnoticed above the room, an opportunity to eavesdrop on the inner thoughts of those at the table, indeed those scattered throughout the Double B. But it was not to be. Try as she might, she could not even draw a cocoon of silence around herself. She envied Mycroft who could.

Big Mike was on his bar stool, paws curled in against his chest, staring placidly at the room and its inhabitants from beneath heavy-lidded eyes. He looked like one of those contemplative statues of Buddha, plump and implacable against the woes of the world.

Penelope stroked his fur gently.

Big Mike looked up at her with his secretive eyes and appeared to smile as if to say, Don't worry, Penelope, we'll get the bastard.

"Are you all right, Penelope?" Pete asked.

"I'm fine. My friends wear me out sometimes."

"Friends do that. Can I get you something?"

"A double scotch for Andy. He needs strength for his friendships."

When she returned to the table, Herbert Fletcher had disappeared, slipping out when Penelope's back was turned. Kathy was preparing to leave.

"Why don't you take the day off tomorrow, Penelope? Spend time with Stormy. I can handle things at the store."

"That's sweet, Kathy. I think I'll take you up on it."

"Okay, see you later, then."

"We're going too," Laney announced. "Drop by for a drink tomorrow. Bring Penelope, too, Stormy."

"My best friend turns on me."

"And Mikey. Alexander misses his little friend."

"That's the kindest thing anyone has said about Mycroft in some time."

"Well, I feel like I have the plague or something," Andy said. "I arrive and everyone leaves."

"I'll get you a bell to ring as you walk through the streets."

"A bell?"

"That's what they did during the plague, you see. You ring the bell and cry, Unclean, unclean. Then people avoid you."

"Unclean!" Andy shouted. This was completely out of character for the mild-mannered editor. Was he going to jump into a telephone booth next?

"Whatever are you doing, Andy?"

"Practicing. I don't want anyone else to disturb me while I'm with my two favorite girls in the entire world."

"Don't get any ideas about Stormy," Penelope warned. "She's remaining chaste until marriage. Or the convent. Whichever comes first."

"But Penny, dear, I don't want to be in a convent. Or married, for that matter."

"Then I must lock you in the wine cellar. Or a chastity belt."

"You don't have a wine cellar. Or a chastity belt."

"I'll build one with a Life Force Machine in it. Perhaps I'll let Andy visit occasionally. You can talk through the little sliding grate."

"How cruel."

"I was a Borgia in a previous life."

"You're going to be an insect in your next life. You have much to answer for, Penelope Warren."

"I have a wine cellar," Andy said.

It was true. Andy did have a wine cellar. The previous owner of Andy's house, a mason by hobby, had built a small wine cellar in the back.

"Then we shall lock Penny in it while we make passionate love. Wouldn't that be fun?"

"It would not," Penelope declared.

Andy, who did think it might be fun, reluctantly agreed with his lady love.

"What an old poop you are," Cassie said to him. I shall have to content myself with that horrid Herbert Fletcher, I suppose. At least, he has money."

"Herbert Fletcher," Penelope said thoughtfully. "I just wonder . . ."

"I was only kidding, Penny. I shall seek the silent cowboy type like Wally."

"What do you wonder about Herb?" Andy asked.

"Why he seems to have such a passion for movies."

"You can't fault him for that," Cassie said. "Movies provide a marvelous escape when you're lonely."

"I suppose you're right."

"Well, now that the paper's put to bed, I'm going to do the same with my weary body."

"Leaving Penelope and me alone? I suppose we shall have to cruise for dudes."

"It's Western dancing night at the senior citizen club," Andy said. "That would be a good place to start. If you're unsuccessful, I will be available tomorrow."

After agreeing to meet Andy for a late lunch, a brief stop at the cineplex revealed that Herbert Fletcher did indeed purchase a ticket for *My Fair Lady* and a jumbo tub of popcorn as well, returning midway through the film for a refill. Popcorn seemed to be

Herb's signature at the movie complex. "I've never seen anyone who can put popcorn away like that old guy," the girl at the concession stand told Penelope.

Disappointed, Penelope returned to the jeep and the waiting Cassie and Mycroft. He may not be a murderer, but he's a lecherous old goat, she thought.

Mycroft seemed disappointed that Penelope returned empty-handed from the concession stand. Perhaps he expected a package of chocolate-coated lima beans. It *was* a long drive home to dinner, at least ten or fifteen minutes.

"What is this penchant you have for discovering bodies?"

Penelope, Cassandra, and Mycroft were finally at home. The two women were at the kitchen table eating Chinese take-out.

"I only found one. Mycroft found Freda's body."

"Poor Mikey. It must have been a severe psychological shock for him."

"He seems to have recovered nicely."

Mycroft was engrossed in lapping up the last of the chicken and gravy in his bowl.

"It's the same thing, anyway," Cassandra said, waving her chopsticks. "You were there. The first human on the scene. Does Muffy know about all of this?"

"Muffy does *not* know, and she will *not* learn it from your lips! That's all I need right now. Muffy hovering around saying, 'Have some more potato salad, dear.' Food is her solution to all problems."

"It's the best potato salad in the entire world, probably the universe."

"Of course, it is, but that's not the point. Muffy would not approve of her eldest daughter chasing around after a murderer. What would the neighbors say? How are the Robinsons, anyway?"

"Busy being the Robinsons." The Robinsons had lived next door to the Warrens forever.

"Naturally."

Mycroft burped.

"Excuse yourself, Mikey."

Big Mike leaped to the table's surface on the chance there was a morsel or two to be had.

There was. Auntie Cassie always spoiled him rotten.

On this occasion, however, Auntie Cassie shrieked before she had an opportunity to begin the spoiling process. Startled when he had been expecting a treat, Mycroft leaped straight into the air and attempted to remain airborne while he inspected the tabletop for dangerous alien creatures. Gravity foiled his attempt, however, so he soared high again, just in case he had missed the cause of Cassandra's concern the first time.

Penelope jumped to her feet, knocking her chair over with a clatter. "My God, what's wrong?"

Cassandra pointed to the kitchen window. "There's someone out there," she cried, pointing. "Wearing a George Bush mask."

Penelope rushed to the door and turned the outside light on.

"Don't go out there alone," Cassie yelled.

"Well, come with me, then." Penelope ran into the back yard.

George Bush was nowhere to be seen. For that matter, there were no other former presidents in the yard either, not even a vice president or a secretary of state or anyone below cabinet rank.

"Do you see him?"

"There's no one here." Penelope turned to find her sister in the guise of Princess Leogfrith clutching the kitchen broom like the sword of doom. Mycroft, who considered brooms far more dangerous than presidential impersonators, cautiously lagged behind.

Cassandra advanced slowly. "Well, he was here. I saw him."

"It's probably just the stress of finding Freda's body."

"Stress, my shapely little behind! George Bush was looking through your kitchen window."

"That old voyeur."

Penelope turned back to the house to discover she was mistaken. There was a former president in the back yard after all. Well, not actually in the yard itself. A gleaming Abraham Lincoln cast in copper was attached to the door.

It was Penelope's turn to shriek.

She turned and yelled into the night. "Damn you, George Bush! I'm going to get you for this!"

CHAPTER FOURTEEN

Mycroft, the little ingrate, slept most of the night and much of the morning away with Cassandra. Penelope missed his furry presence and, when she awakened earlier than normal, considered his absence the reason. But once in the kitchen, with the aroma of coffee filling the room and even penetrating her recalcitrant brain, Penelope slowly remembered the true reason for her restless night. In her dreams she had been pursued by a knife-wielding murderer wearing a rubber George Bush mask. Penelope's escape had been blocked by a growing mountain of slippery copper pennies. Like Sisyphus, she labored and scrambled to climb the penny mountain, but each time she neared the summit, she slipped and fell back to George Bush and the bloody chopping knife.

With such a disturbance of Penelope's night, it was no wonder that Mycroft had curled up with Cassie.

Penelope sipped her coffee and reluctantly admitted the truth: She was becoming just the teeniest bit frightened by recent occurrences. It wasn't big-time fear, not like that engendered by Marine drill instructors, but bad enough for her not to turn her back on anyone, particularly George Bush.

Penelope took her coffee and wandered through the house. It was terrible to be up so early—only ten—without her playmates, Cassie and Mycroft. She stopped at the bedroom door and looked in on them. Mycroft was a big lump beneath the sheets, but Cassie was even more beautiful in sleep than awake. Her golden hair was so artfully arranged on the pillow, Penelope wondered if she did that before going to sleep, just in case someone happened by with a camera and a photo assignment. Hey you, get a picture of Storm Williams for "Sleep-Styles of the Not So Rich and Famous."

Cassie had one arm around Frank, holding him close. She never traveled without Frank. Many a man would kill for the privilege of exchanging positions with that most-favored teddy bear.

Penelope cleared her throat hopefully. And then again, louder.

No response from woman, bear, or cat.

"Well, foo."

Penelope took *Silent Night* outside and compared the cover of the novel with her home. Again, she was struck by the uncanny resemblance, as though the artist had used her house as a model. Except for the Christmas tree. Penelope never put her Christmas tree in that window. And the mountain. Crying Woman Mountain was in front of Penelope's house, not behind it. But everything else was strikingly similar.

What is Louise trying to tell me?

Still baffled by the meaning of Louise Fletcher's message, Penelope got down on her hands and knees to inspect the entranceway and the adjoining cactus gardens closely.

Had she buried something before she died?

Struck by sudden inspiration, Penelope leaped to

her feet, dashed into the house, rummaged through her closet, and cried, "Aha!" as she withdrew a bayonet from a cardboard box. She tossed the scabbard carelessly on her bed.

Returning to the front yard, she knelt and inserted the point of the bayonet at a forty-five degree angle into the sand. This was the accepted method for finding land mines. It was the way Clint Eastwood did it in *Kelly's Heroes.* If it worked for land mines, Penelope reasoned, it would work for whatever Louise Fletcher might have buried in the yard. If she'd buried something . . .

Still, it was a possibility, and Penelope went to work enthusiastically. She was rewarded almost immediately when the tip of the bayonet clinked against something—a buried message from the dead, hidden treasure, a land mine?

Penelope used the bayonet to dig and found a rusted and flattened soup can.

Fifteen minutes later, she still crawled over the desert sand, poking and prodding it with considerably less zeal, as the door opened to reveal a pair of shapely ankles, even shapelier calves, well-turned knees, and perfect thighs which disappeared into a pair of bright red shorts. It seemed that Princess Leogfrith had awakened. At last.

"What *are* you doing down there, Penelope?" Frank the teddy bear was tucked under her arm.

Mycroft appeared next to Princess Leogfrith's legs, probably wondering the same thing. It wasn't often he saw Penelope imitating a cat. That would be a very good thing in Mycroft's scheme of the world, though cats seldom brandished bayonets. Who needed a bayonet when there were perfectly adequate claws available?

"Investigating," Penelope said, looking up at her little sister who towered over her.

"You have an ant on your nose."

It was true. In fact, there were ants on her forearms as well. Penelope leaned close to the ground and gently blew the ant from her nose. She didn't want it to fall very far. Then she did the same for the ants crawling through the burnished hairs on her arms.

Cassie was not at all surprised by the care with which her sister dislodged the ants. She would have done the same thing. Of course, *she* would not have been crawling around the ground with a knife. But then, Penelope always was a little strange.

"You also have a knife in your hand."

Penelope was unable to deny that fact. "It's a bayonet," she said. "I'm looking for something."

"What could you possibly find with a bayonet or knife or whatever it is?"

"I don't know," Penelope admitted. "Something that Louise Fletcher might have buried."

"Why would Louise Fletcher bury something in your yard?"

"I don't know."

"Come, Mycroft," Cassie said, "before the desert sun fries your brain as well. I don't think I could cope with an addled cat too."

"At least, I don't sleep with a teddy bear."

Penelope meekly followed Cassie and Mycroft into the house, bringing the *Empty Creek News Journal* with her. With another cup of coffee at hand, she spread the paper on the table, ready to read Andy's story on the murder. John Fowler wouldn't like the headline, but it was an apt description of the two detectives on the case.

COUNCILWOMAN MURDERED:
POLICE CLUELESS

by

HARRIS ANDERSON III

News Journal Staff Writer

"Read it aloud," Cassie requested. "No, let me do it. I have a much better voice." She pulled the paper away from Penelope and began to read.

" 'The body of Empty Creek Councilwoman Freda Alsberg was discovered yesterday on Crying Woman Mountain. Alsberg appeared to be the victim of foul play, according to Detective Lawrence Burke of the Empty Creek Police Department.' "

"Twit! If a knife in the back isn't evidence of foul play, I don't know what is. Andy didn't write that part," Cassie explained.

"He should have," Penelope said.

" 'The body was discovered by local business-woman Penelope Warren; Kathy Allen, Warren's employee; Storm Williams, Warren's sister and a well-known film star'—wasn't that nice of Andy to say—'and John Bellows, Williams's chauffeur.' "

" 'Alsberg was pronounced dead at the scene.' Blah, blah, blah."

" 'Authorities have no suspects.' More blah."

" 'This latest murder follows the death of well-known Empty Creek resident Louise Fletcher. Authorities believe that the same person was involved in both deaths.' End of blah." Cassandra turned the page. "Oh, look, the hardware store is having a manure sale. We must run right down and get a peck or two."

"It's fertilizer."

"Same thing. I'm going to take a shower." Mycroft followed her from the kitchen.

"No good, two-timing cat. I'll get you for this."

"He loves his Auntie Cassie."

Renewed solitude, even momentary, gave Penelope the opportunity to read Freda's obituary, a sidebar to the main story. It outlined the details of a life that had ended at the age of forty-five—Freda's election to the council eight years ago, her graduation from the University of Arizona with a degree in political science, her married daughter living in New Mexico, her career in real estate. Services were pending. There was little in the obituary that Penelope didn't know.

No mention was made of Freda's brief marriage to a drifter who had disappeared years ago or of the many affairs she was rumored to have had.

The twenty-four/twenty-four rule was close to expiration. It referred to the last twenty-four hours of a murder victim's life and the first twenty-four hours after the body was discovered. Penelope knew those were the crucial hours in any murder investigation. She also knew she could not hope to compete with the resources of the police department. After all, despite their repulsive manners, even Tweedledee and Tweedledum had to have *some* investigative abilities. But she had to do something.

She stared at the photograph that accompanied the obituary. It was a good picture of Freda. She was smiling for the camera and appeared happy, not at all like the sullen fishwife who had berated Penelope only a few days earlier. Although it would make her feel like a snoop again, Penelope decided that Tweedledee and Tweedledum could have the twenty-four hours after the discovery of Freda's body. Penelope wanted the twenty-four hours before Freda died, and she told the coffee pot exactly that. "Maybe Freda had a secret closet too," Penelope added just as Cassie and Mycroft returned.

"A secret closet," Cassie exclaimed. "What fun. Can I look too?"

"It might be dangerous," Penelope warned. "Remember George Bush and the pennies."

"Danger is my life."

Just then the telephone rang. Penelope stared at it for a moment before answering, half-expecting it to be Louise Fletcher calling again, or perhaps Freda Alsberg this time, but it was only Laney.

"It's over," Laney wailed. "This time it's definitely over."

"Don't cry, Laney. What's over?"

"Wally. I've thrown him out. He's turned to a younger woman. He's in love with your sister. You must come immediately. I don't know what to do."

"Did he say that?"

"Well, not exactly, but a woman knows."

Penelope sighed. "We'll be right over." She turned to Cassie. "We have to go."

"What's wrong?"

"Wally's apparently fallen in love with you."

"Oh, good Lord. That was sudden."

Wally sat in the middle of Laney's extremely large, if symbolic, doghouse on the back porch, surrounded by all of his possessions—a pile of jeans and Western shirts, cowboy boots, his stack of Willie Nelson tapes, his guns, a laundry bag, several cowboy hats, and the guitar that he played rather well.

When the sisters and Mycroft arrived, Wally was

reclining against his saddle. Alexander lounged on Wally's stomach, perhaps in sympathy and to offer solace in Wally's latest moment of need, but more likely to escape the maelstrom of Laney's volatile temperament.

"Ow," Wally cried when Alexander used a man's most sensitive area as a launching pad to rush into the yard and greet Mycroft. "Great balls of fire, Alex, I've asked you nice not to do that."

"What did you do this time?" Penelope asked sternly.

"Aw, Penelope, all I said was Stormy's a beautiful woman. Said you was too, but she didn't get mad at that. Started tossing everything out the door. You gonna talk to her for me?"

"That's all you said?"

"Honest to God, except for the part about maybe it might be nice to play a little Cowboy and the Indian Maiden with Stormy."

"And just what does Cowboy and the Indian Maiden entail?" Stormy demanded.

"Well, you see, this handsome cowboy, that's me. . . ."

"Oh, never mind. I don't want to know the sordid details."

"Well, it's only natural. I'm a man. I got feelings too. I told Laney she was much better looking than Stormy anyway. But it was too late."

"Fickle. Isn't that just like a man?" Stormy said.

"I hadda say something at that point."

"I'm going inside," Stormy said. "There may be something Laney forgot to throw out."

"Now everybody's mad at me."

"I'll talk to her, Wally, but only because you said I was beautiful too. That was sweet."

209

"Wanna be my Indian Maiden?"

"Absolutely not!"

Penelope and Cassandra were excellent at sorting out domestic strife, and by the time they had finished, Laney was prepared to forgive Wally, but not without exacting some degree of retribution for his thoughtless remarks. The three women went to the back porch and found that Mycroft and Alexander had demonstrated their solidarity with the male species by curling up with Wally and falling asleep.

Wally looked up from his saddle hopefully. "I'm sorry, my precious."

"I suppose you can't help it," Laney said, "so I'm going to forgive you this time. But—"

"I'll do anything."

"I'll think of something," Laney declared.

Penelope and Cassandra drove away, laughing.

"We should be marriage and family counselors," Cassie said.

Still laughing, Penelope shook her head. "Poor Wally. Laney can be such a bitch."

No doubt poor Wally's life was going to be hell for the next several days. He was quite likely in for a good game of Groveling Male.

Alyce Smith sometimes wished for a good marriage and family counselor. Her secret affair was taking a severe toll on her mental health. When she was with him, all of the planets seemed perfectly placed. When alone, however, Alyce felt that she was astride a shooting star, careening out of control across the night sky, finally plunging to earth in a fiery explosion.

She was determined to look for a sign.

She unfolded the silken scarf that protected her Tarot deck, caressed the cards, closed her eyes, and pulled a single one from the deck.

Alyce opened her eyes and groaned.

The Eight of Swords.

A bound and blindfolded young woman stood in a watery waste surrounded by the eight swords.

Alyce knew exactly what the single card represented. Uncertainty. Restrictions. Bondage of mind and spirit.

Alyce reversed the card. That was the path to freedom and new beginnings. She must take it to maintain sanity.

"Goodbye, my love," Alyce whispered.

Penelope was inclined to cancel lunch with Andy, a proposal that did not sit well with either Cassandra or Mycroft.

"I simply cannot conduct a proper investigation while perishing of starvation. Mikey agrees with Auntie Cassie. We want to go to the Duck Pond."

"Mycroft can't go there. He's been banned."

"How ridiculous. Whatever for?"

"He got into a fight with a duck."

"What's wrong with that? It's what cats do."

"It got to be quite an embarrassing scene." Penelope shuddered at the memory.

"Well, did he win?"

"Of course, he won. He's Mycroft, isn't he? But I really don't like to talk about it."

"Must I torture the information from you? If you trifle with me, I'll run my fingernails across the first available blackboard."

This particular threat had always worked during their girlhood. It worked now.

"It wasn't the fight so much as what happened when the duck retreated. Imagine the *mise en scène*." If the tale was to be told, it should be told properly. "We were all outside on the patio enjoying a placid fall evening."

"And margaritas, I'll wager."

"Please. This is my story. As I said, we were enjoying a most pleasant evening—and margaritas—when this enormous and belligerent duck swam right up to our table, emerged from the pond and squawked at Mycroft, throwing down a webbed gauntlet so to speak. Mycroft, who had been minding his own business, naturally took up the challenge. The duck quickly realized his error and retreated with Mycroft in full pursuit. Unfortunately, the duck used Mayor Dixon's table as his avenue of retreat—right through Mrs. Dixon's enchiladas."

Cassandra was laughing loudly at this point, holding her sides. "Oh, stop, I can't take anymore."

"Well," Penelope continued, "that woman is huge. She must weigh at least three hundred pounds. Still, with wings and feathers and fur flying through her enchiladas—a double portion I have no doubt—she emitted the most piercing scream I've ever heard, arose with astonishing rapidity for a woman of her full figure, knocked the table over into her husband's lap, fluttered her fat little arms as though attempting aerial flight, and fell backward into the pond with a resounding plop. The resultant tidal wave—"

"No more," Cassandra cried hysterically.

"The resultant tidal wave nearly emptied the pond and splashed every diner on the patio. Those inside pressed their noses to the windows and looked on with

212

a mixture of horror and amusement, mostly amusement. I thought we would have to hire a crane to extract Mrs. Dixon from the pond. All the while, she was uttering the most horrible obscenities about Mycroft."

Cassandra wept and shook with laughter.

Mycroft, who had tried to ride out the earthquake that Cassie's lap had become, leaped to the floor of the jeep in disgust.

"He wasn't really trying to hurt the duck. He just wanted to play, liven up a dull evening."

That wasn't entirely true. If Mrs. Dixon hadn't interfered, there would have been duck tacos for all.

"It sounds like he was successful."

"Yes, well, he hasn't had refried beans since."

"Poor Mikey. I guess we'll just have to go to the Double B again."

There was no getting around it. The investigation would have to be postponed until Penelope's partners had eaten.

Thankfully, lunch at the Double B was uneventful, just greasy, fat-filled, cholesterol-laden, delicious cheeseburgers all around.

After lunch, Penelope left the others to dash across the street to Mycroft & Company to check on Kathy and make sure that she was coping all right by herself. Kathy was not alone and appeared to be getting along quite well.

"Oh, my lady," Kathy said. She blushed and quickly brushed strands of hair back into place.

Penelope ignored the lipstick on Timothy's lips. It might be a new style for men, although Penelope doubted it. Without so much to do, Penelope might have considered a little necking herself. It was a more refreshing pause than any soft drink could provide, but it induced lethargy and sleep. And Cassie would be worse than Mycroft, probably wanting to look on and comment on technique.

"We have an announcement," Timothy said. There was no trace of the romantic poet today, at least as that title pertained to the composition of verse. "You tell her, Kathy." Timothy fled, apparently losing his courage.

"He's really quite shy," Kathy said.

"And just what is the big announcement?"

"We're going to live together," Kathy said.

"Well, congratulations, but Andy will be heart-broken."

"Oh, my God, you knew?"

"Of course, I knew. You looked at him like a star-struck calf."

"I'll die. I'll simply die! Did he know?"

"He's a man. What would he know?"

"Thank God for that."

"I'm really quite happy for you, Kathy. Timmy's sweet and he absolutely adores you."

"Yes," Kathy said dreamily. There were those calf eyes again. "We're going to get tattoos."

Penelope supposed tattoos were the equivalent of an engagement ring for the younger generation.

While Penelope was two for two in domestic bliss situations today, she remained zero for two in murder solutions and that was a cause for irritation as she pulled into the lot of the late Freda Alsberg's real-estate office, a small mobile home that Freda had converted into office space. The blinds on the windows were all tightly drawn.

"You know, Cassie, it's funny. I knew Freda for years, and I passed this place probably every day, but I've never been here before."

"It doesn't look like anyone's here. In fact, why are we here?"

"We have to start someplace."

The steps creaked and wobbled as Penelope stepped up to the door. She knocked. No answer. "Hello?" she called. Still, no answer. Penelope turned to Cassie and Mycroft and shrugged before she tried the door. It was unlocked. She pushed it open.

"Isn't this breaking and entering?" Cassie asked. "Mycroft will not look good in one of those horrid orange prison suits. Neither will I, for that matter."

"Fraidy cat." It was a taunt that had earned Cassie any number of skinned knees and elbows during girlhood. Mycroft skipped between their legs and entered the darkness. He was no fraidy cat.

Penelope felt for a light switch. The air was thick and musty. The place needed a good airing out.

She found the switch and turned it on.

The office was a mess.

File cabinets were open, folders and their contents strewn everywhere. Desk drawers had been pulled out and emptied. Photographs of listed properties were askew on the walls.

"My God," Cassie said. "It's just like the movies."

Penelope heard a car start and drive away. It didn't register for a moment, not until a telephone receiver off its hook began a faint insistent beeping.

"Damn!" she cried. She raced through the clutter to the back of the converted mobile home. She hesitated only a second before the closed door. Once through it she was in a bedroom, and a back door was wide open. A distant cloud of dust marked someone's hasty departure.

That someone had been here when they'd entered. "Damn it!"

Penelope started to put the telephone back and then stopped. There might be fingerprints.

It continued to blare its warning. Beep! Beep! Beep!

They had missed the murderer by a few seconds.

CHAPTER FIFTEEN

Three days passed. Three frustrating uneventful days, except for another well attended funeral service. George Bush made no further appearances. No additional pennies appeared on Penelope's door. No other real-estate offices were ransacked. Neither Louise Fletcher nor Freda Alsberg called. Discreet Investigations did not call either, although Penelope had left another message. What was wrong with those people anyway?

In fact, no one called except Stormy's agent wanting to know when she was coming back and why there was no answering machine or service for the telephone number she had left. Stormy put him off on the one and promised to speak to her sister on the other. She planned to remain with Penelope in a protective role until this terrible business was concluded, but she knew better than to tell either Penelope or her agent that.

Penelope was stymied, but refused to admit it.

Mycroft was equally stymied and took to sleeping even more than usual, determined to make the best of what was obviously a bad situation.

Cassandra was, well, alternately Cassandra and Stormy, but a good sport as she traipsed about Empty

Creek with Penelope and Mycroft in search of the elusive break that would lead them to a murderer.

This particular day was not to be an auspicious one for Madame Astoria. The pretty young astrologer looked at her chart each day, but she was not in the habit of checking Penelope's or Mycroft's. Had she done so, she would have seen unfavorable signs for her two friends as well and might have warned them to stay inside or avoid confining places.

It wasn't that the charts lied. But as Madame Astoria always said, it was difficult for her to predict her own future. As she looked at her astrological charts, she could discern patterns and trends, both beneficial and troublesome. Alyce Smith knew, for example, that when Mercury went retrograde, an appearance of moving backward, personal communication would be difficult, since Mercury was a personal planet and ruled communications. This was a basic tenet of the astrological arts and sciences.

And since Venus, also a personal planet and the planet of love, was currently retrograde, Alyce knew that this was a difficult time for relationships. It could be vexatious and disturbing, but forewarned, Madame Astoria would take great care in nurturing current relationships or beginning new ones while Venus gave the illusion—planets do not have a reverse gear—of moving backward across the sky.

In checking her chart, Alyce learned that Mars, the planet of energy, and Pluto, the planet of extremes, were square to each other. In short, they were warring for the upper hand. It was not the time to make changes in one's life.

Easy to say.

* * *

Penelope was outside Mycroft & Company admiring the new window display she had just finished arranging with Cassie's help when Tweedledee and Tweedledum drove slowly down the street in an unmarked car. They were followed by a squad car with two women officers in it. Penelope saw all this in the reflection in the window. She turned in time to see the two-car caravan pull to a halt in front of Madame Astoria's little parlor down the street. The four cops emerged from the vehicles, two of them carrying shotguns, and rushed into the storefront.

Good God!

Penelope ran across the street, dodging behind and in front of two cars that happened to be passing at the moment. She entered Alyce Smith's place of business to find the young astrologer up against the wall, arms and legs outstretched, being expertly, if unceremoniously, frisked by Peggy Norton. Penelope didn't know the other woman officer. Tweedledee and Tweedledum she knew all too well.

"What's going on here?" Penelope demanded.

Peggy drew one of Alyce's hands backward and snapped the cuff on, repeating the process with the other hand.

Tweedledee turned to Penelope, a self-satisfied grin on his face. "Well, if it ain't the head Harpy in person."

What? A flair for wit in the dullard.

"Penelope," Alyce cried.

"Shut up, you," Tweedledee said.

"I will not," Penelope said. "I demand to know what's going on."

"I wasn't talking to you," Tweedledee said.

"Well, you'd better do so."

"They're arresting me for murder," Alyce moaned.

"You can't be serious."

"Shut up. Now, I'm talking to you, Miss Harpy. I gotta read the suspect her rights."

And he did while Penelope fumed, although she noted with satisfaction that he had to read them from the card. What kind of detective was unable to memorize a few simple declarative sentences?

Sensing her growing irritation and hoping to forestall an eruption, Tweedledum explained helpfully, "We don't get much practice."

"Indeed," Penelope replied.

A small group of people had gathered and were peering through the shaded windows of the little parlor. Cassie had followed Penelope across the street almost immediately. She was tempted to barge into Madame Astoria's too, but reasoned that Penelope was capable of driving the two detectives nuts all by herself. Two Warren sisters would be a definite overmatch.

Mycroft was standing in the driver's seat of the unmarked police car when the party emerged. His paws were on the steering wheel, and he was gazing around at the gadgets on the dash with interest. Big Mike had never been in a police car before. No doubt he was looking for the siren.

"Your cat's in my car."

Penelope looked. "So he is."

"So, get him out."

"He's a taxpayer. You tell him that a public servant doesn't want him to see how his taxes are being spent."

Burke went to the door and peered in. He jerked his thumb over his shoulder. "Out, cat!"

Mycroft ignored him as he batted at the Kojack light on the dash.

"I said, out!"

Mycroft turned and stared up at the detective. He didn't like to be interrupted when he was working.

The detective reached in to grab him.

Big mistake!

Leaving the station, Burke had expected no trouble or violence in arresting Alyce Smith. But there was no use in taking a chance, and besides, department rules stated that in any potentially violent situation, bullet-proof vests were to be worn. He and Stoner had therefore dutifully shed shirts and ties, slipped into the vests, and dressed again. Thus protected, the detectives had set off in pursuit of justice.

It would have been better, far better, for Burke had he put a catproof mitt on the offending hand that reached for Big Mike.

"Shit! Ow! God damn!" Burke cried, leaping back.

Big Mike went back to searching for the siren's switch.

"He's had a rabies shot recently," Penelope offered, not without concern. She didn't know the law regarding assaults on police officers by cats.

Despite being handcuffed, in the grasp of two police officers, and surrounded by a growing crowd of her friends and neighbors, Alyce Smith giggled. Peggy Norton tittered despite her official role and tried to hide a smile. Her partner lost it completely and guffawed loudly, thereby endearing herself to Penelope forever. Penelope found out later her name was Sheila Tyler.

221

"Haw," Red the Rat cried, slapping his knees.

Larry Burke glowered. Suddenly he pointed an accusing—and bloody—finger at Penelope. "You're under arrest."

"For what?"

"Obstructing a police officer in the performance of his duties."

"I'm not obstructing. Mycroft is."

"Him, too. I'm arresting him too."

"Larry," Willie Stoner said, "you can't arrest a cat."

"Why not? Vicious goddamned thing."

Down the street, Daisy, who waited patiently at the hitching rail in front of the Double Be, brayed loudly.

"I'll arrest the goddamned jackass if I want."

"You can't arrest my sister," Cassie said, entering the fray. "Or her cat. I'll call the ACLU. I'm a member, you know."

"I'll call the NRA," Burke said, mimicking Cassie. "I'm a member, you know."

"So am I," Cassie said.

"You are?" Penelope and Burke chorused.

"And a member of the ASPCA as well as the RCMP."

"I don't care what you join, lady. Your sister's still under arrest. Cuff her and read her the rights."

"I know my rights," Penelope said angrily.

"Aw, you sure, Larry?" Peggy asked.

"Do it!"

"Sorry, Penelope."

Cassandra watched as Penelope was quickly searched, handcuffed, and placed in the back seat next to Alyce. Cassie was too young to remember the 1960s, but she had watched the reruns on television.

She turned to the crowd and thrust a clenched fist in the air. "Free the Empty Creek Three," she cried.

Red the Rat had spent the sixties either searching for hidden gold or in pursuit of one or another of Debbie's predecessors at the Double B—almost catching one, a memory that still chilled him and provoked the need for hard liquor—but he was a quick learner. "Free the Empty Creek Three," Red the Rat cried, throwing his hand in the air, forgetting that it held a glass of beer, causing those near him to duck before they, too, took up the chant.

"Free the Empty Creek Three!"

The Revolution lived.

Peggy Norton shook her head and laughed. "Move over, Mycroft," she said. "You're going to jail."

And so that's how Big Mike got to ride in a police car, thoroughly enjoying the red lights and siren. He knew his rights too.

In the back seat next to Alyce, Penelope was not quite so happy, but almost. She couldn't wait to see Tweedledee try to take Mycroft's pawprints.

The demonstrators followed in the wake of the two speeding police cars, led by Red the Rat riding bareback on Daisy who brayed excitedly. The marchers now carried signs courtesy of the eminently sensible Kathy Allen, who, when she had seen what was happening, had quickly lettered a slogan on half-a-dozen dismantled cardboard boxes, before locking Mycroft & Company and dashing out into 1968. It was almost as much fun as Elizabethan England, and she already spoke the language.

FREE THE EMPTY CREEK THREE!

The marchers went right down the main street, disrupting traffic, shoppers, drinkers, and other assorted residents and snow birds. They didn't know what was happening, but many of them joined the procession, taking up the chant.

Andy rushed out of the newspaper offices, followed by a photographer who marched backward snapping picture after picture.

"What's going on?" Andy asked.

"Penelope's been arrested," Cassie said. "Mycroft and Alyce too."

Andy's clenched fist flew into the air. "Free the Empty Creek Three!" he cried.

By the time the marchers reached the Empty Creek Police Station, their numbers had swelled to over a hundred. In addition to the signs, many of the demonstrators now carried sixpacks of beer. Rumors swirled among them that hamburgers, hot dogs, and potato salad were on the way for a protest barbecue to be held on the police-station grounds.

When Larry Burke saw them coming, he said, "Oh, shit," and dived into the trunk of the car, emerging with a riot helmet on his head, a long baton in one hand, and a bullhorn in the other.

The crowd swirled over the well-kept lawns of the police station. Burke was ready, standing legs apart, blocking the entrance.

"This is an illegal gathering," he bellowed through the loudspeaker, with some difficulty because the shield on his riot helmet kept sliding down. He pushed it back. "I order you to disperse!"

"Lie down," Cassandra cried. "Go limp when they try to arrest you."

Cassandra marveled at her leadership qualities

when the crowd instantly fell to the ground. She was a regular Jane Fonda.

"Stand up!" Burke shouted.

"Stay down!" Cassandra yelled back.

"Stand up! Sit down! Fight, fight, fight!" Andy pranced up and down before the assemblage.

"What are you doing?" Cassie cried.

"I always wanted to be a cheerleader," Andy said. He led the demonstrators through another cheer. Stand up, Sit down. The crowd jumped and flopped to his commands.

"Go away," Burke pleaded.

Inside the jail, neither Penelope nor Alyce heard the shouts and demands for their freedom. Nor did Mycroft, because Peggy poured a saucer of milk for him almost immediately upon arrival. Although she had to place Penelope in the holding cell with Alyce, Peggy didn't bother to book her. Burke was such a jerk.

Alyce Smith wasn't so fortunate. Still, Penelope had the chance to talk with her while Peggy took her fingerprints and Sheila did the paperwork.

"Do you have a lawyer?"

Alyce shook her head sadly.

"I'll get you one. We'll find the best criminal attorney in the state."

"George Eden," Peggy said. "Looks like an ambulance chaser, but he's very good."

"Yes, he is good," Sheila agreed, "but he doesn't look like an ambulance chaser anymore."

"Where do I find him?"

Sheila took a card from her breast pocket and handed it to Penelope. "He's my main squeeze,"

Sheila said. "When you see him, make sure his numbers match."

"Numbers?"

"I have his ties and suits numbered. If he's wearing a number one tie with a number two suit, he screwed up again. That's what makes him look a little odd."

"Hah!" Peggy exclaimed as she took Alyce's left hand. "You have very nice hands, Alyce. Who does your nails?"

"Sandie, over at the Nail Palace. I had an appointment this afternoon. You could take it, I suppose."

"Would you mind?"

"Not at all."

Penelope shook her head. Nails at a time like this? She looked through the bars. The four women were alone except for a uniformed jailor sitting in his office with a copy of *Playboy*—he appeared to be actually *reading* the magazine—and Mycroft who was exploring the jail.

"Peggy, what's the evidence against Alyce?"

Peggy glanced quickly around. "They lifted a real clear print from the penny on the knife," she whispered. "Had no idea who it belonged to until Burke got an anonymous call telling him to check Alyce's prints. He did, and got a match."

Damn. There were just too many anonymous phone calls in this case. "Was the caller male or female?" Penelope asked.

"Male."

That eliminated Louise Fletcher.

Alyce had been looking back and forth between Penelope and Peggy. Her beautiful blue eyes were glazed with bewilderment. "But I didn't do it," she said.

"I know that," Penelope said, patting her shoulder. "I'll just have to find out who did."

"Who do we want?" Cassie shouted.

"Pen-el-o-pe!" the crowd returned.

"When do we want her?"

"Now!" the supporters roared.

"What the hell is going on here?" This wasn't why John Fowler had retired from the Los Angeles Police Department to become chief of police in the placid little sand dune that was Empty Creek.

Cassie held her hands up for quiet. "Police brutality," she said when her merry band subsided.

"That's a crock, Chief," Burke said, forgetting that the loudspeaker was at his lips.

"Boooooooo!" the demonstrators replied.

"Jesus, give me that!" Chief Fowler took the bullhorn from the sheepish detective.

"Hurray!"

"Now, what's going on here?"

"This oaf arrested Penelope Warren."

"And who are you, miss?"

"I'm Cassandra Warren."

"I thought you looked familiar. Storm Williams. *Amazon Princess and the Sword of Doom.* Right?"

"You've seen it?" Cassandra was pleased despite the absurdity of the situation.

"Not yet. I'm looking forward to it though. I'm a big fan. I'd like to get your autograph later."

"Of course." Cassandra smiled. She was *quite* pleased now. No police chief had ever asked Jane Fonda for *her* autograph.

Fowler turned to Burke. "You arrested Penelope Warren?"

227

"And Mycroft."

"The cat? You arrested a cat?" Fowler groaned. He saw Andy taking notes furiously.

"But . . ." The shield fell over Burke's face again. He left it in place this time. Goddamned defective equipment. What if they started throwing rocks? Burke thought, although there were no rocks handy. Or donkey dung. There *was* a supply of that now available on the police department lawn, courtesy of Daisy. Bloody jackass.

"And Alyce Smith," Cassie added. "Don't forget poor Alyce."

"Alyce I know about."

"The question is, what are you going to do about it?"

"Ms. Williams—"

"Please, call me Stormy. Or Cassie. That's my real name. Cassandra, actually. Muffy adored Greek mythology, you know. She was an English major at Pembroke when she and Biff met. He was at Brown." Cassandra ran down finally. God, he was good looking. And a fan. Oh, dear Lord, he's seen me starkers. She blushed helplessly.

"Stormy." Fowler smiled.

Don't babble. Just smile back. Cassie did. It was a glorious smile. Blush and all.

"Stormy," Fowler repeated, still smiling. "If you'll ask your friends to be patient for a few minutes, I'm sure we can work this out."

"Certainly," Stormy replied. If he said Stormy one more time in that tone of voice, she was going to change her name legally.

Fowler turned to Burke. "Inside," he ordered, jerking his thumb.

"What if they storm the station?" Burke asked.

"Inside!"

"Who is that adorable creature?" Stormy asked.

"John Fowler," Andy replied, not looking up from his note-taking. It had been a slow news day until now. Hot damn. You could always count on Penelope to stir something up. "He's our chief of police."

"Is he, now?"

Willie Stoner entered the jail. "Chief wants to see you."

"What about Mycroft?"

"He didn't say anything about the cat."

"I'm not going anywhere without Mikey."

"Take the cat, Willie," Sheila said. "It's all right, trust me."

When Penelope looked back over her shoulder, Peggy was attaching a plastic identification band around Alyce's wrist. Alyce smiled woefully at Penelope.

"I'll be back," she promised, sounding just like Arnold Schwarzenegger.

Fowler read the riot act to Burke and Penelope. Well, not *the* riot act exactly. That began something like this, "In the name of Her Majesty, the Queen, etc, etc." Fowler's language tended more to the colorfully descriptive. Penelope was impressed and wondered if the chief was a former Marine. If not, he should have been, what with his expert manipulation of the language. Mycroft was less impressed with the chief's linguistic virtuosity. He promptly fell asleep in Penelope's lap until the very end when Fowler made Burke and Penelope stand up and shake hands and promise to cooperate in the future. They did so reluctantly.

"What about Alyce?" Penelope asked.

"Get out of here. This case is closed!"

Perhaps. Perhaps not.

Penelope turned to leave.

"Penelope." Fowler called.

She and Burke turned at the same moment. "Not you, Burke. Go make some coffee or do something else useful."

"Yes, sir." Goddamned brass. Goddamned woman. Goddamned cat.

When they were alone, Fowler said, "Penelope, I'm sorry about all this."

She shrugged.

"And . . . And . . . Well, do you think you could introduce me to your sister later? I mean, formally. We've already met, of course, in a manner of speaking. . . ."

Penelope had no idea what he was talking about. She didn't think Fowler had ever met Cassie.

"Certainly, John, if you'd like."

The chief beamed.

Well, isn't that interesting.

"Today, maybe?" Fowler asked hopefully.

"Why don't you come by the Double B later?"

Yes! Fowler beamed broadly.

Smitten, Penelope thought. Won't that come in handy?

Penelope and Mycroft left the police station by the front door. It was much better than their ignominious entrance through the locked door at the back reserved for criminals and assorted low-lifers.

"Hurray!" the cry went up.

Oh, my God, where had all the people come from?

"Pen-el-o-pe! Pen-el-o-pe! Pen-el-o-pe!"

Cassie and Andy and Kathy were leading the chants, grinning foolishly. Kathy waved her sign. FREE THE EMPTY CREEK THREE!

Penelope pointed to Big Mike hurriedly. She didn't want him to get jealous; it had been a trying day for him. She wondered if "60 Minutes" might like to do a story on the first cat arrest in Empty Creek. Big Mike the Cat and Little Mike Wallace the Interviewer.

Kathy understood Penelope's concern immediately.

The cry went up.

"Big Mike! Big Mike!"

About time.

Back at Mycroft & Company, two of the Empty Creek Three were the center of attention.

"It was glorious, my lady," Kathy exclaimed. "You should have seen Stormy. You would have been so proud of her. Andy, too, he was leading cheers. Timmy was in class. He's going to be so envious that he missed it."

"It just seemed like the thing to do," Cassie said.

Andy groaned.

"What's wrong, sweetie who dashed to my rescue?"

"I think I threw my back out."

"Epsom salts," Penelope said. "You should soak in a hot tub of Epsom salts."

"I have to write the story now."

"The deadline could wait another day."

"I suppose, but I don't have any Epsom salts."

"I do. As a reward, I might even join you. I find that being arrested makes me positively sex-starved."

"My lady!"

"Before you go dashing off to soak," Cassie said, "do you think you could introduce me to that handsome police chief? As a little reward of my own? I find that leading demonstrations piques my appetite too."

"Stormy!"

"Fine indignation from a serving wench who plans to live in sin."

"That's different."

"Hah!" Penelope, Cassie, and Andy chorused.

"Maybe we could just have a nude jacuzzi party," Kathy said. "That might be fun."

"Can John come too?" Cassie asked.

"He's meeting us later at the Double B," Penelope explained.

"What a wonderful sister you are."

"Yes," Penelope agreed. "I am. By the way, what's the RCMP?" Penelope asked.

"Royal Canadian Mounted Police," Cassie replied. "I couldn't think of anything else at the time."

Penelope smiled wearily as she took George Eden's card from her pocket. "Well, I'd better think of something or poor Alyce could wind up on Death Row."

A vision of Alyce Smith strapped to a gurney and being wheeled into the death chamber to await lethal injection flashed through Penelope's mind.

Ugh!

It was better than being burned at the stake as a witch, she supposed, but only barely.

CHAPTER SIXTEEN

It was unusual for a male Arizonian, even an attorney, to wear a tie. Not so very long ago, there had been a great hue and cry in Phoenix when the misguided powers-that-be decreed that ties should be worn while on city business. And when Penelope saw the perfectly ghastly tie, shirt, and jacket combination on George Eden, she felt the reverse should be true for this otherwise handsome man in his mid-thirties. He should definitely be prohibited from wearing a tie, any tie. Penelope thought she might mention it to Mayor Dixon.

Despite the efforts of Sheila, Eden had screwed up again, big time. The tie was an ugly yellow paisley; the jacket was a loud plaid; the shirt was a very nice pink, but matched nothing else. However, Eden did seem very good in matters of criminal law, as promised by both his main squeeze and Peggy.

"A single latent fingerprint," George Eden was saying, "even a partial, identified as that of the defendant, is sufficient proof for conviction, even in the absence of other evidence."

"Does that mean the case is hopeless?" Penelope asked.

"Not at all. Quite the contrary. The prosecution must prove that the object in question, in this case a penny, was inaccessible to the defendant under normal circumstances. Pennies are accessible to everyone. I have several in my pocket at the moment." Eden stood and dug into his pocket.

Good God, the trousers were ghastly.

"You see," he said, holding out his hand. "Seven pennies. I'll bet you have any number of them floating around in your purse. Sheila always has enough pennies in her purse to pay for dinner at any given moment."

"It seems pretty shaky to me that a penny with Alyce's fingerprint on it winds up glued to a murder weapon. Who is going to believe someone took Alyce's penny and carefully preserved the print while murdering Freda and gluing the penny to the knife handle?"

"It's improbable, but not impossible." The defense attorney rose again. His gray eyes twinkled with good humor. "Ladies and gentlemen of the jury. My learned opponent would have you believe that Alyce Smith and Alyce Smith alone had access to this particular penny. But I ask you, ladies and gentlemen, do you know where your pennies are today? At this very moment, is it not possible that a murderer is skulking through your bedroom and carefully removing a discarded penny with your fingerprint upon it?" George Eden turned to Penelope and smiled disarmingly. "You see. Reasonable doubt. Everyone has a pile of loose change around. Does Alyce have a penny collection?"

"I don't know, but—"

"How about this? Ladies and gentlemen, my client innocently made change for a killer. Of course, her print will be upon a penny carefully hoarded by this villainous and cold-blooded killer in order to frame an innocent young woman. What does she do for a living, by the way?"

"She's an astrologer and psychic. You've probably seen her sign. Madame Astoria?"

"Mmm. She probably doesn't make change in pennies then."

"I rather doubt it. I don't think there's a sales tax on fortune-telling."

"Well, no matter. Reasonable doubt. That's all that is required. Is she pretty?"

"Very," Penelope replied hesitantly. Was he looking to trade in his own very attractive police officer for an alleged murderess?

"Good. The men on the jury will not believe that a pretty young woman is capable of murder."

"What about the women?"

George Eden smiled again. "Oh, I know it's not politically correct to say, but they'll be too busy wanting to dress me. You don't think I look like this on purpose?" He lifted his tie. It was labeled number one. He opened his jacket for Penelope and showed her a number seven. "It drives women to madness. Don't you find yourself wanting to make me over in your image of respectable attire?"

"Yes." Penelope smiled and shook her head slowly. It was true. Penelope wanted to join forces with Sheila and burn George Eden's wardrobe and start over from scratch.

"It gives Sheila something to focus on. It distracts her from my real vices."

"Which are?"

"Scotch, cigars, and golf. If I dressed properly—and I'm perfectly capable of matching shirts and ties—she would have time to start in on those. It works for the good ladies of the jury as well." He glanced at his watch. "Well, I'd best get over to the jail and visit my client."

Penelope left the office feeling that Alyce Smith was in very good hands indeed. She also left wondering whether Andy was secreting horrid vices like golf, a silly game by any standards, even those of Empty Creek.

While Penelope was arranging for Alyce's defense, Empty Creek's very own Jane Fonda borrowed the jeep so she might go home and prepare for her evening rendezvous with the police chief. Mycroft, who had thoroughly enjoyed the day's events thus far elected—nay, demanded—to accompany his favorite aunt, no doubt thinking, and correctly so as it turned out, that a repast of lima beans awaited at the end of the road, to say nothing of further escapades with a woman who had suddenly demonstrated a remarkable talent for creating excitement.

Had it not been for the mockingbird who had decided to move into an old woodpecker hole in the large saguaro adjacent to Penelope's front door without so much as a by your leave to Mycroft, everything would have gone quite smoothly indeed.

It wasn't that Big Mike had anything against mockingbirds or any other feathered creatures, with the possible exception of a certain large and rather surly duck; he didn't. But there were proprieties to be followed and the mockingbird, whether from ignorance or arrogance, simply didn't go by the rules.

Big Mike spotted the intruder as Cassie pulled the jeep to a halt. Her mind filled with thoughts of showers, perfumes, and possible wardrobes, all suitable for the seduction of a police chief, Cassandra failed to notice Mycroft's absence until she had unlocked the front door and stood aside for him to enter.

Where was the damned cat?

By this time the cat was shinnying up the trunk of the saguaro, carefully avoiding its thorns, his bright shining eyes focused on the waiting bird. He looked like Garfield climbing the screen door.

"Mycroft," Cassandra commanded sternly. "Come down from there this instant."

The mockingbird, amused by the spectacle of a very fat cat working his way up the cactus, did what mockingbirds are very good at.

He mocked.

That ticked Big Mike off even more. Having quite easily dispensed with a cop earlier that day, Mycroft certainly wasn't about to take guff from any bird that came down the pike.

Ignoring Cassie and uttering little war cries as he climbed—"Mew, mew, mew,"—Mycroft reached the first arm of the saguaro just a moment too late to give the Mockingbird a good what for. The bird simply fluttered way to the very tiptop of the thirty-foot cactus.

All right, if that's what you want, you little turkey.

Unfortunately, as Mycroft started past the hole in the cactus, a nest abandoned long ago, he was distracted by the glint of something shiny. With his right paw still reaching for purchase on the trunk above, Mycroft used his left to reach into the hole.

Oops!

Big Mike realized his error immediately as he did a backward somersault into space.

Had Cassandra been judging his dive, she would have issued at least a 9.5, perhaps even a perfect ten.

As a concerned aunt, however, she screamed and rushed to his rescue.

Without the benefit of having attended jump school at Ft. Benning, Big Mike executed a perfect PLF, a parachute landing fall, that would have been the envy of the most experienced airborne trooper.

But his situation was more embarrassing than falling off the window sill.

The bird hooted louder than ever.

Cassandra scooped Mycroft up before he could consider another climb up the cactus. "Mikey, baby, are you okay? What were you doing up there anyway? Come into the house and rest while Auntie Cassie gets ready."

Mycroft squirmed for a moment, but then succumbed to her entreaties. After all, she was wearing a very nice perfume and she could play the electric can opener to perfection.

Penelope was strolling back to Mycroft & Company after leaving George Eden when she glanced into the window of Potpourri, a shop specializing in assorted junk.

Ron and Nancy Reagan stared out at her.

Penelope quickly backtracked and entered the storefront. "Do you have a George Bush mask?" she asked the proprietor, an old man who still had the freckles that had once accompanied red hair. "I mean, did you have a George Bush mask? What I really mean is, did you sell a George Bush mask recently?"

"Nope," Ted replied in answer to all three questions. Unlike Penelope, he was a man of few words and used those sparingly.

"Oh," she said. Of course, no self-respecting murderer or peeping tom or whatever he was would purchase his disguise in his own theater of operations. But it had been a good idea to check. She wondered how many shops in the greater Empty Creek/Scottsdale/Tempe/Phoenix area sold George Bush masks.

"Nancy," Ted said.

Penelope took that utterance to mean he was offering to sell the Nancy Reagan mask in the window. "Why on earth would I want to be Nancy Reagan?" she asked reasonably enough.

"Don't know. Why would you want to be George Bush?" It was a remarkably long conversation for him. And reasonable.

"I don't."

Penelope decided to browse through the shop so long as she was there. Ted always had some interesting items, and she usually came away with one or more knickknacks that eventually found their way into a storage box.

While Penelope was in Potpourri examining an exercise device guaranteed for breast enhancement, George Bush was peering through Cassandra's bedroom window, watching avidly as she dabbed perfume between a pair of breasts that needed no enhancement whatsoever. Had Cassandra not been so engrossed in seductive wiles, she might have harkened to the mockingbird's warning and looked up to see George Bush.

Mycroft did hear the mockingbird, but still suffering acute embarrassment from his recent belly flop, he misinterpreted the its cries and contented himself with the last of the lima beans and various plots for revenge on the irritating little creature.

So George Bush skulked away unnoticed, but not

until after Cassandra concealed her charms with a robe.

In the end, Penelope discarded the exercise device which required the user to flap her arms like a bird. She decided she could flap on her own if she wanted to, but, of course, she didn't. She was quite satisfied with her chest as it was, so she settled upon a red Detroit Tigers pennant from 1950, thinking that Mycroft would like the portrait of the roaring Bengal Tiger emblazoned on it.

"How do I look?" Cassandra asked, twirling around for Penelope and Kathy. Mycroft had already pronounced his approval by sitting on her lap all the way back into town.

"Oh, Stormy," Kathy exclaimed, "you're gorgeous."

"I thought the simple approach was best."

"You look like the proverbial fresh-faced all-American girl," Penelope said.

"Not too wholesome, I hope."

"Just the right touch of vamp."

"I borrowed your Chanel. I hope you don't mind."

"The blouse and slacks are vaguely familiar also."

"Well, they should be. You have very good taste for a rustic, Penny."

"I suppose the underwear is mine as well? You are wearing underwear?"

"Of course. What do you think I am? And it's mine."

* * *

Penelope brusquely provided the formal introduction of John Fowler and Cassandra Warren. She then spent the next hour unsuccessfully trying to penetrate the romantic aura that hovered around the infatuated couple by asking some pertinent questions concerning the arrest of Alyce Smith.

"Stormy."

"John."

"Call me Dutch."

"All right, Dutch."

Stormy and Dutch. It was enough to gag a goose.

"What evidence did you find in Alyce's files?"

"How long will you be in town, Stormy?"

"At least another week. I'm thinking of buying a weekend retreat. Just a little hideaway."

Oh, really? That was news.

"I'd like to show you around. I know all the best hideaways."

"Do you have any evidence that connects Alyce to Louise's murder?"

"I'll bet you do, Dutch."

"What about the anonymous call?"

"What's your next film?"

"Oh, I'm reading scripts. There are no really good roles for women though."

"You'll make the big breakthrough, I'm sure."

"I hope so."

"Louise Fletcher called me, you know."

"Would you have dinner with me, Stormy?"

"After she was dead."

"I'd like that very much, Dutch."

Oh, foo!

In the ladies' room, Penelope pleaded, "Pump him."

"Oh, I will," Cassie said dreamily.

"I meant for information."

"That too."

It was hopeless. Penelope had seen her sister in love before, but never quite like this. That cute little Cupid appeared to have discarded his delicate arrows for a bludgeon.

Having been arrested *and* ignored in the space of less than eight hours was more than Penelope could bear. With Mycroft and Andy in tow—at least, they were attentive—she retreated to the sanctuary of her remote little ranch, where to the surprise of everyone, including herself, she prepared an excellent spaghetti sauce in less than twenty minutes. Naturally, Penelope used Muffy's recipe—the best recipes came from Muffy's kitchen.

Brandishing the chopping knife as she hacked away at onions and cloves of garlic provided some unpleasant memories, but the glass of red wine that Andy poured for her, carefully staying out of reach of the knife as he put it on the counter next to her, and Mycroft's adoring look—Muffy's sauce was a favorite of his—soon softened her mood.

After putting the sauce on simmer, Penelope turned to Andy. "Feel like a jacuzzi, sailor?" She unbuttoned the first button of her blouse.

"I think that would be nice." He watched as the second and third and fourth buttons came undone. "It's been a trying day," he continued. His voice was much huskier now as he watched her slip the blouse from her shoulders and let it fall to the kitchen floor.

Andy swallowed and gulped when she reached behind her back and unfastened the clasp of her lacy white bra.

"Ah, that's better," Penelope said, crossing her arms modestly. "Don't you think?"

"Oh, yes, much." He followed her naked back into the darkness. Her back turned him on. But then everything about Penelope turned him on.

Since Mycroft was enamored of neither backs nor the jacuzzi, he stayed behind to guard the gently bubbling spaghetti sauce from mockingbirds and George Bush, or anyone else who happened along.

Penelope and Andy bubbled right along with the sauce.

The interlude in the jacuzzi was pleasant as was the candlelight dinner that followed, but once Andy had left, the murderous business at hand quickly intruded on Penelope's thoughts once more.

She took a yellow legal tablet into the living room, brushed aside the books that cluttered the couch, put her feet up on the coffee table, and started to work her way through suspects.

Mycroft decided to help and climbed into her lap. Once he was settled, she wrote the first name on the tablet, using Big Mike as a table.

Alyce. That sweet thing is not a murderess, Penelope thought. It's simply impossible.

Freda. Poor Freda. Why?

Phil Simmons. That buffoon.

Mafia. Not their style.

Spencer Alcott. Bucky Beaver himself.

Casino. Money. Big money. Always an excellent motive. But why kill the councilwoman who was going to introduce the proposal for consideration?

Louise Fletcher. What was she doing out here at my

place anyway? Damn it. Call me again. Tell me what you meant.

Herbert Fletcher. What about him? A lecherous old man with an alibi. Two alibis. Always at the movies eating tubs of popcorn.

Alyce. Who are you sleeping with? Not Herbert. Surely not Herbert.

George Bush. Who the hell are you, and what are you doing in my mystery?

Anonymous woman caller. You and that stupid cat stay away from Herbert Fletcher. Was that Freda? Herb had accused her of stalking him. Could Freda have been so desperately in love with Fletcher?

Louise. Who played the tape of her voice? Damn.

With her mind spinning from so many unanswered questions, Penelope tossed the tablet aside and picked up *Silent Night,* only to encounter another question. What are you trying to tell me from the grave, Louise Fletcher?

"Come on, Mikey, let's go for a walk."

Outside, Penelope again compared the cover of *Silent Night* with her own home. Woman and cat stared at the house for the longest time, to no avail.

Penelope hoped that Cassandra was having a better evening than her own. Well, parts of it had been pretty good, especially when Andy had . . . That had been damned good.

"He was a perfect gentleman. We watched *Amazon Princess and the Sword of Doom.* He loved it, by the way. He called it a wonderful satire of the genre. So there. We talked. Not even a good-night kiss. He shook my hand. Damn. I'm in love."

"On one date?"

"I was in love when he called me Stormy the first time."

"On one word? That's certainly a new record for falling in love. Should we notify the Guinness people?"

"Didn't you know with Andy right away?"

"Andy and I are friends. I'm not sure I love him." Memories of the jacuzzi belied *that* statement.

"Who do you love, if not Andy?"

"No one, really. Sean Connery, I suppose."

"Wonderful. You and twenty or thirty million other women."

"You asked." How did we get on to my love life? "What information did you get for me?"

"I know how he got his nickname."

"I meant about Alyce."

"All in good time, Penny dear. Don't you want to hear about Dutch?"

"Well . . ."

"You see, when he was a young patrolman, he arrested a man for stealing a pair of wooden shoes. As it turn out, this perp had a . . ."

Perp. This was serious if she was already starting to talk like a cop.

". . . shoe fetish and he was carrying this pair of wooden shoes down the street, one in each hand. Dutch thought that was suspicious. . . ."

I should hope so.

". . . And it turned out this guy had a bedroom filled with women's shoes? He'd been in every bedroom in the neighborhood. Thus, the nickname, Dutch? For the wooden shoes, you know?"

Cassie was beginning to sound like Scarlett O'Hara with all those question marks.

"What's the penalty for stealing wooden shoes?"

"Really, Penny, that's not the point of the story."

"I just wondered. I suppose they multiply the sentence times the number of shoes stolen. But do they count a pair as one, or does each shoe count separately?"

"Penny! If you persist, I won't tell you what Dutch said about Alyce."

"You came through!"

"I'm always willing to help my sister, even at the risk of great personal sacrifice."

"No kiss on the first date is hardly a sacrifice."

"Well . . . there was just one kiss. I fibbed. I didn't want you to think I was easy."

"Aha! I knew it. Tell all."

"Well, we were standing at the door and he took me in his arms—"

"You can tell me about the kiss later. What about Alyce?"

"You can be just impossible sometimes, Penny."

"Alyce!"

Even Mycroft heard the warning in Penelope's voice and perked up his ears. He was no fool. Something was going down. Cassie, being no fool herself, relented.

"They found another chopping knife in Alyce's apartment."

"So what? Everyone has a chopping knife. I have a chopping knife. You have a chopping knife."

"Hidden behind the hot water heater with a penny already glued to the handle?"

"That's too obvious," Penelope said finally. "She's been framed."

"Dutch thinks so too."

"Why has she been arrested then?"

"Dutch thinks she might be the next victim. She's in

protective custody. The whole thing was a sham, but no one is to know. Not even Alyce."

Cassie sat back smugly, enjoying the look of surprise on her sister's face.

Gotcha!

CHAPTER SEVENTEEN

Penelope tried Discreet Investigations again. For the umpteenth time, the answering machine went beep. She hung up without leaving a message, then got up and went to Cassie's bedroom door. Cassie and Mycroft were still fast asleep. No help there. Frank, the teddy bear, showed more life than those two.

Penelope returned to the telephone and dialed a second number. When Laney answered, Penelope asked without preamble, "Want to go Bunburying?" Like Algernon in *The Importance of Being Earnest,* Laney was a dedicated Bunburyist, although she certainly didn't need a sick brother as an excuse to run off with Penelope in search of adventure.

The address for Discreet Investigations was a storefront mail drop in one of those seedy areas that all cities have in and around police stations and courthouses. Somehow, urban renewal always manages to elude such places. Around it were a few law offices populated with the kinds of attorneys who advertise free consultations on television, a number of bail bondsmen, an open market with fresh fruits and vegetables, several liquor stores, and an adult bookstore advertising videos, magazines, books, adult toys, and marital aids.

Penelope parked three doors away in front of a bail bondsman's office. "Well, that's a disappointment," she said, looking down the street at the mail drop that was Discreet Investigations.

"Have you ever been in an adult bookstore, Penelope?"

"Mmm?" She was double-checking the address. It was indeed the correct address.

"I said, have you ever been in an adult bookstore?"

"Oh, sure, thousands of times."

"I'm serious."

"Once. After boot camp."

"Well, I've never been in one, and I want to go. It's research."

"First, I want to check this place out."

A sullen two-hundred-and-fifty-pound man wearing a Disneyworld T-shirt was behind the counter. He wore a name tag on the T-shirt: It said Ralph. Despite Tinker Bell and Jiminy Cricket on his chest, he looked like a refugee from a motorcycle gang. A tattoo on one massive bicep proclaimed MOTHER. The word was encased in a red heart. A dagger dripped blood on the other equally massive bicep. Ralph brightened when Penelope and Laney entered the store.

"I'm looking for Discreet Investigations," Penelope said.

"Not here. Call."

"I have called. I'm tired of calling. Who is the principal in the firm? It's really quite important that I contact him today."

"Confidential."

"Yes, I know investigations are confidential, but I wish to hire him."

"Write."

"This is not the way to conduct business."

"Wouldn't be discreet if everybody knew."

"Well, Ralph, thank you so much for your time." Penelope smiled sweetly. That was a mistake.

"Wanna party?" Ralph asked. "Like blondes. Redheads too," he added, leering at Laney.

"Certainly not."

"Show you a good time."

"I'm having a perfectly wonderful time all by myself."

"You ain't alone."

"That's very perceptive of you, Ralph. I'm impressed with your visual acuity."

"Huh?"

" 'Bye, Ralph." Penelope fluttered her fingers in adieu.

On the sidewalk again, she said, "Creep."

"He had a certain animal-like quality about him," Laney replied.

"Animal, yes. Quality, no."

"Well, let's go next door."

"Are you sure?"

"Let's not waste the trip. Just look on it as research."

Penelope shrugged. "Lead on."

Laney pushed through the curtains that hung over the door, took three steps into the store, and stopped abruptly. "Oh, my God," she said.

Penelope would have thought it was impossible for her friend's face to turn a deeper shade of red than her hair. But it did.

"Oh, my God," Laney repeated. Her eyes bounced from one display to another.

"Well, do you want to browse for marital aids or not?"

"Oh, my God."

Ralph's twin was seated on a high stool behind the counter, a cigarette dangling from his lips. He wore an Emily Dickinson T-shirt. He had tattoos identical to Ralph's, but they were reversed. Perhaps that was how "Mother" told her sons apart.

" 'How happy is the little stone,' " Penelope recited, " 'That rambles in the road alone.' "

"Huh?" Ralph's twin said.

"Emily Dickinson," Penelope replied pleasantly.

"Oh, my God, look at the size of that . . . that . . . thing."

"Huh?"

"The poet on your T-shirt. Emily Dickinson. She wrote that poem. 'How Happy Is the Little Stone.' "

"Oh, her," he said looking down at Emily. "I just like thin women. Wanna party?"

"Thanks, no," Penelope said.

"I'm Russell."

"Well, isn't that cute. Ralph and Russell."

"Ralph's my brother. We're twins."

" 'He ain't heavy, Father, he's my brother.' "

"Ain't got no father, but Ralph sure is heavy. Weighs nearly three hunnert pounds. Heavy as hell."

"Oh, my God."

"Hey, this ain't no church, lady. You wanna scare the customers away?"

"You have no customers, at the moment," Penelope pointed out reasonably enough. "Discreet Investigations? Do you know them?"

"Next door. What you girls interested in, anyways?

We got your magazines, we got your vibrators, we got—"

"Oh, my God."

Back on the road again, listening to Penelope's tape of Willie Nelson's Greatest Hits, Laney said of her first foray into the world of adults, "Well, I'm certainly glad we didn't bring Alexander or Mycroft. They would have been shocked."

"How about Wally?"

"He would have come down with a severe case of performance anxiety."

"Oh, I don't know. Wally seems secure enough."

"Did you see the size of those . . . those . . . things." Laney fell silent for a moment. "I wonder if they have a mail order catalog?" she asked brightly.

"Laney, you're impossible."

"Or perhaps you could branch out into other lines. . . ."

Before going to visit Alyce, Penelope stopped by John Fowler's office. She was ready to confess all.

And did.

About Abraham Lincoln and George Bush.

About Bucky Beaver and casinos and secret closets.

About a telephone call from Louise Fletcher.

And, of course, Discreet Investigations. She saw no reason to tell him about those adorable twins, Ralph and Russell.

"You should have told Burke and Stoner all this," Fowler said.

Penelope thought he was only slightly disapproving. That's what comes of a police chief dating your glamorous sister. "They would have thought I was crazy," she said, "especially if I told them I received a phone call from a dead person."

"That's true, but you should have told them anyway."

Unrepentant, Penelope said, "Next time I'll belabor them with every detail, no matter how insignificant."

"Let's hope there isn't a next time."

"Cassie said Alyce is in protective custody."

"I haven't eliminated her entirely as a suspect, but finding a knife in her apartment after an anonymous tip is a little too much for me to accept. I think the killer wants Alyce out of the way. By one means or another. I'd rather have her in here than find her body with a knife in it. After what you've told me today, I'm inclined to put you in with her."

"I've had enough of the city's hospitality. Besides, Cassie would disapprove. You know how she gets."

"Ah, Stormy." Dutch Fowler's eyes glazed over. "I certainly do. She's quite a remarkable and talented woman."

With that, Penelope excused herself, leaving Dutch to daydream of Stormy and their next date.

Despite the shapeless blue dress issued by her jailers and red-rimmed eyes, the obvious ravages of a night spent in tears, Alyce Smith looked angelic as she was escorted into the visitor's room. Her blond hair was carefully brushed, and she wore fresh lipstick and makeup. She was quick to smile at Penelope.

"How are you, Alyce?"

"I'm fine considering the circumstances. Peggy and Sheila have been very kind. They don't think I did it either."

"What did you think of George?"

"I'd like to get him some new clothes."

"Join the crowd. Can I get you anything? I believe cigarettes are traditional. I understand they're useful for barter in the prison setting, a form of currency."

"I don't smoke, and I'm the only woman in the Empty Creek jail." Alyce smiled. "Perhaps some books?"

"That would be a nice title for a mystery. The Only Woman in the Empty Creek Jail. Or a country Western song. I'll bring some books on my next visit."

"That will be nice."

Penelope paused for a moment, took a breath, and asked, "Who is he?"

Alyce's smile disappeared.

"What do you mean?"

"Who is your secret lover?"

"What does it matter? He had nothing to do with this. Besides, it's over. I haven't told him yet. I didn't have a chance. I suppose I don't have to now. Who could love someone accused of murder?"

"Perhaps they permit conjugal visits?"

Alyce brightened. "Do you really think so?"

"You still love him, don't you?"

Alyce bit her lip and nodded.

"Does anyone else know about you and Herbert?"

"You knew?"

"I guessed. I should have guessed earlier."

"We were very careful. I don't think anyone else knows."

"How long were you seeing each other?"

"Nearly a year. He wanted to marry me."

"You know, Freda apparently thought much the same thing."

"I know." Alyce bit her lip again. "What's going to happen, Penelope?"

"We're going to get you out of here."

As she was leaving, Penelope met Herbert Fletcher on the steps of the police station.

"Is it true?" he asked.

"Is what true?"

"That Alyce has been arrested and charged with murdering Louise and Freda?"

"It's true, I'm sorry to say. How is it you're just finding out?"

"I went to Phoenix on business yesterday and decided to spend the night. I've just returned. To this. It's outrageous. Alyce wouldn't harm anyone."

"I think she's been set up to take the fall for someone else."

"But who?"

"That's what I intend to find out." Penelope watched his face closely for a reaction. He seemed genuinely upset about Alyce's arrest, but then he had seemed equally upset over the deaths of Louise and Freda. "Women who are close to you seem to run into disasters of late."

"What do you mean?"

"What do you mean, what do I mean? Your wife is murdered. Your former lover is murdered. Your current lover is arrested for their murders. You don't have a very good track record with your relationships."

"You know about Alyce?"

Penelope nodded. "She told me."

"Did she also tell you I love her, that we're going to be married?"

"We didn't get into that."

"Well, it's true, but we had to keep it a secret, especially after poor Louise. . . . I was going to ask Louise for a divorce, but then she was murdered and . . . Oh, Christ, what a mess."

"Yes," Penelope agreed. "Are there any other women lurking around your life?"

Fletcher shook his head slowly. "Alyce is the only woman in my life. I must see her. I don't care how it looks. I'm tired of sneaking around. I love her, damn it! It's not our fault some madman is going around stabbing people to death. You must find the murderer, Penelope. You must."

"I will," Penelope promised. "You can count on it."

After driving back to Mycroft & Company, Penelope realized that she probably should have told Tweedledee and Tweedledum about Alyce and Herbert Fletcher. She shrugged and dismissed the thought. Let them find their own clues.

"Where have you been, my lady? Stormy's been calling all morning for you."

"Oh, good Lord, I forgot about her. And Mycroft. They'll think I'm terrible. Be a dear. Run out and pick them up for me. I've got work to do."

"Of course, my lady."

But once Kathy left on her errand, Penelope couldn't decide what work really needed doing. There were no customers. The store was lonely without Mycroft and Kathy. I might as well have gone out and picked them up myself, she thought. Just then, a red Cadillac convertible pulled into a parking space right in front of Mycroft & Company. Its arrival was announced by the playing of the University of Southern

California's fight song. In place of a hood ornament, gigantic polished longhorns curved over the width of the hood.

A small apparition in the form of a man wearing jeans and Western shirt emerged from the large car and entered the bookshop. He chewed on a very long, very black cigar which was unlit.

"I'm Beamish," the little man announced, removing the cigar. Without the high-heeled cowboy boots made of snakeskin and the cowboy hat, he would barely top an inch or two over the five foot mark. He doffed the hat and reduced his height considerably.

"Beamish what?"

"Just Beamish."

"Well, just Beamish, what can I do for you?"

"No, *Just* Beamish," he said. "It's short for Justin."

"Oh, Just Beamish. I get it now."

Beamish beamed.

Penelope beamed back at Beamish. "What can I do for you?"

"Discreet Investigations," Beamish said.

"You're Discreet Investigations?" The red convertible, the USC fight song, and the longhorns did not seem very discreet to Penelope.

"Indeed, I am."

"But why didn't you return my phone calls?"

"Instructions of my client."

"Louise Fletcher?"

Beamish nodded solemnly. "A fine woman. Always paid in advance. A very fine woman. You don't find clients like Louise Fletcher very often. Never, in fact." He stuck the cigar in his mouth as punctuation.

"I can imagine. You're not going to light that thing, are you?"

"Oh, goodness gracious, no. It would make me sick.

I quit smoking two years ago with the assistance of nicotine gum, but then I became addicted to the gum. I took up chewing cigars to break my addiction to the gum. Now I'm addicted to chewing cigars. I have a very addictive personality."

"So it would seem."

Beamish still beamed as he looked around the bookshop. "You specialize in mysteries. Perhaps I should write novels. I have adventures to recount. Many adventures." He turned back to Penelope. "But then I suppose I would become addicted to the typewriter."

"I believe most writers use computers nowadays," Penelope said.

"I daresay, you're correct. That would be an expensive addiction. Well . . ."

"Do you have a Louise Fletcher adventure to recount? Is that why you're here?"

"I always try to follow the instructions of my client. She was quite specific. I was to ignore all calls until you were persistent enough to show up at the office. I think she wanted you to meet Ralph and Russell. She was very fond of them. Brought them cookies."

"That was just like Louise," Penelope said. She tried to crinkle her eyes, but succeeded only in making them roll in disbelief. Cookies, indeed.

"Was the message audible over the telephone? I held the cassette as close to the receiver as I could."

"Yes, quite audible—in a "Twilight Zone" sort of way. It was a shock hearing Louise's voice."

"I have another tape to play for you. Mrs. Fletcher was quite specific. You were to hear it only as a last resort, but under the circumstances—"

"It's the last resort."

"Quite so. Do you have a recorder?"

"I'll get it." Penelope went to her desk in the back room and rummaged among the papers on it. She was trembling with excitement as she found the miniature cassette recorder and returned to hand it to Beamish. At last, a break.

Before Beamish could insert the tape, however, Kathy, Cassie, and Mycroft entered the shop by the back door.

Penelope made the introductions. "This is Just Beamish."

"It's short for Justin," he quickly explained, staring up at Cassie. Mycroft was the only creature in the room that Beamish could look down on. "I know you from somewhere," he said.

Cassie smiled down at Beamish. Fans should be cultivated. "Perhaps you've seen my movies. I'm an actress."

"Never go to the movies. I've seen you someplace else. Would you mind showing me your underwear?"

"I beg your pardon!" There were limits to fan cultivation.

"No, I suppose not. I find underwear advertisements very erotic. Bras, panties, slips. I especially like silk slips. I have a vast collection."

"Of slips?"

Kathy was edging slowly toward the telephone, ready to dial nine-one-one at the first opportunity, although the three women could easily pummel the little man into submission, with Mycroft's assistance, of course.

"No, no," Beamish said hastily. "Of advertisements. I just thought I might recognize you if I saw you in underwear. Or your legs. If you modeled for swimsuits, I mean. I've very good at recognizing legs."

"I have done swimsuit commercials."

"That's it, then. Well, I'm glad that's settled. It would have bothered me all day."

"Beamish was just about to play a cassette for me."

"Dear lady, do you think that's wise? My instructions were very clear. For your ears only."

"At this point, I think the more ears, the better, don't you?" Penelope had a sudden urge to pat Beamish on the top of his head. He was rather cute and adorable, kind of like Frank, the teddy bear, dressed up in a cowboy outfit.

"Well . . ."

Mycroft took what Beamish perceived to be a menacing step forward. Beamish took a step back. In reality, Mycroft was only attempting to get a closer smell of the snakeskin boots. Still, Beamish inched away as Mycroft inched forward, wrinkling his nose.

"He won't hurt you," Penelope said, "unless you're also a vet. He doesn't like people who stick needles in his butt."

Thus reassured, Beamish beamed. "We have something in common then," he said. "Nice kitty."

"I don't think he likes to be called kitty either," Cassie said spitefully. She had decided she didn't need fans who wanted to see her underwear. Dutch didn't count, of course.

"His name's Mycroft," Kathy said. "Or Big Mike. He likes lima beans."

"I'm sorry I didn't know that," Beamish said. He was still rather nervous as Mycroft sniffed the boots. "Perhaps I should run out and get a case or two for him."

Penelope demurred. "That won't be necessary. I think we should play the tape. It's important."

"I'm sure it is. Louise thought everything she did was of the utmost importance."

Penelope held out her hand. Beamish sighed and gave her the cassette.

Finally.

The dead woman's voice was exasperated. "Really, Penelope, I simply don't know what is taking you so long. It was a very simple clue, and I'm disappointed that you haven't figured it out yet. You seem like such a bright young woman. Look for the cave. Look for the knot. Mycroft, are you there?"

Mycroft's ears lifted at the sound of his name.

"Mycroft, you simply must help Penelope. Lead her to the cave."

Mycroft set off immediately. All eyes followed him as he went to the back room. Penelope was fairly certain there were no caves in the back room. Before she could follow, however, Mycroft had discovered his bowl was empty and he returned, complaining loudly.

Penelope rewound the tape and played it again.

And a third time.

She looked around at each of the others in the room—Cassie, Kathy, a still-beaming Beamish—he liked being in the midst of three pretty young women—Mycroft. They all shrugged helplessly, except for Mycroft who meowed again. Didn't anyone understand it was time for a little snack?

"Now, what in the hell is that supposed to mean?" Penelope asked finally.

"I haven't the foggiest, dear lady," Beamish replied. "That's why I came to you."

CHAPTER EIGHTEEN

It was worse than the high school prom.

Cassie changed her clothes five times, utilizing her own voluminous wardrobe before starting in on various combinations from Penelope's closets. Penelope quickly grew tired of Cassie's refrain, "How does this look?"

"It looks fine," she repeated. "You looked fine the first time. I'm going to feed the animals."

"I wonder . . ." Cassie said, holding up another blouse.

After feeding Mycroft, Chardonnay, and the bunnies—all had been feeling neglected—Penelope went back to the bedroom where Cassie was changing yet again.

"How do I look now?"

"Wonderful," Penelope said. "Smashing."

"Do you really think so?" Cassie started over. Penelope wandered off to refill her wine glass, leaving Mycroft and Frank as the sole arbiters of her sister's outfit for the second date.

"Aren't you going to get ready for Andy?"

"I am ready."

"You're ready?" Cassie seemed incredulous.

Penelope looked down at herself. "My clothes are clean. I'm clean. I smell nice. I'm ready."

"Penny, dear," Cassie said sternly, "if you take Andy for granted, he will stray."

"He'd better not."

As Penelope went down the hall, she heard Cassie ask, "So, what do *you* think, Mycroft?" Penelope opened her mouth in a silent scream. It was much worse than the high school prom.

Rather than return to the dressing frenzy, Penelope took her wine into the living room and plopped herself down on the couch and turned on "Jeopardy." After watching the first categories flash on the board, she turned it off. Too much science and nothing literary or historical. Had it not been for chemistry and physics, she would have been class valedictorian of her high school, but she had received her only *B*'s in those subjects.

"What do you think, Mycroft? Up or down?" Evidently in the bedroom Cassie had started in on her hair.

Though chemistry and physics had been torture for Penelope, she had rather liked the chem lab when something was fizzing around in violent reaction to something else. What was it that reacted so well to water—potassium, manganese, sodium? Something. Penelope couldn't remember, and there was no use asking Cassie. She had been even worse in chemistry.

Luther Pendross, Penelope's lab partner and a true nerd, had argued unsuccessfully against his suspension after destroying a toilet in one of the boy's rest rooms, claiming to the principal that he'd only wanted to see what the reaction would be if a large block of whatever he'd dumped in the loo was introduced into a larger body of water.

Suspension city.

But it had been a rather spectacular reaction.

"Hey," Penelope hollered, "whatever happened to Luther Pendross?"

"He went into insurance, I think," Cassie hollered back.

That was the trouble with education. It stifled the inquiring mind.

Penelope turned the television on for the Double Jeopardy round.

All right. American Novels flashed on the board.

Penelope suffered through 1955—how could the contestant miss James Dean?—Wines, Famous Animals, and Astronomy. Who knew anything about astronomy? Alyce, of course. She wondered if Alyce had a television set in the jail and if she was watching "Jeopardy." This led her to give the "Jeopardy" contestants a poser of her own. "He killed Louise Fletcher and Freda Alsberg."

"Who is . . . ?" Penelope prompted.

The three contestants—John, Shirley, and Bill—didn't know.

Alex Trebek didn't know.

Penelope certainly didn't know.

Finally, nothing was left but the American Novel. Shirley, who was leading, tentatively said, "The American novel for two hundred dollars, please, Alex."

"This novel was published in 1920 and deals with expatriates in Paris."

"What is *The Sun Also Rises?*" Penelope answered.

"What is *The Great Gatsby?*" Shirley answered. Twit.

Bill rang in. "What is *Winesberg, Ohio?*" Oaf.

John gave it a try. "What is *Moby Dick?*" Dolt. Doesn't anyone read anymore?

Shirley gave it another try for $400.

"Catcher In the Rye." Penelope cried. She usually forgot to make it a question.

"What did you say?" Cassie shouted. "I can't hear you."

"You Can't Go Home Again!"

"Oh."

"Rabbit, Run." Penelope was four for four. The contestants were zero for four.

Shirley finally got *Last of the Mohicans* fifteen seconds after Penelope and went into Final Jeopardy leading. Penelope waited for the last category—Foreign Foods—before turning the set off. That category served only as a reminder of the Old Boy's dictum that the average Englishman's idea of foreign food was to go into a Chinese restaurant for steak, egg, and chips. As a devoted Anglophile, Penelope thought that a rather harsh indictment of the Old Boy's fellow countrymen.

This particular musing was interrupted by the sound of a car and shortly thereafter the crunch of footsteps and the ring of the doorbell. As Penelope went to respond, she wondered if she could get the bell to play the San Diego State fight song, like the horn in Beamish's car.

"Good evening, Penelope, I've come for the wonderful person who is your sister. I will not take no for an answer. Together, we will fly into the night."

"Good Lord, John, have you been drinking?"

"Certainly not. I thought I was being poetic."

"Well, you may have to postpone flight, or go alone. Cassie's not ready. She may never be ready. She hasn't gone through my second closet yet. Would you like a drink?"

"Cops can be poetic."

"I'm sure they can, John. Would you like a drink, or would you rather stand there looking like a lovesick goose?"

"A drink, I guess."

"White wine, all right?"

"Yummy."

"I'll get it." Yummy? What kind of talk was that for a cop? Yummy, indeed.

Penelope returned with the poetic cop's wine. "Cheers," she said.

"Cheers."

"I found Discreet Investigations," Penelope said, "or rather Discreet Investigations found me. His name's Beamish. Cassie can tell you all about it. It'll give you something to do other than play Hello-Good-bye."

"And just what is Hello-Goodbye?"

Penelope gave him her very sweetest of smiles. "Oh, I daresay, you'll find out all in good time. I'll go tell Cassie you're here." Another car pulled in. "That'll be Andy. Let him in, John."

Cassie greeted Penelope's announcement with terror.

"I'm not ready," she cried. "I'm a mess. My life is over."

"It certainly will be, if you're not in the living room in two minutes flat." Penelope left her sister moaning and found Andy and John in the kitchen. Andy was picking bits of cork from his glass of wine.

"It just snapped off," Andy explained. "And the rest fell into the bottle when I tried to get it out."

What a klutz.

Dutch and Stormy finally went out on their second date.

"Have her home early," Penelope called after them.

266

She turned to Andy and opened her arms. "We could stay home or we could go to the movies or we could do both."

"How can we stay home *and* go to the movies?"

"You're so slow sometimes, Andy. We can stay home and play Nibble and Kiss or we can go to the movies and play Nibble and Kiss *and* see the movie. That's both."

"Oh."

Penelope could see that he was perplexed. "You're torn between lust for my body and a craving for artistic enrichment, aren't you?"

"Well, yes. Perhaps we should do both."

Lawrence of Arabia was still playing, one of the movies that Herbert Fletcher had seen on the fateful day his wife was murdered.

"It's a very long film, and there are lots of boring parts in the desert," Penelope said. "I don't mind if you keep your eyes open when you kiss me. That way you won't lose track of the story. You can ravish me later."

Penelope and Andy left the lights on for a very disgruntled cat who was grumping around the living room, protesting loudly at being left behind.

On the way into town, she told Andy all about Louise Fletcher's latest message from the beyond. " 'Look for the cave. Look for the knot.' Whatever could she have meant?"

"Square knot."

"Granny knot."

"Tie the knot."

"Knothole."

"Knothole gang."

"Knotty problem."

"Knotted."

267

"Gordian knot." Alexander the Great had certainly solved that problem with his sword, severing the knot to claim his place as ruler of Asia, just as a modern-day killer had used chopping knives to sever his problems, his relationships. "It's Herb," Penelope declared abruptly. "It has to be Herb."

"He has an alibi," Andy pointed out mildly. "For both murders."

"That is a problem."

"A knotty one."

"Oh, stop it."

Fortified with soft drinks and a large tub of popcorn, Penelope and Andy settled into their seats just as a young man three rows down asked of another couple, "Do you have a napkin I can borrow? Save me a trip to the concession stand."

The woman willingly handed one over.

"Thanks."

"She still has half her coke left," the woman's husband said. "Do you want that too?"

"Is it diet?"

"Afraid not."

"No thanks, then."

Penelope giggled and burrowed into the popcorn.

The lights went down. The haunting soundtrack came up. She snuggled closer to Andy.

A motorcycle roared.

Oh boy, the magic of movies.

As Peter O'Toole was loping across the endless desert on a camel, that magic was interrupted when the exit door next to the screen opened and a figure left the theater. While the door was briefly ajar, the glare of lights from the parking lot blinded Penelope. Little stars and spots danced in front of her eyes. Just as she was growing accustomed to the darkness again, the door opened once more and a dark figure slipped back into the theater. Penelope squinched her eyes shut as giggling came from the front rows along with the snapping of pop tops. Damn teenagers. One of them had probably snuck out to the parking lot for more beer.

Peter O'Toole's camel still loped across the desert. Penelope had ridden a camel once in Cairo. An ugly disgusting creature that had slavered all the way to the Pyramids while its owner trotted along behind, assuring Penelope that the camel had once been in a Cecil B. DeMille film. Must have been the oldest damned camel in cinema history. How long did camels live anyway?

Wait a minute.

Wait just a damned minute!

How did he do that?

The exit door should have locked automatically, but whoever left the theater had returned with no trouble whatsoever.

Penelope disentangled her hand from Andy's. "Excuse me," she said, slipping past him to trot excitedly down the aisle. She opened the door. The parking lot lights flooded into the dark theater.

High above her on the screen, Peter O'Toole and his loping camel were joined by Omar Sharif upon another ugly old loper.

The lock had been taped shut with duct tape.

"Andy!" Penelope hissed. "Come look at this!"

He loped down the aisle. The camels were taking their toll on him.

"Shut the door!"

"Just a minute!" Penelope cried in a loud stage whisper. "This is an official investigation."

"This is an official request to shut the damned door!"

"Oh, blow it out your ear."

"Shut the door! Shut the door! Shut the door!"

Penelope ignored the chanting. "You see how he did it, Andy?"

"How who did what?"

Penelope thought this a strange perversion of the journalistic formula of who, what, when, etc. "Herbert Fletcher, of course. He taped the lock so he could get back into the theater after killing Louise and Freda."

"What's going on here?"

Ushers and concessionaires followed the manager down the aisle.

"Those people are drinking beer," Penelope said, pointing a finger into the darkness.

Camels snorted. Peter O'Toole meditated. "Aqaba," he said. Teenagers fled by the opposite aisle. The manager turned every which way. "Get their names," he cried. Ushers scrambled to do his bidding. "Stop the film!" The projector ground to a halt. "Aqabaaaaaaa . . ."

"I want my money back." A pathetic voice from the darkness before the house lights came up.

"Come, Andy. We'll rent the film and watch it without the utter chaos of this theater," Penelope said firmly, conveniently forgetting that she was the primary cause of the disruption.

Penelope thought it strange as she inserted the key that Mycroft had not come to greet her. Whenever they were apart, he always came to the door. It had started when he was a kitten, and no matter how hard she tried to sneak up on him after being out, he always heard her and was at the door.

Not tonight. Maybe he was still mad. Maybe he was getting old. Maybe he was out looking for Murphy Brown.

Penelope opened the door and stepped aside for Andy to enter.

"Oh my," he said. "I don't think this is the way we left it."

Penelope looked past him.

The living room had been torn apart. Books had been tossed from their shelves. A chair was over-turned. A lamp was on the floor. Sofa cushions were thrown about. Penelope rushed inside and instantly recognized the pungent smell of cordite.

Someone had shot Mycroft!

"Mycroft?" she cried. "Mycroft!"

No answer.

No! Please, God, no!

A bullet had torn into the wall where the hall to the bedrooms began. It was at cat level.

"Mycroft?"

She headed down the hallway turning on lights as she went. "Mycroft?"

She found him in Cassie's bedroom, sprawled across the furry belly of Frank the teddy bear.

"Mycroft, are you all right?"

He hissed in reply. It wasn't a very threatening hiss, not like when he was at Doctor Bob's, just enough to let Penelope know he was upset.

"It's all right, Mikey. I'm sure you did everything you could. You come out when you want to. He's in here, Andy," she called. "He's all right."

Back in the living room, Penelope surveyed the

damage. Well, damn. She went to the telephone and called the police.

"This is Penelope Warren. I'd like you to page Chief Fowler for me."

"I'm sorry, ma'am. I can't do that. The chief left instructions that he was to be disturbed only in case of an emergency. An extreme emergency."

"This is an emergency."

"What is the nature of your problem, ma'am?"

"While Chief Fowler has been romancing my sister, my house has been burgled and someone attempted to kill my cat."

"I don't know. . . . We've got detectives on call. I could send them."

"Trust me on this. Dutch would want to know." The use of the chief's nickname seemed to work.

"I'll page him, but he ain't gonna like it."

"Thank you." Penelope replaced the phone and turned to Andy. "Shall we have a drink?" she asked calmly enough. Then she burst into tears, not for herself or the destruction to her home, but because of the sudden realization that Mycroft could have been killed.

The intruder had gained entry by breaking the kitchen window. The ransacking of the house did not extend beyond the living room.

By the time Dutch and Stormy arrived, both Penelope and Mycroft had calmed. Mycroft remained stretched out on Frank. Penelope was on the bed beside the big cat who alternately complained of the evening's travails or purred in response to his friend's soothing words. As she crooned and stroked Mycroft's back, Penelope used a small pair of scissors to clip away a bit of fur on his paw that was matted with what appeared to be blood. Andy stood by with a sandwich bag, holding it out for the clipping. Penelope dropped the fur into it for sealing. She then picked bits of what appeared to be flesh from his pads and claws. These, too, went into a baggie.

"Good Lord, Penny, what happened? Are you all right?"

"We weren't here. Mycroft—"

"Dutch's beeper went off, and my God, it was you. We got here as fast as we could."

"Here, John."

"What's this?" He took the sandwich bags and held them up to the light.

"Evidence," Penelope replied. "I think Mycroft attacked Herbert Fletcher and was nearly shot. He broke in through the kitchen window."

"Fletcher?"

"He's the killer." Penelope told him of her discovery at the movies. "It's a very long movie," she said, "and we didn't even get to see the ending. He would have had plenty of time to kill Louise and return. It would have been even easier with Freda. She loved him and would have done anything he asked. He simply called and told her to meet him on the mountain. Wham bam, goodbye ma'am. He used Alyce to divert suspicion from himself. It's all very neatly tied up now, except for one thing."

"This is all circumstantial," Fowler said quietly.

Penelope looked around the room as though she had not heard him speak. "There's something here that he wants. Something he needs. First, he thought it was at Freda's real-estate office. Now he thinks it's here. 'Look for the cave. Look for the knot.' "

"You don't know that it was Fletcher."

"I do. Mycroft knows too."

"You are not an eyewitness and Mycroft can't testify. He has to be judged by a jury of his peers. Cats are not peers."

"Well, they should be."

"Penelope, I know how much this means to you. I want the killer too, but this is not evidence of murder."

"Arrest him, John."

"For what? Fighting with a cat in a public place?"

"My home is not a public place, and he wasn't fighting. He tried to kill Mycroft. Surely, it's against the law to kill a pet."

A suddenly weary chief of police looked from Penelope to Stormy to Andy to Mycroft. He sighed heavily. "May I use your phone?"

"Of course, John."

He went to the telephone stand and dialed. "Larry, I want you and Willie to find Herbert Fletcher." Fowler paused. His brow furrowed. "Yes, I'm here, but never mind. I'm going to do it myself. Thanks." He hung up and turned to Penelope. "I'm going over to Fletcher's place. I'm going to ask him to show me his body. He doesn't have to do it. I have no probable cause for any of this. But if he'll submit to a search voluntarily, well . . . We'll see."

"Thank you, John."

"I'll be back as soon as I can."

Stormy walked him to the door. "I'll go with you."

He shook his head, but smiled as she reached up and kissed his cheek. Then he was gone.

The wait was interminable.

Fifteen minutes. He would have been at Fletcher's ranch by now.

Stormy paced through the clutter of the living room.

Penelope replaced the cushions on the sofa and then sat, drumming her fingers impatiently on her knee.

Andy poured wine.

Thirty minutes. He should be on his way back by now. If everything had gone well, if there had been no trouble.

"We should have gone with him," Stormy said.

Penelope shook her head. "He'll be all right. He survived the streets of L.A."

"He wasn't dealing with mad choppers then."

Mycroft came out and settled onto Penelope's lap. She stroked his fur until he fell asleep. At least, *he* was okay now.

Forty-five minutes.

"What's keeping him?" Stormy asked. "He should be back by now."

An hour.

"I'm going to call the police," Stormy declared.

"He is the police," Andy said. "He won't like you interfering."

Finally they heard a car approaching. Stormy ran to the door. "It's Dutch. Thank God."

The Empty Creek Chief of Police was greeted by another quick kiss. That alone made the trip worthwhile.

Holding Stormy's hand, Dutch Fowler looked at Penelope and shook his head.

"No scratches," he said.

Damn, Penelope thought, if it wasn't Herbert Fletcher, then who in hell was it?

CHAPTER NINETEEN

"I'm staying here tonight," Dutch Fowler said. "I'll sleep on the couch."

Stormy smiled. That was certainly an excellent suggestion, but she had her own ideas about the sleeping arrangements.

"So am I," Andy declared. "I'll sleep in the chair."

Penelope smiled, but shook her head. Men. They were so protective. "We're all adults here. Andy, you can stay, but if you do, you'll sleep with me where you belong. Cassie and Dutch can make their own decisions."

It was Andy's turn to smile. The chair had looked really uncomfortable. He persisted bravely, however. "Shouldn't we take turns standing guard, patrolling the grounds, that sort of thing?"

"Good night," Stormy said. "We'll barricade the bedroom." She took Dutch's hand and led a blushing police chief down the hall. Mycroft trotted happily behind them, intent perhaps on a new learning experience, but the door was closed firmly, even rudely, in his face.

He was miffed and let them know it with a loud, "Meow!"

The door opened briefly, and Frank, the teddy bear, abruptly joined Mycroft in the hallway.

Leading her own blushing man down the hallway, Penelope scooped up Frank and said, "I guess you're stuck with us tonight, Mikey. And it's only their second date."

It was always nice to have a few friends in for a sleepover, although if any more showed up Penelope would need a king-sized bed. Still, she was glad to be hostess of a slumber party. She had been shaken by the violation of her home, more than she wanted to admit to either Andy or Dutch—or herself. Propped up in bed, she doubted that anything more would happen that night, but there was certainly security in numbers. Andy was to her left. Frank was on her right. Big Mike was a comforting weight on her feet.

Poor Mikey. What a horrible, shattering experience he had endured. But he must have given as good as he got. Someone had suffered tonight. Who?

"Andy?"

"Yes, dear?" He was preoccupied with lightly caressing the little golden hairs on her forearm.

Penelope ignored the tingling sensation he was creating. "Who was here tonight? I was positive it was Herb." She wiggled her toes. They were tingling too because Mycroft was making them numb.

"I don't know."

"Guess."

His fingers slipped beneath the sheet and walked across her belly doing a little soft-shoe routine as they went.

"That tickles."

His fingers made an abrupt turn to the right and

went mountain climbing instead. It was becoming quite difficult for Penelope to concentrate.

So she stopped trying.

The next morning, Penelope left Andy, Mycroft, and Frank and went past Cassie's closed door into the kitchen. Dutch was already at the table. The coffee was made. That was a pleasant surprise. He might not be such a bad catch for Cassie after all. Cassie made terrible coffee.

"Good morning," Penelope said. "Sleep well? Or should I ask whether you slept?"

Dutch blushed furiously. "Your sister's quite a woman."

"I know."

"You're quite a woman, too."

Penelope helped herself to Dutch's coffee. "I rather immodestly agree with you."

Dutch quickly turned serious. "I want to get some people out here. We've got to find whatever it is that the killer wants so badly."

"The knot. The cave. I agree."

"I'll want them to go through the house too."

"It's all right. I don't have anything here they haven't seen before."

"I'm not sure about that." Cassie stumbled into the kitchen before Penelope could pursue that line of inquiry.

What did Stormy have secreted in her suitcases? Penelope wondered.

"Good morning, darling," Cassie said, ruffling Dutch's hair. "Hi, Sis."

"He makes much better coffee than you do. You should keep him around."

"He has other talents as well."

Dutch blushed helplessly.

Andy appeared, wearing only jeans and clutching Frank. "I got lonely."

"Of course you did, dear. Sit down and I'll get your coffee."

"Why are you carrying Frank around?" Cassie asked.

"He was lonely too."

Mycroft joined them by leaping on the table and looking around in good humor to ask, Did I miss anything?

The little family was all together.

The police went through the house methodically, searching every nook and cranny of the interior. They went through dresser drawers. They went through closets and boxes. One officer even sat at Penelope's computer and searched through her files. The garage was actually neater when they finished than when they had started. Penelope thanked them for that.

But they found nothing.

Except for an earring that had been missing for months. Penelope thanked a young police officer for that too.

They tore up the yard, poking and prodding as Penelope had done with the bayonet. In spots they dug. They sifted through the manure pile at the stable. They tossed and turned the two bales of hay recently delivered to the barn. They went through Chardonnay's oats and her medicines.

Nothing.

Not even the other missing earring.

Tweedledee and Tweedledum were present, although it was difficult to tell. They both avoided My-croft and Penelope, flitting away like ghosts every time one or the other entered a room where they happened to be.

The authorities climbed over the roof of the house and the stable.

They went up and down the banks of the creek that now lived up to its name of Empty.

They found nothing.

No cave. No knot.

Absolutely nothing.

Penelope was feeling very exasperated with Louise Fletcher by the time the police had finished their search. "I don't know why that woman couldn't read something simple and straightforward like Jackie Collins instead of mysteries," she complained.

Mycroft, too, was more than a little put out. The search had disrupted his routine. Every time he went to the kitchen, there were strange shoes clumping around. He growled at each intrusion. Don't tread on this cat's tail, by God. He had just settled in under the bed when the bed was moved. He retreated to the window sill in the living room to watch the activity outside and discovered, to his great dismay, that there were now two mockingbirds flitting around the Saguaro. Count them. Two.

What was a cat to do?

"We don't want police protection," Penelope said. "We don't need police protection."

"I take it all back," Dutch said. "You are not a remarkable woman. You are a stubborn woman."

"I prefer to think of myself as a woman of conviction."

"Ha!" Cassie cried. "Dutch is right. You're stubborn."

"My life has been disrupted enough."

"Think of Mycroft," Dutch said.

"I am thinking of Mycroft. We'll be just fine."

"Do you have a gun, at least?"

"Who needs a gun? I have the Amazon Princess."

"Take mine. You know how to shoot the Beretta?"

"In the Marine Corps, I couldn't hit the target with the damned thing. I don't suppose you happen to have an M-16 handy? I fired Expert with the rifle."

"As a matter of fact, I do. At least, an AR 15, the civilian version."

"You do?"

"At the station. In case of civil insurrection."

"Without civil insurrection, you wouldn't have met me," Stormy pointed out.

"That's true."

Dutch Fowler refused to leave until the AR 15 had been delivered and he was satisfied that Penelope remembered everything she had been taught about it in the Marine Corps.

"The M-16," Penelope recited, "is a gas-operated, magazine-fed, air-cooled, semiautomatic or automatic shoulder weapon." She went on to relate its weight, length, average rate of fire, chamber pressure, muzzle velocity, effective range, and magazine capacity.

Dutch was satisfied.

Cassie and Mycroft were impressed.

Andy went off to work feeling slightly better about leaving the sisters and Mycroft alone.

For her part, Penelope smiled. Rather smugly.

Lock and load.

Ready on the right. Ready on the left. All ready on the firing line. Stand by for targets.

Targets!

Private Warren, get your butt down!

Just like old times in boot camp.

Since Penelope had an AR 15 propped in a corner of the room, she decided she might as well look the part and dug into her old seabag for a camouflage utility jacket with the Globe and Anchor on the left breast pocket and the initials, USMC. Her sergeant's chevrons were still pinned to the collar points. All of her utility uniforms were starched and ready to go. Her boots were spit-shined to a gleaming black. Her greens were protected by garment bags. You had to be ready. She slipped into the jacket and twirled around for Cassie and Mycroft. "How do I look?" she asked.

"Gung ho. Is that the correct term?"

"Damned straight."

The search of the premises had taken the entire morning. Penelope and Cassie fixed a light lunch, and when the dishes were rinsed and in the dishwasher, Cassie announced, "I'm taking a nap."

Penelope would have enjoyed a nap too. Ever since this damnable business had started, she had found herself awakening earlier and earlier. It was just like being back in the Marine Corps. But what good was the AR 15 if you were going to fall asleep at your guard post?

Saddle up! She was becoming downright nostalgic, what with all the Marine Corps memories. If this kept up, she might have to reenlist, ship over. Get up in the damned morning.

Ugh!

Instead, she saddled up by dropping some peppermint candies into the pocket of her jacket, loosening the sling on the rifle, putting it over her shoulder, and moving off at a crisp military pace to the corral where Chardonnay greeted her eagerly.

Mycroft, torn between duty and sleep, decided on duty and followed her down the path for a bit, but then abruptly turned and went back, circling around the house to the front. Cats had certain obligations too, and Mycroft had just remembered one.

Feeding candies one by one to Chardonnay, Penelope had a sudden inspiration. Louise Fletcher had arrived on horseback! After giving Chardonnay the treats, she slipped the bridle on and, riding bareback, went back up the trail to the front of the house. Wearing the utility jacket and with the rifle slung over her shoulder, she felt very much the warrior princess on her trusty steed.

"Mycroft, what are you doing up there?"

Mycroft was in the saguaro, pawing at something in the old nest.

Penelope watched.

It was similar to a cave. There was certainly a knot formed by the saguaro to protect itself when the woodpecker first hammered the nest out. Some people called it a boot. The Indians would use it for a drinking vessel.

Mycroft was pawing at something in a cave! Something in a knot!

"Mikey, you're a bloody genius!"

The mockingbirds fluttering around the top of the cactus didn't think so. He was a bloody intruder, and they were letting him know it.

Big Mike, however, looked over at her. Yes, I am. There was a definite smile in his eyes. Certainly took you long enough to figure it out.

Penelope walked Chardonnay over to the cactus. The hole in the saguaro's trunk was just the right height for a woman on horseback. She reached past Mycroft into the hole. Her hand emerged holding two cassette tapes in hard plastic boxes.

Good old Louise and her mysteries!

The tapes were ninety minutes each, Penelope noticed. One was labeled, Last Will and Testament of Louise Fletcher, the other was—

"I'll take those, Penelope."

Oh, oh.

She twisted around. Herbert Fletcher was pointing a gun at her. A very big gun. She could not get the rifle off her shoulder in time.

"I don't think so, Herb." Penelope slipped the cassettes into her jacket pocket.

"I'll kill you too, Penelope."

"I knew it was you," she said. "I knew it was you all along." Damn. Stall for time. Cassie. Where was Cassie? Scream? No, keep him away from Cassie. And Mycroft.

"You won't know for long." He started to cock the revolver.

Oh, shit!

Oh, well. Do it!

Chardonnay responded instantly to the pressure of Penelope's knees and jumped forward.

The gun went off as Fletcher leaped for his life. It was lucky for him he still had good reflexes because Chardonnay would have run him down.

Penelope looked over her shoulder. Fletcher was up and running. He's got his car hidden away somewhere, she thought, then turned to lean over Chardonnay's neck.

The mockingbirds were forgotten. Mycroft tore across the desert in pursuit of Penelope and Char. Hey, wait for me!

The gunshot awakened Cassie.

Oh, shit!

She managed to get to the window in time to see Penelope gallop off toward the creek and Herbert Fletcher run down the driveway waving a gun. Cassie ran for the jeep.

Penelope leaned over Chardonnay's neck. "Run, Char, run."

Chardonnay did better than run. She flattened her ears and flew down the creek bed right past a startled Laney and Wally who were in their front yard.

"Police!" Penelope cried as she raced past.

Fletcher was on the road above, drawing even with Penelope. He was steering with one hand and leaning across the passenger seat and pointing the gun at Penelope with the other.

This was not good. This was definitely not good for woman or beast.

Before Chardonnay had moved to Casa Penelope, she had competed in Arabian horse shows—in the stock horse class and in the reining class competitions. Penelope hoped Chardonnay remembered her lessons. She also hoped she herself remembered.

Penelope drew back on the reins. Chardonnay responded instantly, rearing up, her back feet dug into the creek bed, skidding to a halt. It wasn't a show ring, but it was a perfect sliding stop. Penelope almost fell off. Without a saddle it was difficult to maintain her seat, but she managed.

Oh, good Chardonnay, good Penelope.

Fletcher was past them, skidding on the dirt road as he attempted to stop. It took him much longer than Chardonnay.

Penelope and Char were already racing back in the opposite direction.

A siren wailed.

That was certainly fast. How did Laney do that so quickly?

Oh, my God.

Cassie was raising dust as she sped down the dirt road in Penelope's jeep. She was on a collision course with Herb Fletcher.

Oh, my God again. An unmarked police car was passing Cassie. Andy was in his own car behind the police vehicle, and Dutch was coming up fast on the other side of the creek bed. Where were they all coming from?

Doesn't anyone trust me? Obviously not, Penelope thought as she heard the USC fight song. Beamish's red convertible now joined the chase, flying over the ruts in the road. Russell—or Ralph—was standing in the front seat next to Beamish, clutching the windshield for support. His twin was in the back seat, brandishing a baseball bat.

It seemed that everyone Penelope knew or had ever met had been secreted in the desert around her house.

By this time, Wally was in the yard with his revolver out. Laney was beside him, jumping up and down.

Penelope was about to fall off the damned horse, she was so busy trying to keep track of everything. *Let's do it again, Char.*

"Whoa."

Chardonnay skidded obediently to another abrupt halt. Penelope slid off while the horse's back feet were dug into the ground, rolled once, and came up running, unslinging the rifle as she scrambled out of the creek bed.

The police car had swerved and stopped, blocking the road. Tweedledee and Tweedledum jumped out of it. For once, Penelope was glad to see them.

Cassie and Herb were playing chicken. Cassie swerved to the left, Fletcher to the right, bouncing once as he hit the ditch, careened back onto the road. He came to a halt inches from the police car.

Burke and Stoner had their guns out and trained on Fletcher. Wally approached from the back. Laney still jumped and skittered along beside him. She had been joined by Alexander who had gone into a barking frenzy, twirling and dancing around his mistress's feet. Cassie was driving cautiously down the road. A very winded Mycroft lagged to a stop at the police car, laid his ears back and growled. Dutch was out of the car, running across the creek with a shotgun in his hands. Beamish was directing the twins and their baseball bats into action. Andy was quickly scribbling an eye-witness account.

Penelope had Fletcher covered with the rifle. She resisted the urge to snarl, "Go ahead. Make my day."

Herbert Fletcher was surrounded.

Tweedledee looked down at Big Mike, said, "Oh, shit," and quickly traded places with Tweedledum.

"What's going on here?" Cassie asked.

A tower of Babel erupted. Everyone shouted at the same time. Mycroft meowed loudly. Alexander barked. Chardonnay joined in with an enthusiastic whinny. Beamish beamed. Ralph and Russell leered happily at Penelope and Laney.

Penelope pointed the rifle in the air and squeezed off a round.

The crack of the rifle shut everyone up.

"I always wanted to do that," Penelope said, looking around and smiling with a great deal of satisfaction.

They played the cassettes on the spot by putting them in the tape deck of Penelope's jeep.

Once more, the voice of Louise Fletcher floated ethereally across the desert. "This is Louise Fletcher," she announced. "Being of sound mind and body, this last will and testament supercedes any of my previous wills. Hear that, Herbert? You're out of it now. You're not getting one damned penny!"

Motive.

Dutch stopped the tape. "We'll listen to the rest of it later." He inserted the second tape and pressed the play button.

This time it was Herbert Fletcher's voice. He was livid. "I'm warning you, Louise. You've gone too far this time. I'll get you for this. I'll get you, if it's the last thing I do!"

"Ha!" Louise had replied.

"We have Big Mike to thank for finding the tapes," Penelope said after Dutch ejected the second one. "I should have known. Louise gave me every clue in the world. The saguaro was right there on the cover of *Silent Night*. It was there all the time, but I didn't see it. The Indians, too, on page three hundred thirty-six. Louise certainly loved a mystery." She scratched Mycroft's chin. "What a good cat you are. You can have all the lima beans you want."

Big Mike agreed with that assessment, especially the part about the lima beans.

"I knew I should have killed the damned cat," a

handcuffed Herbert Fletcher said. "Oh, well, at least I performed a public service in getting rid of Louise."

"Why Freda?" Penelope asked.

Fletcher shrugged nonchalantly. "She suspected me and threatened exposure if I didn't marry her. She was as bad as Louise."

"And Alyce?"

He shrugged. "She was available."

Fletcher was rudely stuffed into Tweedledee's car, ready for transport to the Empty Creek jail.

Penelope returned the rifle to Dutch. "What was everyone doing hanging around my place? You didn't trust us."

"It was Larry's idea. He was worried about you."

Penelope looked over at Tweedledee who shuffled nervously. "Thank you," she said.

The detective smiled shyly. "Hey, you ain't so bad for such an old Harpy," he said.

Penelope smiled and kissed him on the cheek. "And you ain't so bad either," she said.

"Aw." Tweedledee blushed. The Warren sisters seemed to have a definite talent for making police officers turn red in the face.

"Give Detective Burke a big kiss, Mikey."

"I ain't getting near that cat."

If Big Mike was disappointed, he hid it well as he went to check out the two new kids on the block.

"Nice kitty," Russell—or Ralph—said.

CHAPTER TWENTY

Penelope watched as Herbert Fletcher was arraigned the next morning. He entered a plea of not guilty by reason of temporary insanity, but no one thought he would get away with that, not even his attorney, a man imported from Phoenix for the task.

After that brief turn of the judicial wheel, Detectives Burke and Stoner—for the moment Penelope had decided to stop calling them Tweedledee and Tweedledum—made another peace offering by asking if she would like to accompany them on a search of Fletcher's place.

"Mycroft, too?"

"As long as you feed him first," the former Tweedledee said. "I don't want that beast taking a hunk outta my butt."

"He's a very well-mannered cat," Penelope said. She almost succeeded in keeping a straight face as she came to Big Mike's defense.

"Ha!"

"Well, he is . . . most of the time."

* * *

As it turned out, Fletcher had a secret hideaway too. It was nothing quite so elaborate or unconventional as Louise's cubbyhole in the wall of her cottage. Penelope found the safe disguised as a coffee table in Fletcher's study simply because she was looking for a safe, in the desk or perhaps in a wall or the floor. Having examined the desk drawers carefully and turned aside all of the paintings—nudes that would have done a bordello proud—to no avail, Penelope started kicking throw rugs aside.

Nothing.

She pushed a leather reclining chair away from its accustomed spot.

Nothing.

She attempted to lift one end of the coffee table.

Too heavy.

She joined Mycroft on the leather couch and began pushing and pulling at the elaborate wooden panels.

Bingo and *voilà!* A combination safe.

"Larry, Willie," she called. The detectives were in the kitchen searching for a stash of chopping knives. "I've found it."

She fiddled with the combination, moving it from one number to the next. It wouldn't open.

"Willie," Burke said, "call the jail and tell them to get the combination from Fletcher. If he don't wanna give it, tell 'em we're gonna come down there and beat it out of him."

"Okey dokey."

"You're not really going to do that, are you?" Penelope asked.

"Nah, but he don't know that."

Stoner used the telephone at the desk. Burke occupied his time by admiring the nudes. He seemed particularly drawn to one heavy-breasted woman reclining on a wet beach. Penelope thought the model looked very cold.

"Torpedoes?" Penelope asked, offering an olive branch of her own.

Burke turned and grinned at her. "Yeah. Those are definitely torpedoes."

Stoner hung up. "Twenty-seven right, four left, thirteen right."

The heavy steel door swung open to reveal a limp and deflated George Bush and enough chopping knives to reduce the female population of Empty Creek by a considerable number. There was also a pile of shiny new pennies.

"The man was a regular Bluebeard," Penelope said, feeling slightly sick as she wondered who the knives were meant for.

Penelope and Mycroft left the detectives to their work.

For them, the case was closed.

Almost.

Bits and pieces of the murderous tale continued to unfold.

Penelope learned later that Burke and Stoner scoured Empty Creek for the moviegoers who had gone to see *Lawrence of Arabia* on the fateful evening Louise Fletcher was murdered. They found half-a-dozen individuals who would swear to the fact that someone had used the exit door to leave and reenter the theater. They would also testify that it was a tall man. It was circumstantial, but it was another addition to the growing evidence against Fletcher. The detectives also checked for moviegoers on the afternoon Freda Alsberg died and found more witnesses.

The crime lab discovered that bits of rubber taken from Big Mike's claws came from the George Bush mask. That led to an examination of Fletcher's head, and scratches were found on his scalp, hidden away beneath his bushy white hair.

Penelope giggled every time she thought of Mycroft leaping on Fletcher's head, digging in, riding the old man like an apparition from hell. Served the murderous lecher right. Good old Mycroft.

Slowly, things returned to normal.

Until Saturday evening.

Penelope was miffed.

Cassie had borrowed the jeep for her date with Dutch. His car was in the shop, although Penelope didn't see why he couldn't just borrow one from the police department. Still, it was Cassie's last night in Empty Creek for a while as she had tearfully pointed out any number of times in the past two days, so Penelope relented.

That wouldn't have been so bad really, but Andy broke their date at the last minute, saying he was tired and going to bed early.

On Saturday night, for God's sake!

Actually Penelope was feeling rather sorry for herself, even growing a little teary at the prospect of a lonely Saturday night, as she had told Mycroft several times while standing at the window of Mycroft & Company and watching dusk settle over Empty Creek.

"It's just you and me, Mikey. No one else cares."

"But I care, my lady," Kathy pointed out. She was

euphoric at having done well enough at her audition to have achieved the exalted status of gentlewoman for the next edition of the Empty Creek Elizabethan Spring Faire.

"Ha!" Penelope, of course, was pleased for Kathy, but she did wish her assistant would stop being so damned cheery. It was hard to maintain a good sulk when everyone around you was so happy.

"Timmy cares. We're taking you home, and we'd be happy to stop for Chinese food. We could have a little party."

"You young people don't want to be saddled with an old maid. You'd rather be out having fun."

Kathy sighed. Sometimes . . . "You're hardly an old maid, my lady."

Penelope gave Mycroft a little pat on the rump. Woe is us.

Timmy arrived promptly, just as Penelope locked the door of Mycroft & Company. Penelope thought briefly of inviting the young couple to the Double B for a drink, but immediately dismissed that idea.

There would be people there.

Having fun.

Together.

Penelope climbed glumly into the back seat of Timmy's car. Mycroft decided to sit up front on Kathy's lap. Even Big Mike was deserting her. The little ingrate.

The sight of her empty and dark house depressed Penelope even more.

After all, Andy could have gone to bed early here.

"Would you like to come in for a glass of wine?"

"Sure," Timmy replied happily.

Of course, *he* could be cheery. They would leave as soon as decently possible and he would be free to research another ode on Kathy's breasts.

Penelope stuck her tongue out at the Abraham Lincoln twins and opened the door.

They scared the bejeezus out of her.

"Surprise!"

Mycroft leaped straight up, setting a new high jump record for cats in the twenty-five pounds and over class.

"Surprise!"

Cassie and Dutch grinned broadly. Andy held a huge package. Laney clapped. Wally crinkled his eyes. Alexander barked. Alyce winked at Penelope.

Larry Burke and Willie Stoner were there with their wives.

Peggy Norton stood with her boyfriend. Sheila Tyler and George Eden held hands. George's informal outfit was as outlandish as his suits.

Russell and Ralph, freshly scrubbed and resplendent in new T-shirts proclaiming their affiliation with Friends of the Library, flanked the ever beaming Beamish.

Josephine Brooks and Murphy Brown were present.

Sam and Debbie stood shyly behind everyone else.

"Oh, my God," Penelope said.

"You see, my lady. . . ."

Andy thrust his package at Penelope. It was wrapped in Christmas paper.

"What is it?" she asked.

"Open it, Penelope. I didn't have anything but Christmas wrapping, but I know how much you like the holidays, so I thought it would be all right."

Leave it to Andy—Christmas wrapping in March.

Guests crowded around as Penelope looked at the Santa Clause tag: FOR PENELOPE AND BIG

MIKE. She tore at the paper and found the front page of the *Empty Creek News Journal* that told of Penelope and Mycroft's contributions to the capture and arrest of Herbert Fletcher. It was beautifully framed, but the headline embarrassed Penelope. She wasn't sure about Mycroft. He had an infinite capacity for absorbing praise and seemed to like having his picture in the newspaper.

LOCAL HEROINE CAPTURES KILLER:
CAT INSTRUMENTAL IN SOLVING CRIMES

"Thank you, Andy." She kissed him right in front of God and everyone.

Penelope and Mycroft were made honorary members of the Empty Creek Police Department, complete with badges and identification cards set in leather wallets, despite the fact that Big Mike had no pockets.

After the honor was conferred by Dutch, Penelope said only, "It was Mycroft who really solved the case."

Everyone applauded loudly.

From Mycroft's point of view, however, the party was off to a rather glum start. He had been forbidden to sample the hors d'oeuvres, stopped from playing with the ice cubes floating so enticingly in the punch bowl, and threatened with outright banishment if he didn't refrain from provoking Alexander into chasing him around the living room.

How was he going to impress Murphy with all these damned rules thwarting him? This was no way to treat a hero.

"Mikey, you're my favorite guy," Alyce said. She scratched his chin.

At least, she had the proper attitude!

So when Alyce set up shop in a corner of the living room—she had offered to do impromptu readings for one and all—Big Mike settled onto her lap, probably thinking that she needed a familiar to properly practice her various arts. Besides, it was a good place to keep track of people, and Alyce always had such interesting things to say.

The psychic did a brisk business among the guests. Although the atmosphere was not conducive to the concentration needed to ply her trade properly, still she took an object from each person—a scarf, a ring, something personal—held it in her hand, and focused on the aura emanating from that person. It was close enough for party work and little different from when she set up shop as Mistress Alyce Smith at the Elizabethan Spring Faire each year amidst the bustling crowds attending that celebration.

"Hi, Laney," Alyce said. "I see you just completed another novel."

"Amazing. I just finished it this afternoon, and I've told no one, not even Wally."

Alyce smiled, closed her eyes, furrowed her pretty brow, and concentrated as she held the gold bracelet that Laney slipped from her wrist.

"Wally gave it to me for my birthday."

"He'll give you many other presents as well. I see a ring. A diamond ring with baguettes."

"Oh, Lord, is that man going to park his boots under my bed forever?"

Alyce opened her eyes and smiled. "It's possible."

Marriage seemed to be in the air, for Alyce told Cassie that she heard wedding bells and saw Dutch in a tuxedo. "Probably as a groom," she said.

A smiling Cassie led Dutch off to a corner for a quick smooch.

It was ditto for Sam and Debbie.

Empty Creek Wedding Gowns was going to make lots of money if this kept up.

Penelope poured a glass of punch and slipped into the chair across from Alyce. "I thought you might like a little something to drink."

"Thank you. And thank you again for . . . well, you know."

Penelope nodded. "I know."

Mycroft, apparently having forgiven Penelope, moved to her lap, looking up with large quizzical eyes. He purred happily. It was a good thing he didn't carry a grudge for long.

Penelope slipped a turquoise ring from her finger and gave it to Alyce.

Alyce took it and closed her eyes. She hesitated and then said, "There is love all around you, and I see a queen, resplendent in royal finery."

Now what in the hell does that mean?

The party bubbled right along.

Penelope danced with Andy first. Then with Larry Burke and Willie Stoner. They weren't such bad guys, really. Larry told her all about his stamp collection. And then, of course, Penelope had to dance with both Russell and Ralph, who also turned out to be rather decent chaps despite their positions as enforcers for Beamish. As Russell—or Ralph—told Penelope, "Aw, someone's gotta take care of the little guy." Later, Wally swirled her around the darkened living room. Cassie even let Dutch go long enough for him to dance with Penelope.

With such enjoyment pervading the room, it came as a complete surprise when Murphy Brown hissed at

Mycroft. Alexander leaped to his friend's defense and barked loudly, receiving a vicious swipe across the nose for his trouble.

Fickle damned cat.

After this skirmish Wally brought out his guitar and everyone sang along with him as he strummed the old folk songs of Joan Baez, the Kingston Trio and Peter, Paul, and Mary. Penelope marveled at his ability. It was a side of Wally that she didn't know. The man was talented. He could play the guitar *and* crinkle his eyes.

It was close to midnight when Penelope slipped into the cold night to sit on the front porch. Even surrounded by her friends, she felt melancholy. The surprise party had been a wonderful gesture on Cassie's part, but Penelope did wish two other people could have been present.

Louise Fletcher and Freda Alsberg.

Mycroft followed her out and took up his post to stare into the night. The desert was quiet, undisturbed by coyotes or mockingbirds. Everything was right in his world. Except for Murphy. Oh, well.

"Now maybe we can get back to running the bookstore," Penelope said, stroking Mycroft softly.

He purred.

The door opened and Andy came out to sit on the other side of Penelope. "Penny for your thoughts, Penny."

She smiled and took his hand. "I never want to see another penny."

"I'm going to miss having Cassie around," Andy said.

"Oh, she'll be back. She's in love."

"It's nice to be in love."

They sat quietly for a while, holding hands, staring up at a half-moon. Behind them, the house was filled with the laughter of their friends.

"What did Alyce tell you?" Penelope asked finally.

"She said you were a wonderful woman."

"That goes without saying."

"I agreed with her, naturally."

"Naturally."

"What else did she say?"

"Something about love," Andy mumbled. "What did she tell you?"

"Love," Penelope replied. "And she saw me as a queen, wearing royal robes."

"You are a queen to me."

I wonder what it would be like, Penelope thought, to be a queen.

But the queen was dead. Poor Louise. Poor Freda. Long live the queen.

"MIND-BOGGLING . . . THE SUSPENSE IS UNBEARABLE . . .
DORIS MILES DISNEY WILL KEEP YOU
ON THE EDGE OF YOUR SEAT . . ."

THE MYSTERIES OF DORIS MILES DISNEY

WHODUNIT? . . . ZEBRA DUNIT!
FOR ARMCHAIR DETECTIVES — TWO DELIGHTFUL
NEW MYSTERY SERIES

AN ANGELA BIAWABAN MYSTERY: TARGET FOR MURDER   (4069, $3.99)
by J.F. Trainor

Anishinabe princess Angie is on parole from a correctional facility, courtesy of an embezzling charge. But when an old friend shows up on her doorstep crying bloody murder, Angie skips parole to track down the creep who killed Mary Beth's husband and stole her land. When she digs up the dirt on a big-time developer and his corrupt construction outfit, she becomes a sitting duck for a cunning killer who never misses the mark!

AN ANGELA BIAWABAN MYSTERY: DYNAMITE PASS   (4227, $3.99)
by J.F. Trainor

When Angie — a native American detective on the wrong side of the law and the right side of justice — attends a family *powwow*, her forest ranger cousin is killed in a suspicious accident. The sleuth finds herself in deadly danger from a sleazy lumber king when she investigates his death. Now, she must beat the bad guys and stop the killer before the case blows up in her face and explodes in one more fatality — hers!

A CLIVELY CLOSE MYSTERY: DEAD AS DEAD CAN BE   (4099, $3.99)
by Ann Crowleigh

Twin sisters Miranda and Clare Clively are stunned when a corpse falls from their carriage house chimney. Against the back drop of Victorian London, they must defend their family name from a damning scandal — and a thirty-year-old murder. But just as they are narrowing down their list of suspects, they get another dead body on their hands — and now Miranda and Clare wonder if they will be next . . .

A CLIVELY CLOSE MYSTERY: WAIT FOR THE DARK   (4298, $3.99)
by Ann Crowleigh

Clare Clively is taken by surprise when she discovers a corpse while walking through the park. She and her twin sister, Miranda are immediately on the case . . . yet the closer they come to solving the crime, the closer they come to a murderous villain who has no intention of allowing the two snooping sisters to unmask the truth!

LOOK FOR THESE OTHER BOOKS IN ZEBRA'S NEW *PARTNERS IN CRIME*
SERIES FEATURING APPEALING WOMEN AMATEUR-SLEUTHS:
   LAURA FLEMING MYSTERIES
   MARGARET BARLOW MYSTERIES
   AMANDA HAZARD MYSTERIES
   TEAL STEWART MYSTERIES
   DR. AMY PRESCOTT MYSTERIES

Available wherever paperbacks are sold, or order direct from the Publisher. Send cover price plus 50¢ per copy for mailing and handling to Penguin USA, P.O. Box 999, c/o Dept. 17109, Bergenfield, NJ 07621. Residents of New York and Tennessee must include sales tax. DO NOT SEND CASH.